I0822466

THE STARS ABOVE THE HILL

THE WORLD BEYOND DUOLOGY
BOOK 2

ANGELA FUNK

ISBN (paperback): 979-8-9898506-4-8

ISBN (hardcover): 979-8-9898506-5-5

Cover design by Ann Bugarin (@OnyxCatArt on Etsy/Instagram)

Planet artwork by @Akarstudio on Fiverr (Instagram ~ @akar.std)

Character artwork by @SYKOSAN and @sophienova793 on Instagram

For you
My forever

AUTHOR'S NOTE

While this novel is largely a sci-fi romantic adventure full of rich world-building and witty banter, *The World Beyond* duology also covers topics that may be uncomfortable for some. This story contains depictions of anxiety, depression, mention of a parent's suicide (off-screen), and grief and loss (extensively explored).

The overall message of the series aims to be positive, however, these themes are explored throughout, so please read at your discretion.

ALSO BY ANGELA FUNK

Forsaken Destiny Trilogy

The Heroic Facade

The Heroic Fallacy

The Heroic Fall

The World Beyond Duology

The World Beyond the Horizon

The Stars Above the Hill

THE STARS ABOVE THE HILL

THE END
Sundar
Noah's Planet

Fortun
Celeste's Planet

LAST TIME

ON A FATEFUL RAINY DAY...

"Where are you going?"

"Our planets are set to collide in two months, and everything you and I know will be gone."

"Do you want to help me save them?"

To be continued...

1

THE WORLD IS ENDING

"YOU MEAN TO TELL US FISH CAN FLY HERE?"

Mark's voice rang out against the ample chatter of the crowd. He and Noah trailed behind Katalina and Celeste through a section of Mermain City full of skyscrapers and fish swimming through the air. No rhyme or reason; no thoughts or feelings. They simply existed, flickering out of existence when they hit a building, only to reappear on the other side unharmed.

Noah's pale green eyes flickered to Mark as they stopped in the center of a busy walkway, noting the twenty-four-year-old's once short black hair was now beginning to curl around his ears. It'd been a month since they'd jumped off the side of their crumbling planet of Sundar and landed on Celeste's, and their journey was nonstop from there. This was made apparent by everyone's physical states, and they all desperately needed long naps and showers.

"The fish don't fly; they swim," corrected Noah. "And I thought I told you this weeks ago when we first came here?"

Noah combed his fingers through his dusty blond hair; it felt notably longer though they had yet to visit anywhere with a mirror for him to check. He feared the length didn't suit him, and though he knew there was no point in fretting over something he couldn't change, Noah wanted to look his best for Celeste.

He knew, however, that the grime splattered across his black shirt and his tattered jeans did *not* suit him. Not one bit. Celeste and Katalina were dressed in once colorful jumpsuits—pink and olive green, respectively—that were now various shades of muddied brown. Even Mark had a damp maroon shirt and hair stringy with sweat.

Mark was easily two inches taller and stared down at Noah with piercing deep blue eyes and a cocked brow. His mouth remained agape in shock, exposing perfectly straight white teeth, as he turned to Celeste for confirmation. "In the air?"

She nodded, arms folded over her chest. "In the air."

"Is your house close?" asked Katalina. Noah's cousin was the shortest of them all, and the long, intricate dreads cascading down her back were two shades darker than her ebony skin.

"Isn't coming back here a waste of time?" her fiancé added with a stretch, glancing Celeste's way. Her disgruntled, pinched eyebrows twitched at him as she glared, and Mark threw his hands up in defense. "I mean, I love seeing fish outside of water, flying in the sky and everything, but weren't we on the side of your planet we needed to be on and now we're, uh, not?"

Celeste's planet, Fortun, was shaped like a cube, and the

sides shifted at random. The moment they docked their ship and broke free of the desert leading to the city, the sides of the planet changed. They could no longer go back the way they came; the ocean was no longer behind them, and the dazzling stars were no longer ahead.

The stars once littered the entire sky, but they'd been moved by something—or someone. Coincidentally, their group was instructed to retrieve two stars to save their planets from colliding, which they'd decidedly gone out of their way not to do.

"I'd like to see my family one last time, in case we don't make it," Celeste said. Her wavy black hair blew in the breeze gently, exposing the blue highlights underneath that were growing notably lighter. "Thank you very much."

"We don't get the same luxury, you know." Mark trailed off as he looked at Noah, the guy whose mother passed away long before they knew of the planets colliding. Noah spared Mark a chiding for obviously pitying him, instead glancing at Celeste. She would never say goodbye to her brother, Altair, either. There were hundreds of others who sat with similar sadness, and he would stop at nothing to save them all.

Though a thought rested in the back of his mind—even if they protected everyone and everything, one day, nothing would remain. Nature always found a way back to its own demise, and if not nature, then man surely would.

"If we could give you that chance, we would," Noah said with hands on his hips. "We're going to save everyone, anyway. This is just a cautionary goodbye."

"Wow. Since when did you become so positive?"

If only Mark could hear Noah's endless, and frankly, dreadful, thoughts. "When I realized that's all I've got."

Noah peered over at Celeste. Positivity and *her*. Though he wished he could claim his motives for this journey were entirely altruistic, in truth, he was doing so for a woman. She was perhaps the only thing holding him together, aside from the limitless marvels her planet presented. "But I am worried about those shapeshifters that attacked us."

Katalina rubbed her chin in thought before snapping her fingers. "What if they've impersonated one of us again and we can't tell until it's too late?"

"Why would you suggest that now?" Mark asked, bewildered eyes bulging from their sockets.

They were in an odd predicament. Celeste's late brother was a member of a research team studying a black hole that was pulling their planets together. While Altair's research notebook had taken them on a wild adventure to find absurd answers to equally absurd questions, it did not come without naysayers.

"Because we're going back to where we ran into them," Katalina said with a clenched jaw. "It becomes more frightening the more we talk about it."

Most civilians knew nothing of the planets colliding, but there were secret research groups who knew did. A group of shapeshifters was one of them, and they were after Celeste, determined to stop her from following her brother's research. They'd not only attacked her family but also impersonated her and her stepmother, nearly tricking Noah and their group completely. He couldn't imagine what would've happened if he and Luna—Celeste's stepsister—hadn't noticed.

The thought of the gangling, bird-like creatures made him shiver. Katalina had a point. There was something unsettling about returning to Celeste's house. The shapeshifters seemed to want the planets to end, and that terrified Noah most of all.

Noah's thoughts quickly delved into a vat of anxiety, the city of sky fish drifting in and out of focus as he attempted to figure everything out.

It was a game of mental gymnastics, and he was losing. All his thoughts pointed back to something the Ruler of the Deep said. While the ruler was helpful, giving them insight on the next step of their venture, the sea serpent made it abundantly clear he didn't extend help to anyone else. *They were too selfish.*

Perhaps the shapeshifters wanted the worlds to collide because selfishness plagued their societies, and there was no longer any hope of civil survival.

"On our planet, fish *stay* in the water, you know." Mark's voice shocked Noah out of his relentless rumination, and his gaze drifted to Mark.

"I thought we went over this already," Noah grumbled.

When their eyes met, Noah's deadpan expression made Mark stammer, "W-What's on your mind, there? That look of yours is scaring me."

Celeste took a step forward, head cocked, as she examined Noah from head to toe. "I'm inclined to agree."

He took a deep breath before exhaling a string of speedy words. "I'm trying to figure out why the Ruler of the Deep thought everyone who visited him before us was selfish. I mean, how is it selfish to want to save the world?"

"How isn't it selfish?" Celeste's tone was matter-of-fact and airy, as if it was silly to even suggest humanity could be selfless.

"Are you saying the inherent desire to live is selfish?" Katalina asked, astonishment lining her voice. "That's absurd. It's merely human nature."

"Exactly."

Before the debate could go on, Noah pointed ahead. They'd reached the part of the city separating the swimming fish from everything else. It looked to be a wall of nearly transparent blue jelly. When he reached out to touch it, a ripple began like a slim rock skipping atop the water.

A swath of coolness washed over him when he walked through the barrier, the tension evaporating from his shoulders. A small, nervous smile stretched across his lips. If he'd been told this was where he'd be a year ago, he would've laughed. He would've called his prophet delusional. Oh, how thankful he was for such a delusion.

On the other side was a bustling, urban-looking city. Every building was black, accented with neon pinks, and purples, and blues. Celeste's family was somewhere on this side, living in a pointy yet quaint house not too far from where they stood.

There were no modes of transportation on Fortun, aside from paved paths big enough for pairs to walk side-by-side. The walkways were surrounded by patches of teal grass speckled with bright bushes, flowers, and trees. Occasionally, a series of benches or tables would appear, often populated by humans and merpeople alike. Other subspecies drifted in and out of sight, from two-legged fish heads to human-sized snails slowly sliding down the pavement.

"Uh, are you guys seeing what I'm seeing?" Noah asked, his jaw falling open. A cat sat upright and stretched on a small cloud drifting by. Three kittens followed on their own tiny clouds.

Katalina shrieked with delight, a hand over her mouth. "That's the cutest thing I've ever seen. *Cloud kittens*?"

Celeste nodded. "They cannot be tamed, though. They are not pets."

"Good. We can*not* adopt a cat. You promised," Mark warned, wagging a finger at his fiancée.

Katalina's shoulders slumped. "Aw, I wanted to take one back to Sundar with me. For science, of course. Are you sure they can't even be rescued?"

Celeste gently squeezed Katalina's shoulder with a look of solemn understanding. "It would eat you alive."

The group went quiet after that, instead storing that chilling information deep in the back of their minds and marveling at the sweet little animals along their walk. Eventually, the city skyscrapers tapered out into suburban land made up of picket-fenced homes.

Celeste led them to an uneven house painted black and riddled with jagged edges, stopping in front of a red door. Her knuckles rapped against the metal with a hollow bang. At first, there was no response or indicators of life on the other side.

Noah tensed at the sound of turning locks and clanking chains. The first time they'd visited, Luna answered the door, and he expected to see the familiar blue-skinned and gill-covered merwoman again.

His heart dropped at the sight of a short man with a thick,

bushy mustache. The man was balding, and what little was left of his thin, gray hair was parted to the side. A bright grin grew on Celeste's features and she jumped into his arms while exclaiming proudly, "Dad!"

Oh no.

Noah was running on two hours of sleep and he hadn't showered in days, his scent that of dried saltwater and sweat. He wasn't ready to meet her father.

2

MEET THE FATHER

CELESTE AND HER FATHER WERE STILL HUGGING, LEAVING NOAH, Mark, and Katalina to watch on the sidelines. Pevelyn and Luna were nowhere in sight. While they weren't his favorite people—*mer*people—to be around, he'd rather see someone he was familiar with than not. So much for a moment of comfort.

"I can't believe you're in town! Thank the Goddess! I have so much to tell you." Her voice was a rare octave higher, and she spoke quickly with oozing enthusiasm. Noah supposed he should've felt similar. After all, he was meeting the father of the woman he wanted to spend the rest of his life with. Why, then, was it a feeling so far out of reach it wasn't even within eyesight?

His nerves were coiling around him, but as he watched Celeste tell her father the tales of their adventures, her palpable passion sent a wave of calmness through him. The fire in his heart was nearly reignited by her sheer determination—until the fatigue kicked in a second later.

Celeste and her father went on and on, ignoring the blanket of silence surrounding them. Finally, Mark turned his boredom to Noah with a whisper, "Excited to see Luna again?"

Noah rolled his eyes, a light heat rushing to his cheeks as a rosy hue took over his pale skin. Luna made her intentions incredibly clear the first time around; she wanted what Celeste had. Which was, in this case, Noah. It may have been flattering if not for the unreciprocated pining, and the subsequent torturous discomfort it created.

Before parting ways, Luna gifted him with her number and a suggestive wink. He hadn't thought of her since, and her gift had been physically and mentally forgotten during their adventures. But Celeste undoubtably remembered, and he didn't want her to be reminded.

"Really, Mark?" Katalina hissed under her breath. "I thought we all made peace before sailing back."

Though he was fairly certain Luna only developed feelings purely out of jealousy, it was still jarring to think another woman would find interest in him. On Sundar, no one paid him much mind. He liked the solitude to the point he wondered if perhaps his destiny was to live alone forever with his white and orange cat, Henry.

Mark shrugged lazily. "Making peace involves making jokes about each other."

"She was nice," Noah opted to say. He hardly knew Luna, but she'd helped them with their endeavors in the end, despite not fully believing in their cause.

Peering over at Celeste, he wondered if she heard their conversation. Noah could only hope she hadn't. He didn't want to cause unwarranted jealousy.

Celeste and her father finally seemed to remember there were other people in the room. The short man stuck out a hand, his upper lip hidden by his thick mustache. "Sir Rigulas Relanda. As I understand, you've met my wife and step-daughter while I was away on business?"

Noah expected someone else to respond before realizing he was the one being asked. He stuck out a trembling hand and nodded with a close-lipped smile, desperately hoping her father didn't notice his apprehension. First impressions were everything. "Yes, Pevelyn was very kind and hospitable."

His voice was a wavering mess. This was going terribly. He wished he could avoid all eye contact, crawl up the stairs, and hide in one of their spare bedrooms for the rest of their stay. Yes, that sounded nice.

"Ah, she is a much better host than I," exclaimed Celeste's father. "Sorry for keeping the three of you waiting. Please, come this way."

He waved them through the main hallway into a cozy living room. It looked as it had the first time they visited, with two black couches covered in colorful quilts and a canvas hanging above a fireplace. The canvas had a single red and blue dot on each end, slowly moving toward each other.

Noah recalled what Luna told them the first time around—when their parents were spending an intimate moment alone, the colors swirled and merged in the center. A synchronized dance of pleasure. Now the dots rested on their respective sides, calm and distant.

Noah plopped on the couch facing the canvas. Katalina and Mark sat on either side of him while Celeste stared out the sliding glass doors leading to their backyard, arms crossed over her chest. She appeared lost in thought, oblivious to her father gesturing for her to come sit beside him on the adjacent couch.

"Darlings!" came a voice as a tall, azure woman entered the scene. One by one, Noah and the others stood back up, garnering tight hugs from Pevelyn. Her smile was wide and toothy, and a navy blue wig was situated atop her head. A red dress hugged her curves, and her face was splashed with bold blue makeup. "It's so good to see the three of you again!"

"Going out?" Celeste asked, returning the hug with a gentle sway.

Pevelyn beamed. "We were invited to an exclusive dinner, which means we can't visit for long. Luna's staying behind, though. She should be around here somewhere."

Pevelyn joined her husband on the couch. "Now, what brings you back so soon?"

"It's been two weeks. I wouldn't call that soon," said Celeste's father. "In fact, we need to discuss your comings and goings. You do not communicate where you're going or when you're coming back. It's rather frustrating."

"And, importantly, frightening. Young women shouldn't be prancing around without protection," added Pevelyn, a slight frown finding its way onto her lips. Sir Rigulas was a few inches shorter than Noah, but next to his merwife, he looked incredibly short. Their pairing sparked questions in Noah's mind.

Celeste gestured toward Noah, Katalina, and Mark. "It's not like I was alone. Pevelyn knew I had friends with me. And look? We all made it back uninjured."

"Yes, *this* time. Have you learned nothing after what happened to Altair?"

Her smile wavered. "Of course, I learned. That's what I've been doing, actually. Following in his footsteps to finish what he started."

"You haven't learned a thing if you're still pursuing that pipedream," said Sir Rigulas. His voice rose to a shout, and Noah shrunk away, sinking into the couch. "What were those statistics he rattled off again? Twenty-five percent of our planet would be destroyed, if not completely like the other. Such nonsense."

Meeting anyone's family was unpleasant, but this was beyond anything Noah had ever experienced. Yelling was not commonplace while growing up, and it created a deep unease within him. He'd take his mother's discreet jabs any day over this.

Noah raised his hand tentatively. "Um, sir, may I?"

The man stared at him, his pinkish purple, but mostly blue, galaxy-speckled gaze searing holes into Noah's sockets. While Celeste's eyes were more purple than pink or blue, they were still incredibly similar. Noah stuttered through his discomfort, "Y-You have Celeste's eyes. I just noticed."

"Is that what you were going to say, boy?"

"Oh, no—"

"Out with it then, child." Sir Rigulas boomed. Noah gradually sank further into the couch with each syllable. If only he could disappear.

"Noah. Respectfully, you need to square up," whispered Mark. "Not slink back."

Noah shot him a glare before looking over at Celeste, her brows pinched together in hurt shock. Or was it disappointment? Neither was good. This was beyond any socially awkward situations he encountered throughout university or at his prior jobs.

"Altair wasn't following a pipedream and Celeste isn't, either. You should believe in your children, sir. Even Luna helped us when we visited last."

Sir Rigulas stared at him for a moment longer before turning sharply back to Celeste. "So, this is the newest boy?"

"It would appear so," Pevelyn answered for her step-daughter. "I had the boys share a room last time, just in case."

"What'd I help with?" Luna asked, her presence sending a wave of thankfulness through Noah. Finally, the topic could change, and the attention could be on someone else. The phrase 'newest boy' was hard to shake, and he couldn't look at Celeste in fear of her reaction. He didn't want to hear about anything in the past. To think he was worried about *her* being jealous.

What if he stayed on Fortun to be with her, a planet that was not his own, only to be discarded when she grew bored? He tried to erase the questions lurking in the back of his mind, but he couldn't. Not quite.

"My darling! I haven't seen you much today. What have you been up to?" asked Pevelyn, clipping on fake diamond earrings.

"Knitting a new sweater," Luna explained, holding up a bundle of fabric. Pevelyn clapped gleefully and abruptly rushed over to examine the yarn. "For your next sweater night with the girls. I came down to take your measurements before you left."

Luna scanned the room, landing first on Celeste and ending on Noah, their eyes holding for a beat too long. Her full lips were a slightly darker blue than her scaly, cerulean skin. While her mother wore a wig, Luna opted to remain bald, and she wore the look well.

Her outfit was also a stark contrast to her mother's, whose dress was bright and tight, whereas Luna's sweater was baggy and deep green with the head of a brown bear stitched in the front. Her blue eyes widened as she seemed to piece together who they were. "What are you guys doing here?"

Sir Rigulas waved Luna's words away. "Measure your mother first. We must leave in a matter of minutes, and then you kids can catch up."

Luna's gaze drifted to the ground. "Yes, sir."

"Now tell me," Sir Rigulas began while rubbing his hands together. "How did the two of you meet?"

Noah's mouth sputtered. He couldn't speak the truth—they'd met at his mother's gravesite on a different planet. Gravesites didn't exist on Fortun and, for whatever reason, Celeste was keeping her father in the dark regarding her visit to Sundar. He guessed it was because of the man's obvious disapproval of following Altair's research.

Could he be blamed for such apprehension when his son was murdered?

Noah hesitantly shuffled through all the things he could say before uttering, "Through a life-threatening situation."

"Oh?" Sir Rigulas asked curiously. "Did you do something that was against our planet's accords?"

Noah shook his head. "No, no. Nothing like that. It's not worth explaining, though it is still ongoing, unfortunately... but I think it'll all work out in the end. The important part is that I promise to keep Celeste safe."

"That was too ominous to exclude an explanation," said Sir Rigulas. "I can't let you run off with my daughter if you're leading her into danger."

"Yeah, that was a little too much," agreed Mark.

Katalina lightly tapped Mark's chest with a clenched fist. "Don't add fuel to the fire!"

"That's what friends do," he said with a laugh, wrapping an arm around Katalina and pulling her into a side hug. Noah was inclined to disagree.

"Alright, it's time to go, darling," said Pevelyn, kissing Luna on the cheek before rushing toward the door with her head held high, her heels clanking with confidence against the hardwood floors.

"Have a good night, you two," Celeste called quickly. "I'll miss you both!"

Her father narrowed his eyes as he stood. "Don't think this conversation ends here, Celestial. We're discussing this boat stealing and danger nonsense first thing tomorrow. You've overstepped your privileges. You can no longer go *anywhere* without telling us first."

Celeste saluted with a dutiful, stern expression. "Yes, sir! See you tomorrow!"

They hugged one last time, and then Sir Rigulas turned to leave. A hush fell over the room as they collectively waited for the click of the front door. Noah watched Celeste, a single tear falling down her cheek as she stared down the hallway toward the closed door.

"Celeste?" he asked. Her red and puffy eyes snapped to meet his. "Are you okay?"

She nodded, wiping away the few tears daring to fall. "If we mess up, that'll be the last interaction I ever have with either of them."

He walked up to her and wrapped her in a hug. Katalina and Mark slowly stood, joining in on the quiet moment of comfort. Celeste did not shed another tear, and he hoped their love was enough to bring her peace, if only for a few minutes.

"What's going on here, exactly?" Luna's voice interjected the somber scene. The trio pulled away from Celeste. She wiped her eyes again before her lips quirked upward.

"At least we're finally alone so we can *talk*." Celeste pointed at Luna and declared, "You're coming with us."

3

WHAT WOULD I DO?

"I don't know if I have any skills to add," Luna said tentatively, glancing between Noah and Celeste. Mark and Katalina remained on the couch snuggled together, watching the interaction soundlessly.

"You have those breathing bubbles," Celeste suggested. "We'll have to see the Ruler of the Deep again."

Luna snorted. "And I'm guessing you used the ones I gave you perfectly fine without me."

Well, she wasn't wrong.

"To be fair, we don't add many skills, either," Mark stated while nodding between the rest of them. This was also true, as much as Noah hated to admit it. He was surprised they made it this far with how many creatures and obstacles they'd run into. He couldn't possibly imagine what was coming next.

"True, but I'm still not fully convinced there's anything we need to be saving Fortun from," Luna countered.

Celeste gestured toward the patio doors, though it was broad daylight and nothing unusual was happening outside. "You haven't noticed all the stars have disappeared? Or wondered why the shapeshifters attacked us?"

Luna cocked her head. "I assumed it was a mistake. We've been safe ever since, and we've had an overcast the last few days. The stars are just behind some clouds."

"It hasn't been in the news at all? No one's said anything?" Luna shook her head with crinkled brows as Celeste paced. "Something's not right here."

Katalina stood abruptly with hands on her hips and a *hmph* for emphasis. "Things aren't adding up."

"There's something amiss." Noah tossed up a finger with a proud grin. His comment garnered no response, and when he looked around, he was greeted with four blank stares. He shrugged. "I thought we were repeating clichéd phrases."

Mark shook his head in disapproval. "Ever the comic."

"Ever the buzzkill."

"Maybe you *do* need me," Luna remarked, sizing Mark and Noah up. Noah couldn't help the blush overtaking his cheeks at the way she took him in. Finally, her gaze drifted back to her stepsister. "How'd you find the Ruler of the Deep with this group?"

"Rude," Mark and Noah said in unison.

"*Anyway,*" Celeste continued. He wondered if she got her forwardness from her brother, and it saddened him then that he would never know. Much like she would never know his late mother or the friends that came and went in his life. She would never even know his beloved cat.

He ran a self-conscious hand through his hair. Now was not the time to think. Was there ever a time?

Noah was so lost in thought he missed what she said completely. He'd been so preoccupied by the movement of her lips that her voice wafted away. Only when she stopped talking did the world come back into focus.

"—I can only think of the Ruler of the Sky." It was Luna, her bubbly voice a fountain of spurts that took a few seconds for his brain to register and decipher. "But that doesn't make sense, does it? Why would she want to do such a thing?"

A sharp, sudden gasp came from Katalina as she covered her mouth. Mark rushed to her side as though she'd been struck by a sword and desperately needed his aid. "She doesn't want the stars to be found."

"Well, that much was obvious," Noah stated bluntly. "The question is why?"

"Don't you find it odd the Ruler of the Deep told us about the stars, and then they disappeared immediately after? How would she know we were coming for them?"

The Ruler of the Deep was the last lead they had in Altair's research notebook. His research was right so far, but ended abruptly. The sea serpent filled in the missing gaps, telling them of a star that could close the black hole, thus stopping the planets from colliding.

However, the ruler was not without ulterior motives. He requested another star be brought back to him as a gift. The blue star. They didn't know what it did or what he wanted it for, but it hardly mattered when everyone's lives were hanging in the balance.

"The rulers are talking," Celeste said. "Which means we can't trust any of them. None of them cared enough about saving the planets to do anything about it. I doubt they'll start caring now."

"They'll try to stop us," Katalina agreed. "They already are. Otherwise, why would the Ruler of the Sky move the stars?"

Celeste turned to Luna. He could see the wheels turning in her mind. "You're still friends with the Sky Prince, right?"

Luna's light blue cheeks darkened. "W-we may know each other, but I wouldn't call him my friend."

Celeste cocked a brow with a sly smile. "Right. I wouldn't call him your friend, either."

"Celestial, no." Luna wagged a finger at her stepsister, a look of understanding washing over her. "I know you. You're conjuring a plan. A stupid plan. Oh, yeah. I bet you want me to seduce the Sky Prince and learn why the rulers are so set on the planet's supposed destruction. Except we'd have to be in enemy territory to even do it! They don't let just anyone into the Sky Kingdom anymore. You always have the worst plans, and you know what? I'm not doing it!"

"Come on. We need your help."

"No offense, but do we? We did everything without her so far," Mark chimed in. Celeste shot him a dirty glare, her fingers curling.

Luna smirked. "While I enjoy seeing someone rile Celeste up, and I'd normally say yes just to get on her nerves, I can't. I have duties to tend to here."

"What, making sweaters for a season we get once every ten years?" Luna's silence was answer enough. Celeste sighed. "You can knit on the boat. I'm sure we'll be on a boat again at some point. At night there'll be time, too."

"You don't need m—"

"We do. Ideally, we'll avoid the rest of the rulers, but if we run into the Sky Prince, we'll need you to get answers. He trusts you." Celeste didn't mention bringing Luna on their journey until the day they arrived back on land. Her sudden urgency confused him, and he clearly wasn't the only one. There was an underlying reason he couldn't place, and Celeste wasn't giving anything away.

Luna looked down at her hands, wringing a corner of her sweater slowly. "What if he doesn't, and I embarrass myself?"

Noah's eyebrows rose at that. Before anyone could get a word in edge-wise, he said, "You could never. I mean—"

He cut himself off; this wasn't something he should be saying. There was a line, and he was overstepping. Yet, he felt she needed to hear it from someone other than her family. A borderline stranger like himself was even better. "You're a kind person, and kind people shine through in times of great stress. Trust me, you'll do great. If Celeste says you need to come with us, then that's what you need to do."

Luna stared at him, her cheeks darkening further. Noah took a few tentative steps back, bumping shoulders with Mark.

"Now, don't get the wrong idea here, or anything," Noah added quickly, shaking his hands between them. "I mean, I like you and all, as a friend, but uh—"

His eyes flickered to Celeste; she was watching his every move intensely, though her expression was unreadable. Noah jumped at Mark's hand on his shoulder. "Quit while you're behind, friend."

Celeste inspected Noah as though she were seeing him again for the first time. "The Ruler of the Deep was reluctant to help, but did so, anyway. Maybe there was a pact made between the four rulers to refrain from intervening."

"What about the Ruler of the Soil?" asked Noah. "He gave us those tents and other equipment. That's technically intervening. Wouldn't he help us again if we asked?"

She shook her head. "He helped the first time because he was returning a favor. I don't know him all too well. I don't think anyone does, and he's permanently trapped underground."

"Oh, wow. That's so... sad." Noah wasn't sure what else to say. Celeste was still examining him. He must've said something to upset her, and he could guess what.

"Talk about lonely," grumbled Mark. "Noah wouldn't last two seconds down there."

"And you would?" Noah asked, recounting the years he lived alone both before and after his mother passed. For the most part, he enjoyed it. Though there were moments of tremendous loneliness and wondering if he could make it through the night, he found comfort in having time to himself.

"He has the bugs, worms, and animals that burrow underground, so he's not completely alone," corrected Luna, ending the verbal sparring match between Noah and Mark before it could devolve any further.

"I didn't know that," Celeste exclaimed excitedly. "That *is* sad. But, see? This is why we need you to come with us! You know things the rest of us don't!"

"I wouldn't call that useful information," Luna said with crossed arms.

Celeste's shoulders slumped. "Come on. That's not the point! The world is ending, Luna! Two of them! Don't you want to save them?"

Noah watched in awe, surprised by Celeste's pleas. She was nearly getting down on her knees and begging for Luna to help. He didn't understand Celeste's desperation, though he admired her persistence. They'd done just fine without Luna, and oftentimes, she came across as rude. Did they *really* need another version of Mark tagging along?

"I have been alive five hundred years. Hysteria over the end of the world has come and gone time and time again, and yet the planet always remains. I've watched friends build bunkers and spaceships. I've heard how some of them left, only to never return. All in the name of fear."

Celeste grabbed her stepsister by the shoulders and pulled her closer. She stopped only when their noses were nearly touching. Luna was considerably taller, forcing Celeste to stand on her tiptoes. "This isn't one of those times."

"That's what they all said, Celeste! If the stars were truly moved, then the Ruler of the Sky *must* have a good reason. The Ruler of the Deep could use those stars to *end* the world for all we know."

"Then come with us to find out!" Celeste threw her hands up in exasperation, anger and worry lining the creases of her forehead. She tucked a strand of hair behind her ear as she went back to pacing.

"Now, wait. Back up a second," Katalina interjected. She'd

been awfully quiet for the past few minutes, soaking in the unraveling information. "You think the Ruler of the Deep told the other three rulers about our plans, and the Ruler of the Sky immediately moved the stars to stop us from saving everyone? Why would he do that, knowing the others would act against him?"

Celeste nodded. "That's the gist, yeah. I don't have a clue why, and the facts sound even worse out loud. We have the most powerful ruler in our way!"

"So, you don't think the Ruler of the Soil is involved. What about the Ruler of the Wind? Do you think they conspired to move the stars together or is the Ruler of the Sky working alone?"

"I hadn't thought of that," Mark said, rubbing his chin and staring at Katalina with admiration. "You're truly the smartest person I know."

Noah wasn't one to disclose it, but he was also impressed, because he couldn't think fast enough to reach the same conclusion.

"I have no idea," Celeste confessed. "I haven't heard of any recent hijinks pulled by the Ruler of the Wind. He's been off the grid for months now. Have you heard anything, Luna?"

Luna shook her head. "This is absurd."

Noah held his breath to calm himself. He was running out of patience, but he would try to convince Luna to come along if it made Celeste happy. "Think of it this way. At worst, we're wrong, and you go on an adventure with your stepsister. At best, you help us save two planets and explore Fortun with us."

"There's a reason merpeople rarely leave the city borders,"

Luna said with a tsk. “Unless we’re going right back to the ocean, I’m not interested in being fish food out in the wild.”

Noah shrugged. “Well, I tried.”

Luna’s pinched face softened slightly, as though his dismissal was enough to change her mind. “Well... I... if you all truly believe this insanity, then I suppose there is no harm in me tagging along.”

“So you’ll say yes because a cute boy asks you to, but not your stepsister?” Celeste scoffed, and turned away, pausing at the patio doors. The sun beat down on her face, creating a golden glow, begging him to come closer. There was something sharp in her gaze, a hint of distress for reasons he couldn’t discern.

A squabbling, loving familial relationship was not within his expertise, and watching it unfold now only created a pit of disappointment within. How he longed to have a sibling to share experiences with. But he was an only child, and now he was parentless, too.

He tried not to dwell on such a thought, instead making a mental note to ask Celeste about her undoubtably fascinating childhood. One day, he would unravel her story like the yarn Luna used to knit.

“You said he and the other two are from another planet, right? I must say, their faces are slightly more angular than ours, are they not? They could very well be similar-looking extraterrestrials.”

“Altair and I have been warning you since day one, but you didn’t listen to either of us. I see.” Celeste’s eyes were blazing with fresh tears, her lips curling in disgust as she continued to stare outside. "Don't come, then."

"Now, now. Let's not say anything we regret," Katalina urged. She stepped between the stepsisters with her hands out to separate them. Noah could do nothing but watch as his cousin maintained perfect composure.

Katalina held her head high while she explained. "Mark has one older and two younger brothers. You won't believe the amount of damage control I have to do at every family gathering."

"My brothers are crazy," Mark agreed with hands on his hips. "Though we wrestle way more than yell at each other."

"Ha," said Luna dryly. "I'd like to see Celeste try to wrestle me."

"Excuse me?" Celeste snapped. "This is no time to joke! Do you have an ounce of self-awareness at all? You're saying yes to a boy over your own family! Altair would be ashamed."

"That's enough. Let's get some sleep so we can be out first thing in the morning." Mark turned to Luna, his voice stern. He was oddly calm for once. "Luna, if you don't want to come, then don't. If you do, be ready come morning. We're leaving before your father can catch us. He was kind of scary."

With that, Mark headed toward the stairs with Katalina in tow. Noah watched, dumbfounded at Mark's hardened expression. "I'll be taking the room we stayed in last time. See you there."

The pair disappeared upstairs. Noah turned to Celeste. "You're incredibly strong, and I hope Luna says yes *for you*. You deserve it."

Luna and Celeste stared at him, mouths agape. He brushed past them to meet Mark in their room, giving Celeste a small nod as he passed. He saw the corner of her lips curve upward.

Good. He was semi-certain he said the right thing, and Celeste appeared appeased. Everything was ready to be put into motion tomorrow.

Though he wanted Celeste to be happy, in truth, he wasn't fond of Luna tagging along. Oh, well. He'd just have to learn how to tolerate her with a smile on his face.

4

FOLLOW ME

Noah and Mark awoke so early that the next morning had yet to begin, the moon shining high above a sky devoid of clouds or stars. Celeste and Katalina slunk through the patio doors slowly and silently, meeting the men outside. The fenced-in backyard was lush with greenery and there was a long tea table in the center.

The table brought back chilling memories of when Pevelyn and Celeste were knocked unconscious and replaced by shapeshifters. There was no telling if the same thing was happening again unless Luna sniffed it out—but Luna wasn't there.

"So, the plan," Noah started, forcing himself out of his dangerous thoughts. "We should probably have one?"

Celeste smiled softly, though a hint of dismay lingered in her eyes. They were leaving shortly, yet Luna was nowhere to be found. "Naturally. I've been thinking about what we should do every day and night. Remember the island we landed on after meeting with the Ruler of the Deep?"

"How could we forget?" Katalina asked with a grimace. "The rain gave me hiccups for two days straight!"

Noah missed the island. It was a place where everything was okay. Where the waves were calm, the breeze was fair, and there was a cave full of crystals and wonder.

"We'll have to find that side of my planet again," Celeste said. "Luckily, we won't need a boat to reach the stars above the hill. Though we'll need one eventually to find our way back to the Ruler of the Deep."

"I can get you a boat," a bubbly voice said from behind. They all turned to find Luna leaning against the open patio door. Her arms were folded over her chest, her sweater replaced with a knitted crop top and tight pants, both black. "I bought one a few years ago."

Celeste's jaw dropped. "What? A few *years,* and you kept it a secret all this time?"

"Hey, I have every right not to trust your steering ability after—"

Celeste held up a hand. "On second thought, let's not talk about this right now... or ever."

Luna laughed, dropping the subject and leaving Noah to wonder what incident could've occurred for Luna to lie to Celeste for years. She snapped her fingers, gesturing to the pack slung around Celeste's shoulder, of which Celeste was pulling out her brother's research notebook. "I just remembered we *all* need endless bags on us. For my knitting, and food and water, of course. I think I have a few Altair left behind. He always knew how to find the rare stuff."

Luna ducked back into the house as Celeste took a deep, content breath. Whatever animosity there was between the stepsisters was gone—at least for now. For this, he was grateful. "The perks of having a five-hundred-year-old stepsister. She knows the supplies we need without me saying a word."

"You mean we're going to get a bag like yours?" Katalina asked. Celeste's pack could not only hold unlimited supplies, but could also disappear and reappear depending on the straps' placement. "I can't wait to test it out! I wonder if it's truly endless. Could I fit my arm, for example, or my whole body?"

Katalina's giddiness was seeping into Noah as Celeste smirked. "You'll get to experiment soon enough. It'll be fun to see you mess around with it. Though you must be careful, or else you could get lost inside."

"As riveting as this is," Mark interrupted. "What's the rest of our plan?"

Celeste nodded dutifully. "Right. Well, there's a one in nine chance we end up on the correct side right away."

"So traveling to each side is based on luck?" Mark asked with slumped shoulders.

"More like chance," corrected Celeste.

"Those are some pretty slim odds." Luna walked back outside with four packs of varying colors. Noah quickly grabbed the dusty orange one, while Katalina went for green, and Mark picked pink. Luna raised an eyebrow at the option they left her. "Really? Blue?"

Noah held his pack up. "Sorry—I picked this one because

orange reminds me of my cat, and it's the color of our sky back on Sundar, but you can have it."

Luna blushed, waving the offer away. "No, no. That's okay, but that's awfully sweet of you to ask—"

"Don't worry," Celeste said, running a finger along the tea table. There was clearly more on her mind, but all she said was, "We'll head east. East will always take you where you need to go."

"That doesn't sound right," Katalina mumbled.

"We should eventually hit a hedge maze," Celeste continued. "Once we find our way through, we'll be on another side of the planet. It's one of the few ways to know you've made it to another side."

Luna peered up at the sunlight chipping away at the darkness. "We should get going. Mom and Dad will start waking up soon."

"How many days do we have left?" asked Noah, finding his way to Celeste. She was leaning against the table, her wavy blueish black hair hiding her eyes, though her fingers were turning white against the linen.

"A few weeks, if we're lucky. I'm going to miss home, Noah," Celeste whispered. "I'm scared we won't be able to do it. It's taking longer than I thought it would, and two months is almost up—"

"Hey. You can't give up now. We're so close. It's like you said. We'll go east. We'll find the stars and bring them to the Ruler of the Deep. Then you can come home."

"It won't be the same," she countered. "My family will brand me a fool. The planets won't collide, and I'll just be another hysteric doomsayer."

"You are so much more than what your family sees you as. You're so much more than what you see, too. We're in this together, and if they want to call us crazy at the end, then we'll be crazy."

Celeste peered up at him, her small smile returning. She mouthed the words *thank you* before turning to the others with a clap. "Let's get moving. We'll go east until our legs are too heavy. We have to stay sharp in the wilderness. Who knows what we'll encounter next?"

5

AS THEY TRAVEL

The tavern they stumbled upon had outdoor seating, with individual white tents holding a few readily available tables. They were out in the middle of nowhere, yet the place was crawling with patrons. Chatter was heard but hushed, the tents providing privacy from sight and sound, and there was a crisp scent of mint and charred chocolate lingering in the air.

They'd walked until day turned to night, the tavern a bright beacon against a black, starless sky. They had no choice but to stop, the fields ahead hidden behind utter darkness.

"Why do I feel like we're here for dessert and not dinner?" Mark's voice was lined with fatigue, his eyes accented with black bags underneath.

Their trek, though uneventful, proved to be taxing. Hours upon hours of movement through fields of teal grass and a pinkish purple sky, with only the briefest of breaks to relieve themselves along the way. Thankfully, a perfect warmth accompanied their journey with just the right amount of wind to keep them cool. This planet was truly better than his own.

"Dessert is di—" Luna began, but Mark held up a hand to cut her off.

"I know." Mark yawned. "I can't wait to go back home and eat savory foods again."

Katalina nodded solemnly. "I can't go another day without mashed potatoes or pasta. Please. Is there anywhere else?"

"The smell is quite nauseating," Noah agreed, the mint so strong he felt it in his teeth, and his nose burned from the fresh stench of burning chocolate.

"You'll get used to it," encouraged Celeste with a sympathetic smile. "They have the *best* chocolate-filled bread here. You can get other flavors, too! My favorite is strawberry mint rose!"

Noah found her gaze and held it for as long as he could. "Do they have a flavor similar to the ice cream back in Mermain City?"

"They do! I'm happy you found something here you love."

"All I've found here are things I love." His eyes widened as he processed the words tumbling from his mouth, a red hue staining his cheeks. "Except the derithia. That thing was *scary*."

"Celeste," Luna interrupted. "How do we order, again? I can't remember. Isn't this one of those weird places?"

"How do you forget how to order?" asked Noah, his voice low so Luna couldn't hear lest she be insulted.

Celeste released a chuckle. "Luna hasn't left the city in years, so she needs help with these things. It's a little different out here. It's simple, though. All we do is wait for a server to seat us, and then we order at the table."

He nodded along while taking in their surroundings, realizing this was the only structure for miles. They'd probably have to camp somewhere tonight. Hopefully, things remained how they were, and their lives stayed out of danger for another night.

The smell of this place *was* nauseating, though. He couldn't get past it. The source of such bittersweet scents appeared to be a fire pit full of charcoal long enough to fit five cooks, with heavy black smoke billowing into the sky.

Each cook flipped over chocolaty-filled buns, pressing them down on a grill grate to create a sizzle before serving them on long, rectangular plates. Servers picked up the prepared buns, drifting off to the various tents with trays perfectly balanced on their fingertips.

A server rushed over, her loose ponytail slowly coming undone and releasing long brown hair into her lashes. She swiftly brushed the strands away with a flustered pink hue along her tan cheeks. "Table or bar?"

Mark raised his hand. "Ba—"

"A tent, please," Celeste cut him off with a shake of her head. "There's barely any room up there!"

"You're in luck—we have one more tent open for the evening!" They followed the server past a row of tents. While passing the firepit, Noah noticed the bar had a single line of seats with more than half already occupied. There were tall shelves behind the counter, with at least a dozen kegs of ale and wine bottles.

Mark slapped Noah on the back. "I'm very intrigued by what alcohol could taste like here. Do you drink?"

Noah gulped as they entered the tent, noting Celeste was quick to order a red wine. While he wanted to say yes, he shook his head. "There's no need for me. I don't find it particularly enjoyable."

His thoughts grew dark when he drank.

They also grew engaged. Entertained. He would likely either find a reason to laugh at everything or pass out after too many glasses. Or a mix of both. A single sip would lead to a future he saw clearly: he wouldn't stop once he started, and then it would eventually lead to taking some with them on their travels. He'd spiral and start pretending to be sober out of embarrassment while chugging the bottle when everyone's backs were turned.

He couldn't spiral, and he couldn't lie to Celeste. He wouldn't let himself.

"Sounds like something you'd say," Mark said. The hostess rushed over rather quickly with their beverages and a plate of grilled buns. Everyone ordered alcohol except Noah... and Luna.

He met her gaze with his mouth hanging open in surprise. "You don't...?"

"It hurts my stomach. My body is used to seawater and tolerates some juices. That's all I can drink. What about you?"

"Oh, I just don't like how it makes me feel." Every bone in his body wanted to try a glass of Fortun wine.

"I don't normally, but when on another planet, might as well," added Katalina, taking a sip of a cloudy pastel pink concoction with a large ice cube resting in the center. She licked her lips with a smile of satisfaction. "Could be our last."

"Finally, they cooled down enough to eat." Mark rubbed his stomach, taking a long sip of his drink before stuffing one of the warm chocolate-filled pastries into his mouth. He moaned. "While I miss steak and mash *so much,* this is delicious."

Celeste placed her elbows on the table and plopped her chin in her hands. "Please try one, Noah! I want to see your face as the flavors explode in your mouth."

He took one in his hands; the toasted pastry felt like a cozy hug against his palms. He placed it on his tongue, and it melted, sending his tastebuds aglow with a joy he hadn't felt since he was a child. It took him back to a nostalgic, chilly night snuggled up in front of a fireplace with his mother as she read him a picture book, and used zany voices for each character.

His youngest memories tended to be the happiest; he did not sense her sadness then. How agonizing it was to know his middle years were filled with pockets of substanceless drivel, and he would never get that time back.

When he opened his eyes, Celeste was watching him. "I told you."

"Now, we should probably get down to business," Luna said, her face growing serious. "Does this place give you any insight into which side of the planet we're on?"

"The same side we've been on. We'll have to ask the barkeep which way the hedge maze is." Celeste's voice was muffled by the gooey chocolate. "Best to eat and use the bathroom while we're here. Have a good time while we can. It may be our last safe stop for a while."

"Cheers to that," Mark said with his glass raised.

It didn't take Mark long to get buzzed. Noah left to use the bathroom stall around the corner, and when he returned, Mark's cheeks were flushed and his overzealous smile was radiant.

"Noah," Mark exclaimed at the sight of his return, tossing an arm around Noah's neck with another drink in hand. "My man! Have you tried this ale yet? It's—it's the *best*."

His voice echoed through the field as he tilted his head back with a hearty laugh about nothing. Noah imagined every patron within earshot turned to stare, and he was thankful they were hidden away in their tent. "Katalina, I must order this man some ale!"

She winced with a shake of her head at the loudness of his bold decree. "He doesn't drink. Remember, honey?"

"O-ight," Mark continued to mutter, but his words were so slurred that Noah couldn't decipher what he was trying to say.

"How many has he had?" Noah asked, watching Mark drift out of the tent with his head on a swivel. Noah and the rest of their group followed.

"Two cups and a jug," Katalina said meekly. "I thought he could handle it, but… I think it might be stronger here than on Sundar."

The cup in Mark's hand was easily big enough for two glasses. He was undoubtably feeling the effects of the ale. As if to prove this theory correct, Mark smiled smugly. "Tow *and a half* cups."

"Two, darling," said Katalina with a sympathetic pat on his back.

"What'd I say?"

"Tow."

Mark guffawed. His zeal was rare, but welcome, albeit excessive. Noah eyed him up, trying to determine if he should be the voice of reason. He was surprised Mark allowed himself to get this drunk—they should've been trying to stay at their peak health for the journey ahead. There was no telling when danger would strike next. Not only that, but Noah was growing more embarrassed by the second. "I think we need to cut you off."

"Where's the juke?" yelled Mark, bursting from their circle in search of one. "Time for some music!"

Celeste's brows crinkled in confusion. "'Juke?' What's that?"

Noah watched as Mark ducked into a random tent, which was followed by a chorus of shouts. Mark stumbled out backwards a moment later with his hands up in defense. There was no saving this man from himself, was there?

"A music player," Noah explained. "I have one at home. Or had, I guess. We have singers who mostly use acoustic guitars, drums, and pianos, but they re-record their songs for every jukebox made."

Celeste cocked her head, her gaze distant, as though she were deep in thought. "I can't picture what a music machine would look like. We don't have anything like that here. Just bands and solo singers."

Noah traced the rectangular shape of the juke in the air. "It's a bulky machine that sifts through songs using a foot pedal to switch between them. They're everywhere back home, actually. Public spaces like bars, restaurants, stores, even the library."

"Where's the juke?" Mark's yelling was beginning to cause a scene. Well, an even bigger scene, if that were possible.

Katalina cupped her hands over her mouth. "They don't exist here! Wait for the band!" She thrust a flyer Noah hadn't seen wildly in Mark's direction. "There's a band in ten minutes!"

Mark came back, and Noah quickly ushered him inside the tent, forcing him to remain in their enclosure until the band started. "I don't need to wait for some random singer!"

Mark climbed onto the table, belting a popular classic from Sundar and dancing to his own voice, though his moves were too erratic to be classified as dancing. Writhing, perhaps, was the better term for it, but joyful writhing.

Mark paused, reaching down for Katalina's hand. She blushed as she took it. "Sorry, guys."

Katalina joined him on the table, lightly singing along, though incredibly off-key. Noah watched them from his seat with a fond grin. Luna yawned in the corner, clearly unamused and ready for bed, though she did not make a fuss of it.

"It's nice to see you like this," Celeste said, leaning in with a whisper. "I like to see you happy. It's cute."

"Well, I would hope so." He gawked, taken aback by her sudden confession. He hadn't realized she was watching him. "Should we join them?"

"I don't think there's any room left on the table," she said, but her lips were curving upward at the edges.

He smirked, dimples forming. "We'll make room."

Noah stood, fully prepared to show that he could be fun

without ale coursing through his veins. He was more than his cravings.

Celeste opened her mouth, mere seconds from saying more, but then she clamped her jaw shut and offered a close-lipped smile instead. She stood to join him when the table shook, and Mark flailed to the ground. Katalina stopped dancing, hands covering her mouth as she shrieked, "Mark!"

Noah cackled at the sight. Mark was spread along the ground, a cheek pressed against the grass as he released a muffled moan. Noah moved around the table; his giggling subsided, and he flashed Celeste an apologetic shrug before squatting next to Mark. He checked for breathing, bruises, and broken bones, finding Mark was alive and unharmed, but very unconscious.

Katalina hopped down beside them. "Is he going to be okay?"

Noah threw Mark's arm over his shoulder with a grunt. "Should be. We'll have to cut the night short and find somewhere to rest now, though."

"Fun's over, huh?" Luna stood with a lackadaisical stretch, uncaring of Mark's state. "There's an inn a little way back."

"I don't remember passing one," Katalina challenged, her jolly demeanor evaporating into a stern glare. Her hands were shaking as she brushed Mark's black hair from his eyes. He was snoring, his features relaxed and peaceful. "You don't think he has a concussion, do you?"

"It's one of those inns that hides in plain sight," explained Luna. "And he'll be fine. His breathing patterns are stable."

"How do you know that—" Katalina began, but Celeste cut her off.

"Oh, good! I must've missed it. Let's go there. Those are the safest since they're so easy to miss!"

"Can somebody help me?" Noah pleaded. Mark's tall and muscular limp body was weighing him down.

Celeste jumped into action. "Of course—sorry about that!"

A sigh of relief escaped Noah as the pressure was released from his shoulders. Luna and Katalina led the way to the inn while Noah and Celeste trailed behind, with Mark between them. Noah caught Katalina glancing over her shoulder every few minutes to check that Mark was still okay. He found it odd she would walk ahead of her unconscious fiancé instead of with, but Noah wasn't about to question a moment alone with Celeste.

"Thank you," he said, breaking the silence. "For showing me this world and encouraging me to try all this new food. And for, well, everything."

"Of course," she said tentatively, dragging out her words in timid confusion. "But why bring this up now?"

Noah took a deep breath. Truthfully, there was a sinking feeling swirling in his gut, but he didn't want to alarm her, so he said, "I just thought you should know."

She chuckled. "Well, *I* should thank *you*."

"Me?"

"For coming with me, and for making the end of the world so fun. Mark and Katalina aren't such bad company, either." It was too dark to see, but he could've sworn she was blushing as she added, "Though I sometimes wonder how much more fun it would be if it were just the two of us."

"Or, as Mark would say, tow of us."

Celeste giggled. "I'm so lu—"

"Please flirt when I'm not in between you," grumbled Mark, his head slinging back and forth sluggishly. Noah jumped at the sound of his voice.

"Right," Celeste said through another flurry of giggles. "Sorry, Mark."

"I liked it better when you were unconscious," Noah grumbled. "Say, want to take one for the team and pretend?"

Her happiness made his heart flutter, her laugh a melody escaping her chest and filling his. When Celeste finally settled down, her eyes found Noah's, and her smile stole his breath away. "I'm so lucky."

6

Noah was never one to believe in luck. He didn't feel lucky when a bolt of lightning cracked against the roof of his apartment and sent rain down on everything he owned. He didn't feel lucky when he was fired from his first job for something a coworker did, and he certainly didn't feel lucky that his mother took her life.

Yet Celeste's wistful words echoed in his mind as he lay wide awake on an inn cot next to a snoring and drooling Mark. *I'm so lucky.*

He didn't think himself lucky at all, but if she were to consider their paths crossing as luck, then who was he to deny it? He couldn't fathom that someone out there could meet him, hear his voice and jokes and gloom every day, and still consider themselves *lucky.*

But Celeste did.

How could he explain to her it wasn't luck at all that pulled them together, but the bond of their souls?

How could he explain it was not luck he believed in, but fate?

What would she say if he told her every muscle beneath his skin, every thought uttered in the trenches of his mind from morning to night, always led back to her? He both knew the answer and feared it.

7

WINDING WAYS

"This is it." Celeste gestured toward a towering wall of beautiful green vines and leaves spanning left and right with no straightforward way around. There was an open archway leading in, speckled with tiny purple flowers. It looked to be the *only* way in. "The hedge maze."

Celeste bounced on the balls of her feet and shook her arms wildly. He looked her up and down. "Are you excited or scared?"

The lush hedge wasn't endlessly high, but looked close enough. He didn't spot a way to climb to the top, either, eliminating the option to see how far the maze stretched. Noah took a hesitant step through the archway to further examine their options. Inside, there were only two ways to go—left or right.

"Both."

"Both?" asked Katalina. "Is there something lurking in there we should be afraid of?"

"Honestly, no." Luna stepped up beside Katalina, stretching high as if measuring her height against the hedge. She was taller than all of them, yet the hedge made her look small. Luna tilted her head. "Animals rarely live here. That being said, you never know."

"Although," Celeste began, only to trail off. Noah's heart pounded at the implications of her hesitation. "There *is* a chance we wind up stuck in this maze for days, *but* we'll hope for better luck than that."

There she went, throwing around that word again. There was no *luck* pulling them toward the tavern or maze. In fact, it was all because of *her.*

Mark, who was already pale from his copious drinking the night prior, turned a stark white. "Nope. Don't think I can do it. Claustrophobic."

"The maze isn't harmful or full of harmful things," Celeste clarified. "I don't think so, anyway."

"You don't think?" Mark asked.

She ignored his question and continued, "On the bright side, the leaves can both heal and take away life force, depending on whether they deem you good or bad. Only hedge mazes have this ability."

"And they're technically going extinct now," Luna chimed in. "There's only two or three left in the world."

"But why?" asked Katalina. "Wouldn't you want to preserve the mazes? To keep them prosperous if nature created them, and with such a unique gift to cultivate?"

Celeste sighed. "Those who understand the power of the mazes want the leaves for themselves, so they harvest them until there's nothing left. The Goddess weeps her losses, I'm sure."

"Are we going to keep ignoring the part where you said the leaves can also 'take away life force?'" Noah asked with a hand half-raised. "Isn't that risky? If we're attacked and pushed into the leaves, we could, well... I don't know what happens when your entire life force is drained. Do you?"

"I understand all of your worries, but it'll be okay. The leaves are slow acting unless they're crushed up into a paste. So, even if one of us accidentally fell into the hedge somehow, we'd likely be fine."

"Likely?" Mark repeated, rubbing the back of his neck.

"Besides, there's no point in debating it." Celeste stepped forward with hands on her hips, and stood directly in front of the arch with her eyes trained ahead. The leaves shifted in the light breeze, creating an ominous rhythm. Noah couldn't look at the looming structure for long, a shiver running along his spine. "This is the only way we can go."

"Have you ever felt it?" Katalina blurted out, curiosity burning within her brown gaze. "Have you ever had your life force drained? Either of you?"

"Of course," Luna admitted a bit too quickly, her expression neutral. She didn't give specifics nor make eye contact.

Celeste nodded. "I've been here twice before. The first time, yes. I was twelve. Again, at twenty, I was healed."

"Oh?" The noise left his lips involuntarily, the surprise of her admission taking hold. He couldn't fathom an ounce of wickedness was inside her.

She shrugged. "It happens to most people. We can all grow

or devolve at any point. Regardless, merely touching the leaves shouldn't do any harm."

"What warranted the hedge taking your life force, though?" he asked, desperate to uncover every detail of her life. Noah wished he could pull out a notebook and write it all down. He didn't want a single word to fall through the cracks. "What'd you do that was so wrong?"

Celeste flashed him a mischievous grin. "You'll have to unlock that part of my story."

Noah smirked. "Do I, now?"

He took a step closer, their eyes never drifting from one another. "With pleasure."

"Alright," Mark said, stepping between them and holding out his arms. "Your flirting has officially become too bold as of late."

"Says the guy who made out with my cousin on the stairs of someone else's house," Noah accused.

"Yeah, *my* house," Celeste said with a thumb thrust toward her chest. "In front of *my* step-mom."

Luna glowered. "Oh, yeah. I forgot about that. Gross."

"Should we take some leaves in case one of us needs healing down the line?" Katalina asked; her words were rushed in a likely attempt to divert the discussion away from her and Mark's public displays of affection.

Celeste's brows shot up. "That's an excellent idea. We should all grab a handful."

Noah ran a finger over a clump of leaves as he plucked them, waiting for a rush of warmth or pain, but feeling an underwhelming amount of nothing instead. He debated crushing some up, curious about whether he would be deemed good or bad by a plant.

"I have a bad feeling about this maze," Luna said as they filed in. The leaves rustled faintly in response. The wind was picking up, creating a gentle howl. Noah used to enjoy the quiet, but it was too often eery on Fortun. Rubbing her forearms, Luna added, "It's so chilly."

While Noah's growing goosebumps may have been a cause of concern, they were not what was bothering him. Celeste was looking progressively more nervous each time he looked at her. "What are you thinking about?"

She jumped at the sound of his voice and shook her head vigorously. "Oh, it's nothing. I just hope we don't run into any more of the rulers. They may not be as forgiving as the Ruler of the Deep was."

He meant to ask what she meant—the rulers were far from his mind until now, their journey lackluster since leaving the island—when a gasp came from behind them.

They'd barely started their trek, and his heart was already in a panicked frenzy.

Noah and Celeste turned just as branches wrapped around Luna and Mark's midsections, forcefully tugging them backward. Katalina grabbed Mark's wrist and pulled on him feverishly, but he was yanked away with another branch covering his mouth. In a split second, he disappeared into the hedge.

"I love you," she yelled, but she was too late. Her hand was still reaching for her fiancé, but he was no longer there.

Noah took a startled step back, a scream lodged in his throat. He watched with wide, terrified eyes as Celeste's fingers grazed Luna's, missing by mere centimeters. By the time Noah's mind caught up to react, Luna was sucked into the hedge, too.

A stark, stunned silence fell over the scene. Katalina fell to her knees, her trembling hands slowly climbing to her mouth as she held back a wail.

Mark and Luna were gone.

"Thi-this is no time to mourn," Noah stammered, though he couldn't get his legs to move. Worse still, they were begging to buckle. No. He had to remain calm. Luna and Mark were fine. They were alive and well... somewhere. He just had to remain *calm.* "We have to run—"

Celeste's sharp intake of breath was hot on his ear, cutting his command off. Noah whirled around, grabbing her extended arm. He pulled as hard as he could, but the wretched plant was stronger, and she slipped through his fingers. Her face was overtaken by thick vines, her eyes the last to go, staring at him with tears threatening to fall.

Noah's body trembled, his thoughts reeling. She was fine. They were fine. Everything was *fine.* He repeated this over and over in his mind, but he couldn't get himself to believe it. They'd been abducted by leaves. How could he remain calm when there was a high likelihood the love of his life was gone forever and he was stranded on a foreign planet alone?

He held his breath with eyes clamped shut, mentally preparing to be yanked in next. A few seconds passed. Then a few more.

Nothing happened.

He opened one eye, then the next, realizing the hedge was done doing its dirty work.

"What just happened?" Katalina asked, tears streaming down her cheeks as she sniffled. "Is he—"

"Don't say it," Noah snapped, his tone harsher than intended. "Don't even think it. They're fine."

He and Katalina stared at each other. The surrounding scenery grew hushed. There was not a dash of wind or rustle of leaves. Only the sound of their heavy, worried intakes of breath as their new reality settled in.

Luna, Mark, and Celeste were swallowed by the hedge.

8

KATALINA CRASH COURSE

"So," Noah said. "Here we are."

Noah and his cousin walked side-by-side in uncomfortable silence, eyes focused on the perpetual greenery surrounding them. They'd been estranged until the day he ran into Celeste, and started their journey off with a rather rocky relationship. Though they'd made up over their travels, they still didn't make it a point to talk outside of gatherings. Even in social settings, the cousins seemed to drift toward anyone else except each other.

"Where do you think they went?" she asked, her voice lined with distress. He couldn't look at her, afraid her anxiety would spill into him. If he were walking with Mark, he'd make a lukewarm joke and they'd walk around until Celeste undoubtably found them. If he were with Celeste, they'd flirt and figure out the solution quickly.

With Luna—well, he couldn't picture what that would entail, either. She and Katalina were wildcards in his mind.

"I'm trying to channel my inner Celeste," Noah said, punching a declarative fist into his palm. "Everything will be fine. I'm sure of it."

Katalina peered up at him, her worry exemplified by the crinkle between her brows, and he attempted to encourage her with a half-smile that dipped a little too low at the edge. Katalina grimaced. "I don't think you believe what you're saying."

"I guess that shows how little you know me." He regretted his words, but he didn't want to apologize either. Instead, he changed the subject briskly. "I hope they weren't eaten."

"What a comforting thing to say." Katalina's comment was drenched in sarcasm. "No wonder you and Mark get along so well."

He nodded, allowing the quiet to fester once more. This was precisely why they avoided each other.

"I hope he's okay," Katalina said after a moment.

"He is," Noah assured with a hand pressed lightly on her shoulder. "He's with Luna, Celeste, or both of them. If anything, he's lucky to have someone who knows their way around. *We're* the ones *they* should be worried about."

"If they weren't eaten."

Noah paled. "True. There is that."

His attempt at optimism wasn't filling him with much hope. Fear of losing Celeste and Mark forever seeped into the crevices of his mind. Fear of failing, the planets exploding and turning everyone into dust.

"Thank you, Noah." Katalina's voice made his ears perk, and he turned to her in surprise. "You're right. Celeste and Luna told us the hedge wasn't dangerous. Sometimes my nerves get the best of me."

"I hear that." He paused, hesitant to continue. Giving away details from his life wasn't his forte; he didn't like to feel as though he were under a microscope, ready to be dissected by eager scientists. Scientists like, well, Katalina. "I think my nerves have gotten the best of me every day of my life."

"Well, that can't be true," she said with a startled chuckle. "You followed Celeste all the way here without a second thought!"

"Didn't you do the same?"

"No, I put a lot of thought into it. I just thought quickly. Going to another planet isn't something I could pass up as a scientist, you know, and I needed a moment of adventure. Or, at least, I thought I did. It's been amazing, but I'm not a fan of being put in so many near-death situations."

"What about you?" she added quickly. "Do you still love it here?"

"I do," Noah confessed. "This place is everything I could've wanted it to be, and so is Celeste. I can't imagine leaving it all behind to go back to... boredom, I guess."

They turned a corner, and at the very end was a wall of bright blue flowers hanging from vines. They reminded him of Celeste, and he had the sudden urge to pluck one for her. He nodded for Katalina to follow.

Katalina raised a brow, but her eyes were fixed on the sky above. Curious, Noah followed her gaze toward a pair of white birds with their wings spread wide, though there was something off about them. Their heads were pointy and swan-like, but as they neared, he noticed they were devoid of eyes or beaks or feathers. He could've sworn they looked like paper cranes.

Noah tilted his head at the strange sight; one seemed to shoot upward, only to soar straight back down. In fact, it looked like it may have even been coming toward them—

"Speaking of danger," he cried, swiftly grabbing Katalina's arm and tugging her closer seconds before the bird landed on her head. The creature hit the ground where Katalina had been standing, scattering into a squishy white blob of splatter, reminiscent of pudding. The pair stared down at the mess; Noah's hands were shaking, nerves pulsing with every beat of his heart.

"I think there's more coming," Katalina exclaimed, pointing up at the sky. "Look."

He followed her finger; two more white birds were circling above. He noticed movement in the corner of his eye, and his attention snapped back to the blob on the ground. The mound twitched and twisted before morphing back into its original shape.

A *swoosh* grazed his ear as something whizzed past, but his focus never wavered from the first white bird on the ground, watching as it flew back into the distant air. Dozens filled the sky now, and another pile of white goo was at his feet. The cause of the swoosh, no doubt.

"Oh," said Katalina. "That's a lot more."

"Come on." Noah grabbed Katalina and pulled her along, weaving through countless twists and turns with no end in sight. All the while, wings crinkled with each flap behind them.

Noah didn't dare look over his shoulder, knowing it would only lead to despair.

"Duck," he yelled, a sudden plan forming. A long shot, but it was the only plan they had. "Lay flat!"

Noah belly-flopped onto the ground harshly, Katalina following suit with a pained *oof*. He held his breath, terrified of what was to come. Would the paper cranes notice Katalina and Noah stopped running, or—

The birds flew past, hitting the hedge wall ahead before dissipating into dust. Noah's harsh breathing gradually softened as he flipped himself over and took in the blinding bright sky. He was surrounded by such beauty. Such life.

If only Celeste was lying next to him instead.

"That was weird," Katalina said between light gasps for air. "I think my entire chest is bruised."

Noah nodded with a meek groan as he held his ribcage. His flesh was throbbing, bruises forming along each bone with a pulsating pain. His legs were exhausted, and the adrenaline coursing through him was coming to a crashing halt, his eyelids growing heavy. "I wonder if getting hit by one would've hurt, or if it would've turned to dust on impact."

"I'm happy we didn't have to find out," Katalina said as she stood and brushed herself off. "Celeste and Luna didn't seem to know these would be in here."

"What are you suggesting?"

"That we aren't alone." Her eyes were a piercing river of knowledge waiting to be unleashed.

They kept walking, turning the corner hesitantly. He prepared himself for another sudden attack, but there were no paper cranes or other entities to be seen. Still, his shoulders did not relax. "You think someone is watching over us?"

They turned another corner, and Noah immediately stopped in his tracks at the sight of movement. Terror struck at the idea of more creatures to evade, and his heart dropped at what he saw.

It was *them.* Celeste, Luna, and Mark, walking together like nothing had happened. Celeste noticed him first, giving Noah a wave.

Katalina put her hands over her mouth, and Mark's shock morphed into a broad grin before he jogged over. His black hair flowed effortlessly in the breeze as they met in the middle, and he scooped her up in a swooping hug. They spun in a few circles, their lips meeting with a cascade of passion.

While it was sweet, it was also incredibly stomach-churning to watch. Katalina was his cousin, after all.

Noah jogged past the pair toward Celeste and her stepsister, only to look between them awkwardly. While he didn't know Luna particularly well, he still felt bad she was the odd one out in their group. As much as he wanted to pull Celeste in for a long, lingering kiss, he didn't want to make Luna feel any worse than she probably already did. So he didn't.

"How did you guys escape?" he asked. "And did you encounter anything odd while you were stuck in here?"

"The hedge spit us out on another side of the maze," Luna explained. "I guess it still led us back to you."

"*That's* your choice of words?" Celeste crossed her arms over her chest with a glare, though she didn't expand on her thoughts. She turned back to Noah. "Anything odd? No. In fact, it was much too quiet for my liking. I could feel the wind, but the leaves didn't rustle. It was strange. You?"

He nodded. "Actually, we were attacked by birds made of paper."

The two women stared at him with blank expressions. Celeste usually had an explanation for whatever crazy thing was attacking them next, but not even a name for the paper-like birds was uttered. Instead, Celeste asked, "How did you survive?"

"That's the strange thing. They simply stopped attacking us. They ran into the hedge and burst into nothing."

Celeste scratched her chin. "I've never heard of such a thing."

"Me neither," said Luna. "Come to think of it, I've never heard of an instance where the hedge maze absorbs people, either. Are you sure they were made of paper?"

"It looked awfully like it. There were no eyes or feathers or mouths."

"Well... it could be someone who controls the wind," Luna suggested hesitantly, as though she didn't want to say whatever she was about to.

Celeste continued to ponder, ignoring Luna completely.

"What do you mean?" asked Noah. "People can control the wind?"

"Not people. Not a person. A being," Luna said.

"The Ruler of the Wind?"

Celeste nodded. "He has a mostly human-presenting form, but he's made entirely of wind."

"He also presents as a cat-human hybrid," Luna added. "With ears and a tail… and he's incredibly handsome."

"Makes sense," Noah said dryly, glancing briefly toward Celeste to see if she agreed. She remained stoic. He wasn't sure he could compete with another handsome man who liked cats, much less a ruler. "If he can look however he wants."

"He's the only ruler that can willingly change his form," said Celeste. "It's quite a feat to be formless, too. That would explain the wind without rustling leaves, and paper birds flying by themselves."

"Very good," praised a voice. No—two voices at once. The group turned toward the sources at the same time.

Two beings blocked the direction they were heading. Noah wasn't sure what else to call them other than beings, as they were made of brown twigs and leaves. Their green hair was thick like vines yet flowing and free like moss. They had no obvious trademarks of gender, and their eyes were beady and bright blue, relentlessly penetrating Noah's soul.

"Ah, crap," Luna said.

9

RIDDLE ME THIS

CELESTE TOOK A STARTLED STEP BACKWARD, A HAND TO HER chest. "You were right. The Ruler of the Wind is here."

She regained her composure quickly, gesturing toward her stepsister. "See? That's why I invited you. You can have some smart moments here and there."

"*Some?*" asked Luna with a glare.

Mark raised a hand. "Um, who are these people supposed to be?"

"People?" they asked as one, tilting their heads. It was jarring to see two beings with the basic structure of humans, but wrapped in branches instead of skin, and with thin, long twigs instead of fingers.

"We are children of the Forest Goddess," said the one to the left. Their voice was pitched slightly higher than the other and wispy, chilling him to the bone. It was uncomfortable, such a feeling. "I am Tysven, and this is my sibling, Rosvel."

"Goddess? I thought you only worshipped one goddess on Fortun," Katalina said.

"There are many false goddesses. The Forest Goddess is a powerful nymph, but certainly not the one, true Goddess," whispered Celeste.

"*I* believe in the Goddesses of the Three Seas," Luna added. "And they are *not 'false.'*"

"The Forest Goddess' children often remain by her side to protect the forest," explained Rosvel, ignoring the bickering stepsisters. The only physical difference between the pair was the missing twig fingers on Rosvel's left hand. Otherwise, they were identical. "We've chosen the brave task of branching out to help someone in need instead."

"Someone in need?" Celeste asked, her voice lined with accusation. "The rumors say you've worked with the Ruler of the Wind for years to create havoc on civilizations that don't worship him."

"He's nothing more than another man obsessed with himself," agreed Luna.

The twins nodded. Their emotionless nature was putting Noah on edge. "We are his loyal subjects."

Rosvel's blue orbs shot toward Luna. "As a merperson, you have no say on this subject. You have plenty of cities and towns already named after you. Thousands of loyal subjects."

"What? Are you telling us the Ruler of the Wind is jealous of merpeople?" Luna scoffed at their lack of a reaction and waved a hand in dismissal. "What are you lot doing here, anyway? You could've let us pass peacefully."

"We will help you find the other side of this maze,"

promised Tysven. "If you answer a question. A riddle, if you will."

"Why would you do that?" asked Celeste. "What's in it for you?"

"Whatever happens with our planets, we will serve him until the end," the twins said, ignoring her question entirely.

"Great," Mark grumbled. "What luck."

"Better than a deadly animal," Noah contested, thankful to be rid of another wild chase from an evil deer or any other Sundar-adjacent creatures turned horrific.

Mark shook his head with a cross of his arms. "Alright. Let's get this over with, then. What's the riddle?"

The forest beings smiled wide, their mouths filled with rows of cramped thorns, as though each layer had two too many. They looked rather evil, now that Noah thought about it. What if they presented an unsolvable riddle before a brutal, choreographed attack? He could only take so many more before the trauma of the events finally caught up to him.

"If one equals two, and two equals eight, what equals us?"

Noah's eye twitched; the way they spoke at the same time was like a chair scraping against a metal floor. He nearly asked if it was necessary, but he didn't want to upset them. Instead, Celeste and Noah exchanged a nervous glance. He shrugged, his thoughts unrelentingly vacant. He didn't know what to make of the situation, landing on a mix of confusion and fatigue. Celeste didn't speak, either, an unusual state for her.

Luna tsked. "I thought the Ruler of the Wind and the two of you were off in the middle of the desert somewhere?"

"We moved," said Tysven. "We moved to find you."

"If one equals two, and two equals eight, what equals us?" Rosvel repeated. "You should feel special. This is a riddle designed only for you."

"The Ruler of the Wind thought long and hard about this day."

Something about that sentiment made Noah squirm.

"Now wait a minute." Katalina took a step forward. "What happens if we can't figure out the answer? Will we be allowed through?"

"Of course not," said Tysven. His branch-like fingers were growing longer and sprouting flowers at a slow yet precise pace.

"You certainly wouldn't be allowed to leave," Rosvel added, peering down at their sibling's moving appendages. "The hedge wants you, Ty." The forest child frowned, their voice filled with genuine curiosity. "Why do the hedges always choose you and never me?"

"Well, any guesses?" Mark asked, eyes jumping to each member of their group before landing on Noah. "You've been awfully quiet. Thinking hard?"

"Harder than you, I'd wager," Noah retorted, turning his attention back to the twins. "Is there any other way you'll let us pass? Any at all?"

An awkward silence ensued as the twins appeared lost in thought. Finally, Rosvel said, "We like flower or vegetable seeds. Do you have either of those?"

"We would accept those in exchange for your lives and guesses," agreed Tysven.

"What about fruit seeds?" inquired Noah, garnering confused stares from the others.

"No," said the twins in unison.

Mark put his hands on his hips, appearing genuinely stumped. "Why would you—?"

Noah cut him off, his words directed at the twins. "We don't have any of those, either, but I wanted to cover all the bases."

Luna snapped her fingers with a peppy spring in her step. The group's focus switched from Noah to her, and he felt the tremendous pressure release from his shoulders. "What if it's literal? There are two letters in the word 'us.' Therefore, the answer to the riddle would be two."

"But one equals two, and there are two letters. So it would be eight plus eight," said Katalina. "Therefore 'us' equals sixteen."

The twins smiled, clapping for a full five seconds before finally saying, "Very good. You're correct."

The afflictions in their voices remained one grating note, never staying on-key.

Mark slung a fist in the air before enclosing Katalina in a swaying hug. "That's my smart scientist for you! You're perfect, Katalina! Absolutely perfect!"

"So far, I feel I've been rather useless," Luna stated.

"You're not the only one," Celeste said, her narrow eyes pointed at Mark.

Mark furrowed his brows with a wag of his finger. "Hey, I didn't hear you make any guesses. Besides, I'm a genius for marrying a genius. A genius by proxy."

The twins pointed to the left. "That is the way."

"I thought you were going to lead us to the exit?" asked

Celeste. "There's obviously way more ground to cover before we make it to the end."

"We said we would show you the way out," said Tysven. "It's that way. Though, that's not necessarily true, is it? The hedge maze chooses when to let you go."

"That can't be," said Katalina. "We entered from somewhere. At the very least, we could find our way back."

The twins shook their heads. "The hedge closed the entrance after you crossed over."

"So we solved that riddle for nothing? There wasn't even a hidden message?" Mark asked with fingers balled into fists.

The twins continued to grin, making Noah shuffle awkwardly in his spot. Tysven asked, "Is anything ever pointless?"

A question that would surely leave Noah awake tonight, staring at the ceiling of the inevitable tent he'd be sleeping in.

"Focus on those who lead the way," said Tysven, their lipless mouth opening until their jagged teeth were on full display.

"Though some may try to lead you astray," finished Rosvel, mimicking the other's expression. They took a few steps backward until they were leaning against the hedge. The vines and leaves furled around their arms and legs slowly, as though the vines took great pleasure in doing so.

"No—no way. You're just toying with us?" asked Celeste, utterly exasperated. "What was the point of the riddle, then?"

There was no answer. The twins seeped into the wall of leaves and branches until nothing remained.

10

RULER OF THE WIND

"WELL, THAT WAS A WASTE OF TIME," LUNA GRUMBLED. HER FACE was scrunched in either thought, mild frustration, or both. There was a sense of panic brewing in the pit of Noah's stomach, like the walls could cave at any minute. Everywhere he looked, there were green leaves bristling in the light tousle of the wind.

"I don't like this," Noah said, glancing over his shoulder. A soft breeze wafted over him, the wind whistling faintly while creating a layer of goosebumps over his exposed arms.

"I agree," Katalina said. "It's spooky in here. What did those twins say again?"

"They basically said we aren't escaping." Noah's mouth grew dry. "This maze has locked us in. It's inescapable."

"I wonder if it's unpeckable, too?" Mark pondered, referring to the shapeshifters that'd attacked them a little over a month ago. He was met with three glares, and he shrugged sheepishly. "It was just a question."

"Even if the maze was unpeckable, how would that help us? Unless you're a shapeshifter or something?" Luna said with a chuckle before her smile gradually dissolved. "Are y—"

"Don't even joke about that. Of course, I'm me."

Celeste tilted her head upward, sniffing the air. "He's telling the truth. I don't smell a shapeshifter near."

Noah looked up at the dimming sky. They'd been stuck in here longer than he'd expected, and now the day was almost over. He raised a curious brow at the light draft that pushed him forward as the wind seemed to whisper in his ears.

"Celeste," murmured the wind. Noah gasped, peering around the spacious walkway the group paused on, his heart ricocheting against his ribs.

"Did anyone hear that?" he asked, relieved to see Mark's head bob up and down, followed by Katalina's.

"Celeste," the voice said again, clearer this time. Noah couldn't help but notice it had a sultry smoothness to it, one that made him question how the wind knew Celeste.

Noah peeked at her from the corner of his eye; her jaw and fists were clenched as she stared ahead. Noah blushed despite himself and the situation. She looked so cute when she was frustrated. Her nose was scrunched in a way that made him instantly want to make her feel better.

"What's going on here?" Noah asked no one in particular.

"I could be your worst nightmare." The voice brushed against his ear like a set of plump lips. An unease pooled within

Noah, a jittery jump of nerves crawling up his spine. No matter where he tried to go, the wind could catch up.

"It's him. The Ruler of the Wind," Celeste confirmed under her breath. While Celeste appeared flustered, Luna looked terrified, with palms trembling at her sides.

He looked down at his hands, wondering why they weren't doing the same. Only weeks ago, they were running from tiny lizard people labeled city protectors, and being attacked by a deer-like creature. All of which made Noah quake in his shoes, and while he was still anxious, he couldn't help but feel a sense of eager anticipation. Perhaps it was because they had already won over another ruler, or perhaps because he had Celeste, Katalina, Mark, and Luna at his side.

He was no longer alone.

The thought shocked him back to reality, and he spoke to the wind. "Could you? Could you be my worst nightmare? You don't seem all too scary to me."

It was a bluff, of course. The wind could knock the oxygen clean out of him. He didn't want to suffocate because he accidentally made the Ruler of the Wind angry, but he couldn't seem scared, either.

A mischievous chortle ebbed through the air before a person materialized in front of them, beginning with a top hat resting on a mop of black hair. His eyes were violet and wide as his lips curled into a charming smirk. He looked young—perhaps in his mid-twenties, and tall, perhaps a little over six foot one. He was much too tall and handsome for Noah's liking.

The man wore a plum suit and violet tie, with a black tail

swishing behind him. His delight never wavered as he bowed and exposed his purple-gloved hands to take off his top hat.

"Hey, I thought you said he had cat ea—" Mark began with a thrust of his arm toward the man. He briskly cut himself off once the top hat was removed and two pointy, dark purple ears popped out against the Ruler's wild and curly hair.

"Xyrus Velham," said the man. He appeared wispy at the edges, turning nearly transparent as swirls of purple and black slunk against his skin. Was he merely a form made of wind, or a tangible, living thing? Was it possible to be both yet neither at the same time?

Xyrus narrowed his violet eyes with a growing grin; his pupils danced with intrigue and mischief. He walked around Noah and Mark toward Katalina and Celeste, examining them one by one with his face a little too close.

"You know what? I take it back. An attractive man interested in stealing the woman of my dreams?" Noah asked, looking Xyrus up and down. He hadn't known a man could look so good in splashes of purple—or with cat ears and a tail. "You're not wrong—you *could* be my worst nightmare."

Xyrus chuckled, making a show of his movements with the exaggerated use of bobbing shoulders and a head tilted back as his amusement morphed into full belly laughter.

Noah tsked; even his maniacal laugh was sexy—Noah was screwed. Xyrus only laughed harder.

"What are you doing here?" asked Celeste. "Of all the places for you to be?"

Noah analyzed every word and mannerism she displayed, attempting to decipher how they knew each other so well.

As if to torture Noah, Xyrus winked at her. "I'm everywhere, darling. That's why I'm called the Ruler of the Wind. I hear and see everything, at any time."

"Everywhere?" questioned Mark. "Wouldn't that give you a headache, hearing *everything* all the time?"

Xyrus massaged his temples. "Worse—relentless migraines. It can be a curse to be as powerful as I."

Celeste took a step forward with a deep, nervous breath. "Does that mean—?"

"I know what the four of you are up to? Of course. All the rulers know—our sea serpent friend made sure to tell." He walked over to the hedge and plucked a handful of leaves before crumbling them in his fingers. They turned to glittery dust in his palm, sparkling as they fell to the ground. So he was tangible, or at the very least, could become so when he wished. "I wanted to see firsthand who convinced the serpent to help, and who agreed to steal the blue star for him."

"Steal?" asked Luna. "From who?"

"You know who."

"The Ruler of the Sky," Celeste pieced together. "Our theory was right—she moved the stars. She doesn't want us to save the planets."

"Do you know why she would do something like this?" Mark queried suddenly, his voice surprising Noah so much so that he jumped. Mark ran a shaky hand through his jet-black hair before he regained his composure; he straightened his back with a crack of his neck and puffed out his chest. Was he threatened by Xyrus' beauty, too?

Xyrus' grin expanded as he tilted his head in an inquisitory nature. "Why, of course I know, dear boy."

"Then tell us."

Xyrus snorted. "Humans are always the same, aren't they?"

Noah couldn't discern who he was talking to, and that unnerved him almost as much as the notion that humans were always the same. If that were true, Noah would fall in love with Mark right about now, too.

"I see." Xyrus squinted at him. "Your thoughts are loud."

Noah looked over both his shoulders before pointing to himself. "Me?"

"There's always someone, isn't there?" Noah wasn't sure what Xyrus meant. "I was surprised the Ruler of the Deep would change his mind like that. We agreed to remain neutral on the matter. Allow nature to take its course. The question I have is—why you? Surely it was not for your humor or style—"

"Hey now," Noah said, hands raised in defense. "I have style, and I'm funny. Right, guys?"

He peered around at the others, realizing they were all avoiding eye contact. Mark shrugged. "On a good day, yes. There just aren't many of those."

"I think you're funny," Celeste assured. "That's all that matters, right?"

"Ah, this makes much more sense now," said the Ruler of the Wind. "I expected your taste to be different, Celestial, but he suits you well."

A pang of pain shot through him as his ego was destroyed. Shattered. Possibly forever, considering Pevelyn had a similarly unimpressed reaction toward Noah. Was he not good enough for Celeste? Had she brought home countless others that *were* good enough? When she'd first invited Noah, she'd done so because he looked *lonely*. She never said it was because he was *attractive*.

He couldn't handle the wondering any longer. "How do you know each other, exactly?"

"I have known Celestial and her family for many years. Since she was a child. I know of all the families in all the lands, but I cannot pinpoint yours, or theirs," Xyrus purred, eyes flickering past Noah. He'd almost forgotten Katalina and Mark were there, his attention fixed on Xyrus.

"Why are you really here?" Celeste asked again. "To stop us?"

Xyrus sighed, tucking his hands behind his back while straightening his spine.

"Are you admitting you *all* knew there was a way to stop the collision?" Celeste's fingers curled into fists. "Yet you did nothing, knowing innocent people died trying to find the truth? Knowing so many more were *still* going to die?"

Xyrus had moved on from Noah back to Celeste, circling her like a cat to a rabbit. His slender figure was fluid and free with each step, a cloud struggling to remain whole.

"Of course," the man said matter-of-factly, giving no further insight into why. Noah couldn't explain his sudden need to look at Celeste, and he noticed Xyrus was quick to follow. It was becoming bothersome, the way Xyrus seemed to view her as a toy in need of smacking.

"It's getting darker out by the minute," Mark exclaimed. "We should be going. Not listening to some guy who wants everyone to die."

"He's right," Luna said. "This is a waste of time."

Xyrus chuckled, though his eyebrow twitched, and his jaw clenched. "You've brought an interesting crew with you, Celestial. Far more entertaining than any of the people your brother brought around."

Noah watched Celeste intensely, waiting for her demeanor to reveal her thoughts. Xyrus inevitably knew her entire family, a side of her life Noah would never truly understand. A pang of jealousy spiked within him at the notion of this man knowing Celeste's brother before he passed, and her mother before she left Celeste behind. Selfish, he knew, but he couldn't deny how he felt.

"Altair was here?" she asked, her voice wavering. Her mouth may have been a straight line, but he could tell she was only trying to hide her emotions. She was far better at it than he. "When?"

"Shortly before traveling to the other world, I believe. He came with a few others, asking if I knew how to stop the planets from colliding. Of course, I said yes, and then I turned them away, as I and the other rulers agreed upon. What I *thought* we agreed upon." Xyrus cocked his head, staring Noah down with a slight squint. "You must've said or done *something.*"

Noah shrugged, his nonchalance further appearing to irritate the man. "He thought I was cool, I guess."

"If you'd told Altair about the stars, he wouldn't have gone to Sundar," Celeste began, her voice breaking. "He wouldn't have—"

"Does it matter what would happen when what was meant to happen already happened?" Xyrus asked with a twinkle in his eyes, as though his joy was resuscitated by the sour expression Celeste gave.

Through gritted teeth, she said, "Yes. It does."

Xyrus waved her words away. "When you have lived as long as I, you find it doesn't."

She tsked. "I pity you."

"Well, what's new? You were always judgemental in that head of yours. It's a shame you've locked it away."

"Is it?" She crossed her arms. The rulers could read minds, but Luna and Celeste knew a way to shut them out. If only the practice could be shared and honed by the others. Instead, their secrets and unchecked thoughts were running rampant.

As their conversation persisted, Noah couldn't help but wonder where this vitriol was coming from. Partly because of her brother's passing, surely, but there had to be something more between them. He wasn't sure if he wanted to know. No, probably not.

But, *yes*, he did. The mind was a treacherous place to be.

As though Mark could read the creases in Noah's forehead, he leaned in and whispered, "I'm picking something up here. Romantic tension?"

It was Noah's turn to tsk. "I know we're all thinking it, but why'd you have to say it? I don't want to know."

Mark stared at Noah before he said, "Yes, you do."

Noah's shoulders deflated. He didn't need to say anything for Mark to know he was right. Of course, Noah wanted to know every detail of her past, but that's precisely why he didn't want to know. To know was to think, and he'd rather be blissfully ignorant than think anymore than he already did.

"He watched her grow up," interjected Katalina with a lip curled in disgust. "That would be weird."

"But unsurprising," Mark asserted. "He's an attractive immortal being."

Noah grimaced. "Please stop. Celeste has better taste than that."

Xyrus' abrupt snickering cut Noah's thoughts off. "You've picked quite the crew, Celestial. I dare say I like them."

The Ruler of the Wind walked around Noah, staring him down with their noses inches from each other. "I like the way he fears me whilst also hurling insults."

"Why does the Ruler of the Deep want the blue star?" Noah asked, hopeful of redirecting their conversation away from whatever this was.

Xyrus appeared dumbfounded by the question, if only for a mere second. His lips quirked upward again. Did this man do anything else but smirk? "You don't know, yet you agreed to help him?"

He tossed the top hat from his head into the air with a sudden flick of his wrist; it landed upside down with an almost inaudible *thump.* At the same moment, Xyrus' body dissipated like steam on a hot day, becoming one with the wind.

11

A TOP HAT BELOW

THE AIR WAS STAGNANT AS THE TOP HAT HOPPED FORWARD LIKE A bunny. The hat stopped beside Celeste, and she jumped back with a squeak, grabbing Noah's arm for support.

The top hat started vibrating, releasing a low, slow hum before reaching a crescendo. A beam of golden light shot up from the center, funneling outward. The sky transformed from dusk to a stark night—with stars speckling the scene.

The stars looked to be crudely drawn by hand and they created different constellations with single lines connected to each other. He was unfamiliar with the designs; there were but two constellations on Sundar, and they were circular with names to match the moons—Tivinis and Lynoli. Yet another dull thing to add to Sundar's roster.

Of what he saw now, there was a bow, an arrow, the wings of a draegon, and a hammer.

"Is the hat... projecting these images?" gasped Katalina as she spun in circles. The projector spanned the entire sky above them, and while he appreciated the star show, he wasn't sure what this had to do with anything. All the stars were the same color and shape.

He squinted—no, there was one off in the distance that was pale blue. Noah reached up as if he could touch the star, but when he tried, he was too far, and his fingers slipped through the air.

"I don't understand," said Celeste. "What's the purpose of showing us this?"

His sense of doom returned rather quickly as he realized they'd reached another night closer to the end of life as they knew it. On any other day, during any other quest, it would be exciting to see something so new and bold. But now, all he wanted to do was scream at the ruler to stop messing around and get to the point.

The projection went black before being sucked back into the hat. The dim, graying sky came back into view, the hat stopped vibrating, and everything went still. Noah and the others stood motionless, staring at the ground with mouths agape.

"At this point, we could just walk away and find the exit without his help," Luna suggested with a twinge of frustration in her voice.

The others nodded, with Mark proclaiming with a point, "I like that idea."

Without warning, the top hat slid against the ground before

flying into the air. Noah watched as it landed in a gloved hand. The Ruler of the Wind chuckled while placing it back on his head. "You don't understand? Perhaps you will in time."

The ruler walked around them, stopping only to ruffle everyone's hair like they were his little pets. When he reached Noah, he lingered, leaning in to whisper, "The actual test is if *they* like you, too."

Noah gulped, wondering whom Xyrus was alluding to.

Something chimed in the air, three hollow cords that made the ruler's ears perk up, and he looked at his wrist, though it was blank. "Ah, I must be going. It's our daily Remembrance Well water and tea time."

He turned to Celeste with a warm smile. "It was most wondrous to see you, Celestial. I'm sure I'll see you again sometime soon."

His gaze turned sharp and cold toward Luna. "And you."

With nothing more to add, Xyrus turned and continued down the path their group was headed. He dissipated at the edges as he became transparent, starting with his feet, then legs.

"Wait! Why is the blue star so important?" yelled Katalina, her hands cupped over her mouth. "Why would the Ruler of the Deep want it?"

Xyrus' torso was next to drift away. His words were carried with the wind, swirling around the group. "The blue star and the star the shade of hope should stay in the sky, but if it's the only way to save the planets, what else can you do?"

"Most importantly, why would you willingly drink the

Remembrance Well water?" cried Noah. When he tried some all those weeks ago at morning lunch, the water had only filled his head with sorrowful memories of the past. Nothing tasted good enough to go through that again.

"That didn't answer my question," Katalina said.

"And it won't. I won't reveal more than I already have, either. Unlike the Ruler of the Deep, *I* keep promises." His words tapered off at the end, becoming distant as the last piece of his body disappeared. The wind picked up once more before growing stale altogether. The Ruler of the Wind was gone. In his place was a dark purple bag tied closed with gold string.

Celeste picked it up, reading the inscription on the side. "'For use when the going gets small.' Huh."

"What's inside of it?" asked Noah, coming to her side. His cheeks grew hot as their shoulders touched, and he edged even closer. She opened the bag, revealing a dark pink powder.

"Not sure what purpose that served," Mark grumbled, scratching the back of his head. "Felt like he wasted even more of our time."

"He's taunting us," Luna said, rubbing her chin. "He must've been hinting at something we missed. But what?"

Noah looked between Katalina and Celeste, certain one of them would've come up with the answer by now.

Celeste shrugged. "The projection showed constellations written in the stars. That's all I've got."

Katalina tapped her foot rapidly, mumbling to herself. When she glanced up, her eyes were wide with surprise at the others watching. "I have no clue."

"Well, did any of them mean anything to the two of you?" asked Noah as he attempted to picture what had briefly flashed across the sky. "There were wings of a draegon, a bow, an arrow—"

Luna waved away his words. "We don't need a recap. We need an answer."

"I don't see you giving one," countered Celeste. "And, no. The hat showed all the constellations we have here. They have no significance other than the symbol of spiritualism and the observations of some bored fairies."

"Maybe the stars we're looking for are hidden within one of those constellations?" Mark suggested. "I saw a blue one, but not a star resembling hope, I don't think."

"That might be the best guess you've ever made, Mark, but why show us all of them if we only needed to know two?" combated Celeste. "It makes no sense."

"To confuse us," Luna said simply. "To have a good laugh about everyone dying. I bet he even had the hedge separate us just for the fun of it."

Noah raised a hand, and they all turned to him. "Isn't this something we can talk about *after* we escape this maze? I can barely see in front of me."

It was fully night now, and the hedge was creating dark shadows along the ground and their faces. They were running out of time. They were always running out of time. Two months were turning into mere weeks, and their crew was nowhere closer to finding the hills. If only the Ruler of the Wind decided to actually help them, instead of play a game.

Celeste sighed with her hands on her hips. "I guess you're right."

"But it is curious, isn't it?" Katalina asserted. "That the other rulers don't want the Ruler of the Deep to have the blue star? What if the end of the world is a better option?"

The question hung in the air.

12

NO TIME TO REST

It was eerie without the stars sparkling above. He hadn't realized how much he would miss them until they were gone.

Growing up, his mother hated the dark. She refused to let him go outside at night because of it, so he never had the chance to lie under the stars and moons. Now, the opportunity was still so far away. He feared he'd never get the chance, and he desperately wished he could've convinced her all those years ago that there was nothing to be afraid of. They took the stars for granted.

How odd that the memories of her brought about a fleeting sadness, one where the pang was powerful, yet not a tear was shed.

Their group decided not to rest until they found the exit of the maze. Incidentally, the path the twins initially took them down had arrows made of leaves glowing like yellow lights, leading the way. It took a few more turns, and they were greeted by an open field followed by a mass of trees.

Noah exhaled, as if he'd been holding his breath the entire way, and collapsed to his knees. The grass was short here, and yellow instead of the typical teal. The trees ahead looked to be pine, and the hills were just a little further. He smiled. Though they couldn't see much from here, a faint glow rose from the hills. "We found the right side of the planet."

Celeste turned to him with a light chuckle, though he didn't know what for. "We did. I guess we're lucky the Ruler of the Wind helped us after all."

"If there's any luck, then it's in the form of you," said Noah.

"I wonder why," pondered Luna, brushing past his comment. "He's always out for himself, sure, but usually he and the Ruler of the Sky are friendly, no?"

"Maybe he's just sensible and doesn't want everyone to die," suggested Noah.

"It could also be that," agreed Celeste. "Actually, it's probably that."

"*I* still want to know why the Ruler of the Sky moved the stars in the first place," tacked on Katalina, pointing broadly at the landscape before them. "And what the blue star does."

"Can we sleep soon?" piped up Mark. He bent over, his disheveled black hair stringy with sweat. "My legs can't take it much longer."

Instead of responding, Celeste sat next to Noah on the ground, trailing her fingers over the prickly yellow grass. "I couldn't have done any of this without you."

Noah's face turned red immediately, the heat sending his

temples into a sweating frenzy. He hadn't expected such a declaration, and he looked away quickly with a stammer, "I-I wouldn't talk like that yet. We still have so much further to go."

"Is there time for rest?" inquired Luna. "How many days do we have left?"

Celeste sighed and pulled around her disappearing-reappearing pack. From there, she took out Altair's research notebook and thumbed through it. She pointed to a page. "Ah. Here it is. Yes, we have fourteen days until the end."

Two weeks. That was it? Really? Time was moving far faster than he anticipated. His anxiety peaked. "We can't stop!"

Mark cleared his throat, grabbing Noah's attention. He looked around at their crew. Katalina climbed onto Mark's back, her legs wrapped around his torso, and arms around his neck, as she rested her tired head on his shoulder. Mark was clearly struggling to keep his eyes open, though he tried to hide it with a straight posture and a determined, hard face.

Only Luna appeared functionally awake, already taking steps toward the lingering forest ahead. Noah couldn't deny his dislike for forests. They always led to trouble, like a cave with wings or protectors of a city determined to shoot him full of arrows.

They made it a few steps past the treeline before the branches creaked to life, sowing the openings of the forest shut until utter darkness consumed them. There was no hope of turning back, nor was there light to guide them forward. They would have to stop for now.

"What's happening?" Mark asked with a quiver in his voice.

Katalina had fallen asleep on his back, and his words made her eyes flutter open for a moment before they closed again.

Celeste took a startled step back. "I don't know!"

"Is it the Ruler of the Soil?" asked Noah.

Luna put her hands on her hips. "Really? The Ruler of the Soil *still* owes you favors?"

"I don't think so! It could be the Forest Goddess—"

A growl came from underneath them, the ground shifting and pebbles bouncing. Celeste gasped, falling to her knees and placing both palms on the dirt. He watched curiously, remembering their time by the river on their quest to find the Ruler of the Deep.

At first, nothing happened. Then, something appeared to sprout from where her hands rested. The object began folded up, popping open once it was pushed out of the soil. A fully formed tent was set up and soon came another.

Next came a set of wooden logs stacked on top of each other inside a pit of rocks. There was even a box of matches beside it. Thick logs rolled through the trees horizontally, stopping around the firepit for them to sit. Everything else came from the soil, pushed through by worms and slugs and other small rat-like mammals that burrowed in the dirt. They largely kept underground, but he saw a fuzzy brown tail here and there.

A full-fledged camping ground was set up before them. Noah's shoulders fell with a heavy sigh of relief. "Oh, good. I wasn't ready for another bout of running away from something."

"I guess... I guess the Ruler of the Soil is helping us," Celeste said with surprise.

Mark nodded. "As much as I'd love to chitchat, I don't think I can hold Katalina much longer."

He headed into a tent, ducking and disappearing with a close of the flap. Noah turned to Celeste with a suggestive shrug. "Well, should we sleep or make a fire?"

Celeste glanced between him and the firepit as Luna tore open a bag of marshmallows and popped one into her mouth. Luna moaned. "That's the stuff."

"Where did you get those?" he asked, surprised at such a commonality between their worlds. He loved marshmallows, but they were highly expensive on Sundar because of their rarity.

"They came from the dirt, of course."

As Luna prepared to devour the next one, the stepsisters locked eyes. Celeste offered a half-smile. "I think I'm going to make a fire. I haven't made one in such a long time."

Luna jumped away from the unlit firepit as if she'd been burned. "Are you insane? I'm a merperson! Fire will dry me up!"

Celeste stuck her tongue out with a playfully scrunched nose. Luna huffed, hastily stomping over to the empty tent and disappearing inside with a bag of marshmallows clutched in hand.

With Luna gone, Celeste clapped her hands enthusiastically and turned to Noah. "Are you hungry?"

He cocked his head in thought. "I can't tell. Why? Are you going to have me try another dessert?" She nodded, and he smirked. "Good. I love when you show me new foods."

Celeste turned her head away, tucking a strand of hair behind her ear. Though it was incredibly dark, he could've sworn he saw a light blush dusting her cheeks. Alone together, he watched with bated breath as she lit a match and held the flame to a log. She nodded for him to join her, and so he did.

Standing side by side, he watched the fire shift and shadows move along her face, catching her skin in a golden hue. She was a luminous light among the darkest caverns of his mind.

"What are these marshmallows for, exactly?" He held one up, inspecting it before tentatively taking a bite. "I've only ever used them for hot milk."

"Don't you mean hot chocolate?" she asked with crinkled brows.

"Chocolate?"

Her mouth fell open. "Wow. Every time you tell me about Sundar, it sounds stranger and stranger."

Celeste reached around for her pack and pulled out two tiny expandable metal sticks, topping each off with a marshmallow. He watched as she pulled out a container of white fluff —presumably whipped cream—four square crackers and two tiny wrapped chocolates. "You've really never had a Delicious Delight? They're divine! Here, copy me."

She handed him a stick, pointing the marshmallow end at the fire. They sat on one of the log-shaped seats beside each other. He'd been alone with her a handful of times now, and yet a flutter erupted within him like it was the first time again. Words were distant as his mind drew a blank.

"Hold it closer," she whispered, placing a hand on his and pointing the stick downward. Sundar lacked such an activity. Though marshmallows and fires existed, no one ever thought to put them together. Celeste looked up and found his eyes. "There you go."

A breath was lodged in his throat, and he couldn't help the slow pull of his body toward hers. Leaning in, he was sure their lips would touch, and then a bright shadow erupted against her face. They both jumped from the movement, and Celeste released a mischievous giggle at the marshmallow she set on fire.

She waved it around, blowing on it for extra measure before the small flames burned out. The marshmallow became bloated and black around the edges, but she happily placed it on a cracker with a piece of chocolate and topped it off with the whipped cream. "My parents were out of the teeny tiny chocolates. Altair and I used to use them to make eyes. We'd call them our Delicious Delight Spiders."

"That's really cute," he said. "And it looks incredibly tasty, albeit unhealthy."

"Maybe for you. But we live off of sweets here, remember?" she asked.

"Hard to forget," he said, pulling his marshmallow from the flickering flames. She helped him assemble his Delicious Delight, and he took the dessert from her fingers hesitantly. The marshmallow and chocolate melted along with the whipped cream in a haste, sliding down his hands and arms.

She laughed. "You're supposed to eat it quickly!"

He did as instructed, the gooey goodness melting in his mouth. An involuntary moan of pleasure came from his lips. She mimicked him, the tender noise sending an intoxicating shiver throughout his body. If he looked at her now, he was sure he'd have no choice but to kiss her. To hold her in his arms and never let go.

"I knew you'd like them," she continued. "I miss the days my mother, Altair, and I would camp together. Luna and Pevelyn hate forests and fires and all things outdoors, really. My father couldn't care less about any of it. Thank you for staying up with me."

Noah watched as her eyes welled with fresh tears, and somehow that made him want to kiss her more. "Of course. Thank you for showing me. We have nothing like it back home. Only normal cookies and cupcakes and occasional donuts. This is unbelievable."

He devoured his cookie quickly and used a cup of water he'd stashed in his endless pack to clean off his hands before taking a swig.

"Your eyes are so beautiful," he whispered, the words replaying in his mind finally coming loose.

"So are yours," she said, her voice lowering to match his. "We should do this again. After we save the planets."

He nodded, slowly closing the gap between them. "We could stay in a safe forest, go hiking, make meals in a cabin somewhere."

"Live far away from everyone yet have the means to visit whenever we wanted," she agreed. They grew closer and closer until Noah couldn't take his feverish need any longer, and he leaned in with a hand resting on her cheek.

Their lips clashed, and he found his hands trailing her body as he pulled her closer. She grabbed him by the collar of his shirt, drawing him in as loving, lustful hunger consumed his thoughts.

"I've never seen someone so beautiful," he said. He couldn't stop saying it. He didn't want to. Noah wanted her to know she was as perfect as he saw her. "So kind. So thoughtful."

Her blush seemed to deepen, and she pulled him in again. They'd known each other for over a month now, on an adventure he'd never thought could be had, and finally, *finally,* they had the privacy to connect for longer than ten seconds. *Finally.*

"I need you," he said, kissing the crook of her neck and trailing up to her ear. "But we should wait. My cousin and your stepsister are a little too close for my liking."

Noah ran a finger along her jaw, kissing her again before she could respond. He savored each stroke of their lips, and every inch of him grew aglow, an effortlessly glorious yet torturous feeling wrapped in one.

She leaned into his ear. "I never thought I'd say this. It always sounded so silly in my head, but it's the truth, so here goes." Celeste sucked in a deep breath. "I'm yours. I think about you—us—together all the time. Sometimes I fear I think about you more than saving the planets. Of course we can wait. I would wait forever if you asked me to."

Noah pulled her in once more, certain he would never let go again. At this moment, he knew there was more in the universe than planets and subspecies and stars. There was no other explanation for his and Celeste's encounter. It wasn't luck at all that brought them together.

It was fate.

13

AFTER

NOAH LAID AWAKE DEEP INTO THE NIGHT, EYES TRAINED ON THE canopy of their tent. Celeste was curled up in his arms, her mouth parted slightly; Luna was snoring on the opposite side, cuddling with a dirt-speckled pillow.

Celeste was a beautiful sleeper, even with her cheek squished against his chest and leg wrapped around his torso. Occasionally, she would mumble something indiscernible to herself while snuggling deeper into his arms. Absolutely adorable.

Yet the idea of after crawled into his thoughts. After they saved the planets. After they found salvation. What would they do? What would they see?

What if there was no after?

What if saving their planets was nothing more than a fruitless endeavor?

He wouldn't be surprised.

He hoped there was an after for them. An after and a forever and an always.

Despite his happiness, there was a lingering nudge of numbness beneath it all. He was still the same aimless man he'd been at the start of their adventure. He feared there was a hole inside him nothing could fix. No matter how hard he or anyone else tried, he'd always have a piece of him that was missing.

Even after.

14

INTO THE FOREST

The following morning, they were packing up the campsite and cooking a batch of fresh eggs the soil provided them. The air was chilly, and he was grateful for the limited sunlight peeking through the trees. He and Mark were in a heated debate on what color the grass was—Noah insisted it was yellow whilst Mark proclaimed it was neon orange—when Luna suddenly straightened, head darting around in confusion. "Did you hear that?"

Noah scanned the area; Celeste was standing by the fire, tending to the last of their breakfast before the start of another incredibly long and painful trek. He looked around but saw and heard nothing out of the ordinary. The forest was quaint, with birds chirping above, a breeze ruffling his blond hair and swaying the trees.

Katalina stuck her head out of her tent while holding

scrambled eggs placed on a leaf instead of a plate. "Did someone say something?"

"That answers that," muttered Luna as she tapped her foot in aggravation before wincing suddenly, her hands feverishly reaching up to cover her ears. "Really?"

"Well, what do you hear?" asked Celeste. "You *do* have super special hearing compared to us."

"Yeah. *Underwater.* On land, I'm just as useless as the rest of you."

"Thanks," Celeste said tersely, folding her arms over her chest. Noah admired how cute she looked, her stubbornness nothing short of endearing. Her cheeks were growing a soft rosy color, the kind that came with being flustered. How desperately he wanted to cup her face in his palms and feel the warmth of her lips—

"Noah," Mark said, waving a hand in front of Noah's face. "You're staring again."

Noah frowned. "Can't a man admire?"

Mark's eyes narrowed. "There's a time and place."

"Yeah, like right here and now."

"I swear someone said 'come here,'" Luna interjected. "And they won't stop."

This way, came a whisper, brushing against Noah's ear. He took a sharp intake of breath with a shiver, expecting a flesh-eating monster to pop out of the trees, but there was no one there. The voice was high-pitched and distant, a stark contrast to the Ruler of the Wind's deep, sultry tone. In fact, he could've sworn it sounded like his mother.

But no, that was silly. It couldn't have *really* sounded like her. His mind was playing tricks on him. Besides, her voice wasn't typically *that* high-pitched. Yet he couldn't shake the feeling she was calling to him.

Noah took an involuntarily surprised step back. "I heard it, too! More telepathy? I can't take much more."

"The Ruler of the Wind again?" Katalina suggested, garnering a shake of the head from Celeste.

"He wouldn't keep following us around. This has to be something else."

"We need to find the source," Luna stated wistfully, weaving through the nearby trees and checking under bushes. She must not have found much, because she kept creeping deeper into the forest until she was nearly out of sight.

"Uh, guys... not to be the common sense around here, but I don't think following a random voice is a good idea," Mark interrupted with a shrug. "Does that need to be said?"

"I haven't heard anything," agreed Katalina. "It could be a trap."

"She's right, Luna," called Celeste with a point toward Katalina for emphasis. "Remember what the twins in the maze said?"

Noah drifted closer to her, watching the woods with scrutiny to make sure there were no strange movements or sounds. The birds stopped chirping; the trees stopped rustling. Silence fell over the scene, and there were no signs of life anywhere. Something was off.

"'Focus on those who lead the way,'" Luna recited with a dazed, distant voice. "That's what I'm doing."

"Yes, but they followed it up with, 'though some may try to

lead you astray,'" Mark emphasized. He cupped his hands around his mouth as Luna continued to search deeper into the forest and yelled, "*Astray!*"

Luna bent down as though she were inspecting another bush, but she didn't come back up.

"What the—" Celeste jogged a little way ahead before coming back to the campground with hands on her hips and a chest heaving in panic. "I don't understand. She couldn't have gone far. We lost sight of her for just a second! How could she just be... gone?"

Noah turned in circles, hoping to catch a glimpse of Luna and save the day. Instead, all he saw were the same tall trees and thick branches littering the forest. Panic set in as an odd sucking noise ripped through the air. The tents and firepit disappeared into the sinking soil a second later.

"I heard it once," Noah said with a snap of his fingers and a nod to the right. "It sounded like it was coming from that way."

"Why do you always get to hear everything?" mumbled Mark. "It's not fair."

"Consider yourself lucky." Noah still couldn't shake the thought that it was his mother calling for him, trapped in these woods for all eternity.

He refrained from saying anything more and pointed ahead, though he couldn't be sure if he was pointing in the right direction anymore. He'd spun so much that he'd grown confused; the camping equipment was no longer there to use as a marker.

Great. He was useless yet again. There was an insurmountable pressure that came with being the only one who was continuously, inexplicably chosen by everything. Something the others wouldn't understand. To them, it must've looked like a luxury.

"Let's go. We'll have to run. She could've gone pretty far by now," Celeste said. Her voice was shaking along with the rest of her.

They ran in the direction Noah pointed, having no other guidance. He didn't want to be the one responsible for taking them toward danger. The pressure pinched his throat as he gasped for breath.

It was hopeless. There was nothing but trees. After a few minutes, they collectively stopped. It felt notably harder to breathe, though he couldn't pinpoint why. Was it the running, the fear, or the forest itself?

"We need to regroup," Katalina said, waving for everyone to gather around. Noah noted there were bags under her eyes. "We're obviously not finding her this way."

"Luna," Celeste screamed into the thick void. Her voice bounced off the trees, and he hoped the sound was enough to attract a response. They waited until the echo grew stale, and then a moment more. There was no answer. Celeste's shoulder's slumped. "I don't know what to do."

He'd never seen her look so defeated.

"I don't know what to do at all, Noah. It's my fault she's even here with us. I can't believe I dragged her along, and for what? Merpeople are revered by some species but hated by others. I should've known this was too dangerous. I'm so... so stu—"

Noah grabbed her by the shoulders and looked into her beautiful, pinkish-purple eyes. "Don't go denouncing yourself over one minor hiccup. Luna can handle herself. She'll be fine, and we'll find her safe and sound."

He wrapped Celeste in a quick hug, stroking the back of her head. He wished he could hold her forever, but there was never enough time for forever.

When he pulled away, a tear was slipping down her cheek. "I don't want to lose my stepsister, too. I can't."

"You won't."

"You can't promise that." Her voice was a barely audible whisper.

"Technically," Noah said with a light chuckle. "I can promise whatever I want. So I promise. Now, come on."

He held out a hand and offered her a comforting smile. She stared at him a moment longer before returning the gesture, and he could've sworn his heart was going to beat out of his chest at the way she looked at him. The sun was hitting her hair in such a way that she seemed to glow around the edges, and her eyes were magnificently bright.

Celeste took his hand, and they were off, sprinting through the forest. All the while, he hoped to hear the whispers once more, a hint to point them in the right direction. But if this species could read minds, they weren't doing Noah any favors, and the forest remained eerily quiet, aside from their footfalls.

Noah forced himself not to slip into thinking the worst, that Luna was abducted and eaten or killed. There was no such thing as a forest back home, just a treeline along the single mountain separating the two sides of his planet. One was crumbling and empty, whereas the other held a large city. Needless to say, there was nothing as dense as this on Sundar. Perhaps, in other circumstances, it was a sight to behold, but now he found the overcast of branches and the shadows they created unsettling.

“This is feeling like the wrong way,” Mark shouted, but he cut himself short when the treeline broke. Human-sized huts filled the small clearing. They were made of interwoven branches with blue leaves peeking through every few strands. Circular windows dotted the walls, and they were all sealed shut with their curtains drawn. He noticed the grass was taller here, too, and seemed to grow into the walls of the huts. “I stand corrected.”

Luna was still nowhere in sight, nor was there another creature or person about, yet dozens of these small homes speckled the area.

“Does anyone else find this strange?” Katalina asked. “An entire village deserted?”

Noah tried to look through the nearest window, but the curtain gave nothing away. A knock came from behind him, and he jumped, but it was only Celeste trying the house across the way.

They all waited with bated breath.

No one answered.

Celeste jiggled the door handle, and Mark tsked with a hand out to stop her. “Hey, I don’t think that’s a great idea.”

“I’m going to find my stepsister. If the people here don’t want to show themselves, then I’ll make them,” Celeste snapped over her shoulder. Noah gulped before speedily joining her side. It wasn’t often she lost her temper.

“I don’t normally agree with Mark,” Noah started gently.

"But I think I'm inclined to agree. We don't know who or what lives here. We'd be cornered in their territory and likely punished, at the very least, for trespassing."

She ignored his warning and squared her shoulders, fully prepared to step into a stranger's home. Just as she leaned forward to push open the door, it swung open on its own. No—there was someone was on the other side.

Celeste lost her balance and stumbled forward. Luna reached out, catching her by the forearm and breaking her fall. Their wide, surprised eyes connected before Celeste regained her composure.

"What are you doing?" Celeste hissed, her breath hot with anger. "Leaving us behind and then hiding away in there? We have to stick together!"

She craned her neck to look inside the home behind Luna, and Noah felt obligated to do the same. The house looked otherwise dark and empty. "Do you know who lives here?"

Luna shook her head and moved over so the four of them could enter. "Of course not. I'm hiding."

"Hiding? From what?" Noah asked as he and the others filed in. The house was accompanied by a wooden, rotting smell, one that curled along the edges and sent bile up his throat. He wondered if anyone had lived here in the last few years, or if they were dead. Perhaps this tiny town was overrun by the very creatures that lured Luna here.

He vaguely wondered if they should trust someone who disappeared from the group, only to reappear a bit too easily. But she looked and sounded like Luna, and he didn't think shapeshifters would be all the way out here.

The furniture inside was regular, human-sizes, but there were smaller versions connected to each. He cocked his head, picking up a tiny stove with a pan, burner, buttons, and everything. "This is cute. Are there dollhouse furniture collectors on Fortun or something?"

Celeste's eyes widened at Noah's words, though her gaze was focused on Luna. "No."

Her stepsister nodded solemnly, her azure skin turning pale. "Fairies."

Celeste scowled as she repeated, "Fairies."

15

FIGHT, FLIGHT OR FAE

"What would fairies want with us?" Noah asked, leaning against the kitchen counter of the empty home they'd technically broken into. He fiddled with the small fairy version of the dining table and chairs.

"Will they try to kill us?" asked Katalina. "Or are they nice fairies?"

Luna let out a sharp bark of laughter.

"Remember how I told you merpeople are rude and unhelpful?" Celeste asked. Noah nodded. "Well, fairies are worse."

"Why'd you follow the voice, then?" Mark added, throwing his hands in the air with a glare thrown Luna's way. "We shouldn't even be in this situation right now!"

"It sounded like my mother," Luna explained. "Calling for my help... I can't explain why I believed she was out here. Her pleas just sounded so... so real."

"I should've known." Celeste shook her head. "Some forests are populated with them. I guess we were lucky until now. They enchanted you. To taste your blood, no doubt."

"Excuse me." Mark gulped. "To do what now?"

"But I heard a voice, too," Noah exclaimed. "It sounded like my mother, too, but I didn't feel compelled to follow."

Celeste took a deep breath, dodging eye contact with him. "They can't enchant those with deceased or completely estranged parents. The blood isn't deemed worthy enough."

"Rumor has it merpeople are the tastiest to them," Luna confirmed. "They must've targeted me. I sure am an idiot. My body moved without thought, and next thing I knew, I was drawn here, to this house."

Celeste grabbed her stepsister's shoulder with a reassuring smile. "You're okay. That's all that matters."

"To *this* house?" Noah asked. His thunderous heart reverberated through his chest, traveling up his spine and to his brain. A mild headache of nerves emerged. "So we're standing *in* the trap right now? Shouldn't we, you know, go? Especially since I was also targeted?"

"Maybe they wanted a taste of you, too," Celeste suggested with a wink. "Who wouldn't?"

"Gross," Mark said with a nose crinkled in disgust. "And if that were the case, they'd be trying to lure me, too."

"There's a difference between inner and outer beauty," Noah countered.

"Where are they?" Katalina asked, ignoring their squabbling. "The fairies? If they tricked you into entering their house, then where are they?"

Celeste pointed to Katalina. "Right. Well, they're a little shorter than the average human in their daily lives, but when they're around other species, they shrink and sprout wings."

"Huh," Katalina said. "I wonder what the science is behind that."

"I don't think there is any."

Katalina gawked. "There's a scientific explanation for everything."

"Maybe where you're from, but there is no here nor there on Fortun, no rhyme or reason for many—if not most—things," Celeste said with a shrug before providing Katalina with a sly wink. "If you decide to stay with us on Fortun, you could try to prove me wrong."

Her bold proposition made Katalina's mouth fall open.

"We should be careful. They could be somewhere inside right now, listening in," Luna warned. "And don't make any sudden movements. They hate that. Think they'll get swatted at or squished."

The idea of accidentally crushing a tiny person with wings made him squeamish, and he shuddered. He didn't like the idea of people-adjacent creatures the size of bugs lurking about.

"Hiding?" asked Katalina. "Why would they lure us here just to hide?"

"For the added challenge, probably," said Celeste, twirling a dark blue strand of hair around her finger. "They're hunters."

Katalina crept toward the door. "Not to state the obvious, but can't we just... leave?"

"Uh... I think it might be too late for all that," came Mark's voice. Noah's heart skipped a beat; he hadn't noticed Mark was peeking out of the front window. "I think they're all standing outside."

Noah rushed to his side, nudging his way toward the opening in the curtain. The waning glass distorted his view, but there was definitely a large group of people standing outside. People who were certainly not there before.

Noah ducked below the window, white-hot panic consuming him and blinding his vision. He scurried back to the kitchen, where Luna was muttering obscenities under her breath as she kept her eyes trained on the wooden floor below.

Celeste, on the other hand, was opening cabinets and checking under furniture for any potential fairies who may have been eavesdropping.

"Is there anything we *can* do?" Noah asked, his mouth running dry.

"Probably not. There's nowhere to run or hide. Fairies are incredibly strong. Probably from all the blood and fear," Luna stated with a tremor in her voice. "I'm really sorry, everyone. I guess it was a mistake to invite me, after all."

"They feed off of fear, too," Celeste added, popping open each cupboard for alternative exits or weapons. "If we can't go out the front, we can try these back windows."

The front door rattled before anyone could move. Katalina screamed with a hand over her heart; Luna and Celeste shushed her in unison, though it was too late. If they had any chance of secrecy, it was lost now.

Mark was nearest the door, staring down at the jiggling handle. "Well, that can't be good."

Celeste ran toward the door, slamming her side against it to make sure it stayed shut. "There's no lock! Impossible. How is there no lock, yet they're struggling to get in—"

The rattling stopped. Celeste cocked her head. "How odd."

"Look," Noah shouted, eyes bulging as he thrust a finger toward Celeste's hand. Her palm was becoming transparent from the inside out. She followed his gesture and gasped, shaking her arm frantically as though movement could bring her back to a solid form.

It was no use.

She was disappearing. It started with her hands before traveling up her arms and to every limb until she was entirely see-through. Celeste met his gaze with quivering lips, her skin growing pale. "Better me than Luna, I suppose."

"No," he yelled, running up to hold her, to feel her warm embrace, but he was reaching for something that wasn't there. His grip slipped through her fingers. "Wait! You can't go. I never told you I lov—"

In a puff of smoke and colorful confetti, Celeste was gone.

Noah yelped and fell backward, landing on the ground with a harsh thud. He scooted away from the door hastily, his stomach churning. He only stopped once his back hit the cupboards.

There and then gone. Just like his mother and father. Just like everything and everyone if they failed. If they succeeded, it wouldn't matter because she wouldn't be there. It never truly mattered to him if they failed or not, as long as they failed *together.*

Celeste couldn't be *gone.* "No. No, no, n—"

"It's okay," Luna said. "Well, actually, it's not, *but* she's alive! It's a lame thing the fai—"

She never had the chance to finish her sentence, because she disappeared next, bursting into blue and green confetti. Noah's mouth hung open as he gasped for air that would not come.

"Mark, Katalina, run!" It was the only thing he could think to say, though he knew there was nowhere to go. They were surrounded, and he couldn't even get himself to stand up. Did he want to escape when she hadn't?

Something inside him cracked. Perhaps it was the dread of always being alone. Or perhaps it was the fact he could've had everything—*her*—and now it was all gone. In the blink of an eye.

"Noah, hurry," cried Katalina. "I found a secret door."

She and Mark were crouched beside an open cabinet with a hidden crawlspace leading outside. Noah dragged himself over, though everything looked and felt hazy, and his limbs were growing heavy as fatigue seized control.

A strange concoction of nausea and numbness washed over him. His head lolled to the side and his body hit the ground harshly before he could think of bracing himself. He'd landed flat on his face; a throb shot through his nose instantly.

He forced his weak head up to find Mark was reaching down for him. "What's wrong, Noah? Hurry, take my hand! Who knows when we'll be next?"

As if on cue, Mark's hand became transparent until his entire arm was gone. In seconds, Noah was staring at nothing but a wall, confetti gracefully falling to the floor. His colors were red and yellow.

Noah was out of screams, his mind so overwhelmed he turned to autopilot as he looked around for Katalina, but she was gone, too. There were no last goodbyes. There was simply 'the end', followed by a long line of blank chapters of what could have been.

He was so, so tired, his body perpetually glued to the ground. Noah vaguely heard the door whack against the wall before a persistent buzzing filled the room. Though he couldn't see them, he could hear the fairies snickering between whispers as they hovered above. It hardly mattered that they'd cornered him, because his fingers were growing transparent now, too.

What colors would his confetti be? Would they be as melancholy as his life back home, or bright from new knowledge and love? He hadn't a chance to see Katalina's, either. What a shame.

Yet Noah smiled to himself. The end was near, and that was okay because he would see all his loved ones again in the great beyond.

16

CAGED IN

"OW!" MARK'S PAINED PROCLAMATION SHOCKED NOAH AWAKE. His face was squished between two metal bars, his cheeks flaring with agony from the pressure. "Your knee is digging into my back!"

Noah tried to take a deep breath, but the more his chest expanded, the more uncomfortable he became. He couldn't complete the action and let out a suffocating wheeze in surprise. The snug metal bars were digging into his ribcage, threatening to shatter his bones and squeeze the life out of him. If Noah could turn his head, he would provide Mark with an agitated glare. "How do you propose I fix it?"

He tried to move, but that only made his knee dig deeper into Mark's boney back, and Mark released another groan. Noah gave up with a huff and asked, "Hey—what's going on? Where are we?"

They were in the smallest enclosure that could hold them,

stuffed in a vast and empty crack on the planet's surface. The cage bars curved upward and over, with a small platform underneath. The group of five were essentially shoved so close together that not a muscle could move beyond an inch without someone else becoming collateral damage.

Straight ahead of Noah was a rushing waterfall cascading down from the cavernous crater into an even deeper orifice below. Plumes of steam rose from the underbelly of the planet, creating a flow of damp coolness along his skin.

"Oh, good! You're awake! I was worried," Celeste said with a sigh of relief. "I've been calling your name for a good five minutes."

Noah blushed at the worry expelling from Celeste's lips, and he wondered where she was in this jumbled mess of bodies. Gratitude filled his heart, though the pain from his squashed face brought him back to reality rather quickly. He hoped she was somewhere close. "Are Luna and Katalina here, too?"

"Present," came Luna's meek, bubbly voice.

"What happened?" Katalina asked groggily.

"Katalina, thank the Goddesses you're alright," cried Mark. Noah could feel him wiggle around to look at his fiancé, only to stop with a groan of frustration.

Noah's body was horizontal, crammed between Mark and the metal bars, and he could vaguely see Katalina's hand resting on the ground. She may have been upside down for all he knew, but he couldn't see anything else from this angle, including Luna or Celeste.

He felt like a bird stolen from flight, only to be stuffed in a claustrophobic nightmare. "We were abducted? I thought I watched all of you disappear one-by-one. Unless that was a dream?"

"It wasn't a dream. That was one of many illusions the fairies can create," stated Celeste. "A way to instill fear, since they thrive off of it."

Noah shuddered at the memory of Celeste's body waning before turning into smoke and confetti. "I thought everyone died. I thought *I* was dead."

"Well, lucky for us, we're still alive," Luna said with an aggravated huff. "Except we're stuck in the den of blood-sucking fairies, and it's all my fault."

"All fairies are blood-suckers," Celeste corrected. "That's a redundant statement."

"Not only that," Luna continued. "But we can't move *and* we're stuck with Mark."

"Hey! What did I ever do to you?" Mark asked, hurt laced with irritation lining his voice.

She ignored him. "This is insane. Who would want to go on an 'adventure' like this? It's basically torture—"

"Please don't insult my fiancé when you're the reason we're stuck. Technically, we *were* trespassing their forest, *and* we broke into one of their houses," Katalina argued. "Maybe we look like the bad guys."

"So the answer is to resort to this?" Noah scoffed. "The worst we do to criminals on Sundar is send them to the Reform Apartments. Are there *any* nice species here?"

Luna cleared her throat. "Merpeople, for one."

"Ha," came Celeste. "I find species are much like people. So, no. There are only kind individuals."

"How do you suppose we get out?" Katalina asked, bringing them back to the task at hand. "I don't see hinges or a door handle for an opening anywhere."

Noah tried to gauge their surroundings further. Aside from the sparkling waterfall, the walls were made of jagged rock, and there didn't appear to be a ceiling, only a long way upwards. The moon, though hidden behind clouds, provided a faint sheen of light for them to see. Somehow, the sky had already drifted into darkness, and they'd once again lost another day to an unnecessary obstacle.

He noticed dark passageways were etched along the sides of the rocks spanning in all directions; the holes were big enough for fairies to walk and fly through. There were no fairies to be seen, however. It was eerily hushed aside from their echoing voices as they continued to bicker in the open cave-like crack.

"Stop blaming yourself, Luna," came Celeste.

"Oh, no. You should blame yourself," interrupted Mark. Noah imagined him wagging a finger at Luna for being tricked so easily. "You could've gotten us killed!"

"True, but beating ourselves up isn't the answer," Celeste countered.

"Shh," Katalina released harshly, and the group grew quiet. "Do you hear that?"

There was a faint buzzing, like the whizz of a bug too close to an ear. The noise started slow and distant, but quickly morphed into a thrum of thunderous wingbeats. Noah's muscles grew tense as he prepared for whatever was coming.

He held his breath at the sight of the first dozen—there were hundreds, if not thousands, of beating wings with tiny people connected to them. They were no larger than an index finger, and they had pointy ears and pale pink skin. Their hair was less remarkable, ranging from brunette to blonde.

"Good evening." A fairy with a voice full of ecstatic wonder flew through the crowd with two male fairies on either side. Her dress was a shimmering gold and cascaded well past her feet. Her dark pink hair was wrapped in a bun with a tiara atop, its small golden gems gleaming when struck by the moonlight. "I was told we caught quite the crew."

"Listen," Noah began, skipping the formalities. The fairy was hovering in front of his face with an eyebrow ticked upward. "It might sound crazy, but our planet is crashing into another—my planet. We *need* to get through this forest and save them both. Please, let us go. We have less than two weeks left. There's no time for all this."

The fairy squinted, her nose notably turned upward. "I'm the princess, you know. Or the queen now, I suppose. Queen Iridessa."

He furrowed his brows. She looked to be no older than sixteen, yet her gaze was worn. Her cheeks were dusted with freckles, and though her silver eyes were narrow to appear intimidating, she looked too much like a little sister to truly be so. "You don't look like a ruler."

One of her male minions zipped forward and smacked Noah's nose with a tiny hand. The motion felt like a cat's paw trying to nudge him awake. Her henchmen were wearing suits made of mint green leaves, and their wings were a similar see-through shade. "How dare you speak to her that way!"

Noah suppressed a laugh at the attempt to hurt him. Instead, he quickly skimmed over the other fairies, realizing they all had the same transparent green wings, too. The Queen's, however, were light pink. He'd certainly put his foot in his mouth. Every part of her differed from the rest—it was glaringly obvious she was the Queen. No wonder her subjects were offended.

The Fairy Queen held up a hand. "Sire Donald, I did not grant permission for violence."

The fairy's pale pink cheeks turned magenta, and he flew backward with a head held down in shame. Queen Iridessa found Noah's eyes once more. He expected to see anger staring back, but there was only an overwhelming sadness. "My mother's death was untimely. She was eaten by a bear a few weeks ago."

Noah frowned as embarrassment flooded his thoughts. "I'm sorry to hear that, and I apologize for making such a brash observation. I've also lost my mother."

"Noah, this isn't the time to bond," Luna hissed.

"It's always the time," countered Noah. "That's how we convinced the Ruler of the Deep to help us."

"Using the word 'convinced' makes us sound like liars," Mark pointed out. Much to Noah's dismay, Mark wasn't wrong.

"Was she eaten, too?" Queen Iridessa asked, a little too joyous to bond over such depressing details of their lives.

Noah tried to shake his head, but the metal bars kept him locked in place. "No. She... well..."

He hadn't said it in so long that he wasn't prepared for the lump in his throat. The taste of tar lined his lips, the words coming out slow and uneven. "She took her own life."

Queen Iridessa gasped with a hand flying to her mouth. "The Forbidden Act."

The audience of fairies turned to each other with inaudible whispers. Noah sucked in a deep, nervous breath. He was being judged. His family was being judged. He could feel his fingers curl into fists, his lips drawing into a sneer. He knew it was wrong to yell at a queen while he was being held hostage by them, but he couldn't stop himself—

"Regardless," Celeste said. Her fingers lightly brushed against his, and a wave of calmness washed over him, bringing him back to a reality where he didn't burst. "What Noah said before is true. We're all going to die if you don't let us go."

"The Collision isn't set for another three hundred years, my child," the Fairy Queen said with a chuckle, garnering an explosion of robust laughter rippling through the crowd.

"The Collision?" Celeste asked, her voice riddled with confusion. If only he could see her now and wrap his arms around her shoulders while muttering words of comfort.

"Yes. It's written on our calendars to happen in four hundred Y.B. That's 'Years Beyond.' We're currently in year one hundred Y.B."

He could feel Katalina's chest fill with air. "Why lure us here in the first place?"

"To suck your blood, of course," said the sire who'd slapped Noah. "We must eat, and it's been a while since such a delicacy has graced our presence. Don't worry. We don't need much." He exchanged a ravenous glance with the other fairy flanking the Queen's side, and they guffawed at the same time. "Oh wait, we do!"

"I only wanted the merwoman, but the more the merrier," agreed the Fairy Queen with a clap of her golden-gloved hands.

"There can't possibly be enough of our blood for all of you," Mark stammered. "Let us go, and find something bigger to feast on."

"They taste through me," Queen Iridessa snapped with a broad smirk.

"You aren't listening," Celeste urged. "*Everyone* is going to die unless you release us!"

"How about this?" Luna offered. "If you let us go now, we'll donate our blood to you. An endless supply for our entire lives. You just have to let us go now, and we'll come back later."

Queen Iridessa scratched her chin in thought. "Interesting proposition. You'll need to leave something here as leverage, so we know you'll return."

Noah gulped. He hadn't a single thing to hand over. "Uh... does anyone have something of value on them?"

"Just a picture of our kickball team," Katalina said with a sigh. "I miss them greatly."

"I have my mother's necklace," Luna added. "Would that work?"

"It has to be more sentimental than that," said the Queen. "Something you couldn't live without."

There was one thing that came to mind, and it was the notebook given to Celeste by her brother. It would certainly be more sentimental than a living mother's necklace. Although he desperately wanted to, he couldn't bring himself to suggest it. He didn't want to offend Celeste.

The five remained silent.

The Queen let out a *huff.* "Well, then I guess we shall feast."

She fluttered forward, pausing above Noah's nose with a smile, and revealing two small fangs he hadn't noticed from afar. Her eyes turned from silver to golden-red.

"But what about all the bonding we just did?" Noah asked. His heart rate was progressively picking up. The fairies had the wings of bugs but the teeth of bats, and the hive mind of bees. Tasting blood. *His* blood. She was terrifying, yet he couldn't look away. He had no choice but to watch as the fairies did whatever they wanted. "We have so much in common."

"We all encounter tragedies in life. It's not worth putting an end to our feasting." Queen Iridessa did not come closer, however, and instead glanced over her shoulder with a snap of her fingers. "Sire Arnold must take the first taste to make sure no poison runs in your veins. Then I will drain you until you are even paler than you already are. Until your heart stops beating and your body falls limply to the ground with wide eyes full of despair and *nothing.*"

"You don't have to do this," he pleaded. "Let us go. You can show mercy. Everyone will die if we do!"

"I am a queen. I do not know mercy." A glint of elation flashed across her face.

"Why not?" he asked. "Were you not shown love as a child?"

The Queen's lips curled in disgust. "Of course I was. Being a queen *is* love. An unwavering love for one's people. My parents showed me what is best, and what is best is the demise of intruders like you. Pillagers who think they can enter our forests, sleep on our soil and tell us what to do."

She snapped her fingers, and the second of her underlings approached, his extra pointy teeth gleaming in the dim light. Noah heard Sire Arnold's tiny wings fluttering in his ear as the fairy landed on his shoulder.

"No—you're really going to suck my blood?" He nearly shrieked at the thought, but his body gave way to shock instead.

"Among many other things," growled Sire Arnold. A sharp pain radiated through Noah's neck, and he gasped. His cheeks flushed at the icy flow of the blood leaving his veins.

"Wait, wait," he said, his voice growing softer as his body became weak. "Celeste, what about your notebook? It proves what we're saying is true, and it's sentimental—"

"No. There has to be something else. Anything else." Celeste's tone left no room for arguing. Noah would've gasped if he had the energy. He wondered what look was overtaking her face. Was it one of fear? Of resignation?

"Please—" He couldn't help the sense of betrayal he felt as he grew weaker. She was choosing a notebook over his life? Surely, she wouldn't. He couldn't be what Pevelyn claimed he was—just one of many boys Celeste plucked for an adventure, only to discard when he was no longer needed.

Right?

"I—" A sigh overtook the room, and when he tried to open his eyes, he couldn't. A bright light was weaseling its way into the back of his eyelids.

He was tired.

Oh, so tired.

"It looks like Sire Arnold is getting carried away. There might not be any left for the rest of us," Sire Donald noted.

The Queen shrugged. "Let him. There's plenty more to go around."

"Here." He heard the word as something shuffled against his back. From the corner of his eye, he saw she'd somehow gotten her hands through the bars with the notebook out. "Take it and get your disgusting fangs out of his neck."

Vitriol lined her voice. It was low and threatening, and he couldn't help but smile faintly as another sharp tug ripped at his neck. Cool air wafted over Noah as Sire Arnold's wings pushed away from his shoulder.

"Disgusting?" cried a fairy in the audience. "How dare you talk about the Queen's sires that way!"

"Keep them in the shrinking cage!" cried another.

There was an uproar within the cave, drowning out his thoughts, but not the pain. He was much too tired to move, and his emotions had long since grown stale. The cage was so small that his head didn't loll to the side, instead remaining stuck between the bars. Sleep was threatening to take hold. Still, he meekly forced out, "Thank you, Celeste. I—love—"

His lips became too numb to move.

"You can't be serious," Mark exclaimed. "Is he dead? It sounds like he's dying!"

"Is he going to turn into a fairy now that he's been bit?" asked Katalina, a question Noah hadn't thought of. He could hear their voices in a far-off way, as though he were underwater but somehow still breathing.

"Enough, my children," Queen Iridessa declared. Noah

forced his burning eyes open, watching as she waved her arms in broad strokes. Altair's notebook was too big for just one fairy to hold, so a crew of ten flew down and picked it up, hovering with the book above for all to see. "A sentimental sacrifice has been made. We shall free them in the morning. The cage may crush them by then, but it will be worth the wait to see! Place your guesses with Sire Donald."

The room was filled with cheers, and all the fairies slowly filtered out of the cavern through the tunnels in which they arrived.

"Hey," yelled Luna. "That wasn't part of the agreement!"

The Queen turned, her pale pink wings shimmering when catching the light. She giggled, covering her mouth with a wicked gleam in her eyes. "You should know to never make deals with fairies, you pesky sea dweller. You're lucky we don't drain you here and now."

Once again, Noah was left to wonder how lucky they'd actually been.

17

CAUGHT IN THE MIDDLE

"THAT WAS FAR DARKER THAN I THOUGHT IT'D BE," MARK announced with a shaky breath. "How does anyone stay alive on this planet?"

"We steer clear of forests," Luna said.

"And we never leave the city without excessive protection," added Celeste.

The crowd of fairies had long since left, and while there were likely guards loitering about, they were nowhere to be seen. Noah was still tired, his neck throbbing from the sharp stab of fangs, and words were lost on him. The chilly air nipped at his freezing flesh. He was in limbo, caught between the things he had to say and no way to say them.

"Are there fairies in every forest?" asked Katalina.

A body readjusted behind him with a groan as Celeste explained, "Fairies only live in very warm forests, and they cannot leave. Something to do with the sky. They need the shade to survive or something."

"That, and they can be squished or eaten easily by non-fairies," Luna tacked on.

"By Goddesses—that's awful!" Mark exclaimed. "And you want to stay here, Noah?"

If Celeste stays, I stay, he thought. All that came out was a weak groan. The inability to speak would've been frustrating if he wasn't so tired. Noah strained his eyes, forcing himself to stay awake with what little energy he had left. The thought slowly leaked from his ears like string cheese, replaced with the memory of Celeste's hesitation toward handing over Altair's notebook. Noah could've died.

What if their love was one-sided? The question lingered in the back of his mind, never straying far enough to forget.

"He can't talk," Luna stated. His ears perked at that. "Fairies can choose how fast they drain their victims. Doing so quickly can cause a numbing effect. Makes it easier to kill."

There was a pause in the conversation as the implications of this settled in.

A sudden low screech scraped his eardrums. The metal bars moved inward, pushing his head back until it slowly ran into another. They were being squished.

"What is this?" Katalina's voice was full of distress, the kind that was often followed by a scream of panic. "Some twisted example of what happens to them?"

"Is there a way out?" Mark grunted. "Don't either of you know the secret to escape this thing?"

"Do you think anyone can escape a cage without a door?" Luna snarled. "It's not possible."

"A sentimental item," came a voice. It was familiar, much like—

"But there's another way," said another, this voice slightly lower. His heart sank. Tysven and Rosvel. The riddling twins. "A way you clearly do not know."

"Otherwise you'd be gone by now, surely," agreed Tysven with a shake of their head.

"Yes. There is one last thing. A riddle," Rosvel said. The pair were circling the cage with narrow eyes, inspecting their newest toys.

Mark groaned loudly, exaggerating his aggravation tenfold. "Of course, there's another riddle. Can't you just be helpful and let us out?"

"How did you find us?" asked Celeste.

"And why would you want to?" Luna's displeasure was highlighted with a scoff.

"For a little entertainment before the end of days," Tysven remarked.

"And maybe we don't want the planets to collide." Rosvel tucked their twig fingers behind their back with a close-lipped smile.

"Then help us escape," Luna begged. "Skip the preamble and riddle nonsense and break open the cage. You're both wasting our time, not helping it!"

"Easy, there," Celeste said under her breath. "We don't want to upset them."

"There's no joy in that," sneered Tysven. "You of all species should know that."

There wasn't ample time to unpack Tysven's words, and Mark was quick to fill the spaces with another question that hadn't crossed Noah's mind. "Isn't the Ruler of the Wind going to be upset if he finds out you're helping us?"

"He knows," said Rosvel. "But he lets us do as we please from time to time."

"He does not think our interference will matter," added Tysven. "He thinks we are doomed, no matter the move. A game designed to lose."

"'Lost planets or lost freedom,'" they recited in unison.

"We do not see it that way," Tysven said. "Nature can be defeated."

But could it? Could it be defeated? The question had admittedly popped into Noah's head a handful of times, but he didn't want to contest their claim and reverse their possibility of survival with pessimism.

Rosvel nodded. "So can a big fish."

It was possible that no matter what they tried, their fates were sealed, yet the twin's reasoning was the same as his—they had to at least *try*. Noah may have had his many nights of doubts and depression, longing for the end to draw near, but that didn't mean everyone and everything wanted or deserved the same fate.

"The Ruler of the Deep might use the star to reign," explained Tysven. "But what does it matter if everyone has perished? A silly squabble between kings and queens is not leading to the loss of Mother's life nor our many siblings."

"This is our forest, you know. Mother is here," Rosvel agreed. "The Forest Goddess."

"Where is she, then? Can she help us?" asked Celeste.

The twins shook their heads. "She must not know we're here. We abandoned her in pursuit of freedom."

"Alright, alright. Can you spit out the riddle or what?" Luna barked. He imagined her staring daggers at Tysven and Rosvel. She must've had a feud with half the planet, by the looks of it. "I can't stand all these damn guessing games."

"Language." Noah's eyebrows rose as he realized he was the one who'd said it. His voice sounded inhuman, mouth stuffed with gravel. Of all the times to speak up, he'd managed to for a joke. He tried to say something else, but his jaw went slack. Of course.

"Noah," Celeste exhaled excitedly. "I missed your voice. I'm sorry I didn't hand over my notebook sooner."

He tried to release forgiveness from his lips, but the words did not come.

"Tell me," Tysven said, ignoring Celeste with their head tilted to the side. "Did any of you think about how you could capture the stars? Did you think you could grab them with your bare hands and put them in your pockets?"

Noah waited for Luna or Celeste to speak, but they didn't. He realized then how much hope he put into the stepsisters, and how dismaying it was when they didn't have the answers. It was becoming abundantly clear none of their group thought through much of their plan, hoping they could simply grab the stars and go.

"Look," Mark interjected. "We aren't the best people to save the planets. That's been established enough, I think."

The twins gravitated toward each other, standing side by side with their gangly arms dangling at their sides. They both had tight-lipped, expressionless faces. "None of you thought about it at all?"

Noah presumed everyone collectively provided them with blank stares.

The pair shared a look, and Tysven asked, "Should we even help them?"

"Should we even tell them about the room with the object made of stars?" asked Rosvel.

"You mean the ones—yeah, you're right. We shouldn't."

"They wouldn't think about it."

"They *didn't*." Tysven released a drawn-out tsk.

"I think I understand Mark's anger issues," Celeste grumbled, breaking the tension. "I don't know how much more of this I can handle."

"Thank you." Mark's tone was surprisingly smug for someone who'd just received a backhanded compliment.

Noah felt a bubble of laughter erupt in his chest, but his lips barely parted, and the noise came out as a mix between a cough and a groan. He still couldn't move his mouth, no matter how hard he tried. It was agonizing to have so many thoughts swirling in his head with the inability to utter a single one.

"A sister and a brother had a bond," began Rosvel.

"But one died, and the sister grew sad," continued Tysven. They continued to alternate between each other, telling a story Noah was struggling to follow.

"So tragically sad, she fell into deep despair. One where not a tear was shed for a hundred years."

Tysven began walking clockwise around the cage. "Then one day, she found a photo of them. A photo she'd thought she'd thrown away long ago. She didn't like being reminded of him, you see. And so she cried and cried."

Rosvel joined, walking around the cage counterclockwise. "She trapped her sadness in a jar, allowing her sky-colored tears to fill the container until it overflowed. She vowed that day to no longer despair. To instead be joyful, and hope to see him again after this life."

"When she finally passed away, she was sent to the stars, where her brother awaited, becoming the constellation of hope."

"It is said this jar is the only item that can hold a star, much less two."

"That wasn't much of a riddle," Mark blurted out.

"Respect your saviors, boy," Rosvel said in a low, primal tone.

Mark gulped. "Right. Sorry."

"The riddle is as thus. 'If the left is right and right is wrong, which tunnel should you take? The answer will lead to the jar."

"There are at least fifteen tunnels surrounding us," snapped Luna, effectively ignoring their demand to respect them. "There is no left or right here!"

The twins met back together in front of Noah and stopped walking with heads cocked to the side, befuddled looks on their wooden faces. It was Tysven who asked, "There's no hope for your crew at all, is there?"

"None," agreed Rosvel. Noah desperately wanted to point

out the waterfall directly in front of him. He wondered what was behind the cascading water. If there was a waterfall on the parallel side, he wagered there was a secret tunnel behind both, an element of confusion in case prisoners were to escape.

His suspicion was proven even further by a sign shoved into the ground that read, 'look this way for the riddle.' When had that gotten there? He reckoned he was the only one who could see it. Surely, it wasn't the fairies doing—?

"Alright, enough," Celeste barked. "We have to hurry and figure this out. Noah is likely losing consciousness, and he hasn't spoken in minutes."

"You're not wrong," agreed Tysven. "He is not looking particularly well."

Noah's heart fluttered at the sound of Celeste's concern. It reminded him that the brief kisses they'd shared were as passionate as they'd felt.

"What do you mean?" she asked, her voice lined with concerned urgency. A piercing ache whirled through him, laced with such longing that he was nearly shocked back to his senses.

It was love. It was Celeste. She captivated him with every word. If only he could look at her now as he was possibly taking his last breaths. But she'd hesitated to save him.

The pain in his neck zapped through his body in such a sudden way that he groaned again, his heart palpitating and organs twisting. He was certain the agony would kill him, yet he held on by the thread of his love.

"Do you think they took too much blood?" Celeste asked. She was panicking; he didn't have to see her to know. He could vaguely feel someone shuffling behind him, followed by ferocious tapping against the cage.

"It's no use," said the twins. "You must answer the riddle or we'll leave you in there."

"But the cage is going to crush us," cried Katalina. "Where is your empathy?"

Though he expected the twins to look at each other and laugh maniacally, they didn't even smile. "There is no fun in making the right choices without getting your hands a little dirty."

"You've officially won as the worst of the species we've met," Mark grumbled. "Aside from the fairies."

"Stop insulting them," Luna snapped. "Read the room! We're in a cage that's shrinking and they're our only way out! Now, someone repeat the riddle back to the group, please. I don't remember it."

There was a moment of silence before Celeste said, "Aren't merpeople supposed to have an amazing memory?"

Luna tsked. "We aren't all the same, you know."

"If the left is right and right is wrong, which tunnel should you take?" Katalina repeated. "The answer is obviously the right tunnel."

"But right is wrong," Mark countered.

"Yes, but no. Right is right. So that's the answer. Let us out now," Katalina said plainly.

"All of you must agree with one answer," the twins said. "That's the only way we'll let you go."

The bickering had long since begun, but somehow he knew it was about to get so much worse.

18

ESCAPISM IN ITS TRUEST FORM

"LUNA. RESPECTFULLY." HE'D NEVER HEARD THIS SIDE OF Katalina before, her voice seeping with unchecked rage. "You're going to get us killed if you do not agree."

"You have lived for hundreds of years," Celeste yelled. "And yet you cannot agree with an answer that's so obvious it's painful!"

"Excuse me?" asked Luna, aghast. Though Noah had no siblings to experience such a tiff with, he supposed he'd acted similarly cold toward Katalina for a long while—but for much different reasons. "An answer that could get us killed!"

"I think I have to agree with Luna on this one," Mark joined in. "The riddle clearly states the tunnel to the left is the right way to go, and the right tunnel is wrong."

Celeste scoffed. "Of course you would think that."

"Mark, I love you," Katalina began. "But that wouldn't make it a riddle. 'Left is right' means the right side is actually the left.

Since the right side is wrong, we still go right. Because *left* is right."

"This is ridiculous," contested Luna. "I have lived for so long that I know false beings when I see them. No matter what we guess, right or wrong, they won't let us out. It's a little game to watch us squirm. I wouldn't be surprised if the fairies or Ruler of the Wind put them up to this."

"Are you being argumentative for fun? Because it's not fun, Luna. It's cramped in here and Noah is dying!" The urgency in Celeste's voice was growing. Noah would've smiled to himself if his lips could move. They'd long since been tingling, and all he could think about was the drooping of his eyes with each passing second. "You could take the left tunnel after we all agree that the *right* tunnel is the right tunnel!"

"There is another issue," Katalina warned. "Noah can't agree *or* disagree right now. We can't escape until he can talk."

"We're screwed," came Mark.

Noah feared Mark was right. He tried to speak, but his mouth was just as numb as it was two seconds ago, and drool was slipping down his chin. Not even the pain of the cage bars digging into his face could keep his eyes open.

"I'd say you have more or less ten hours before they decide to drain or squish you all," said Tysven.

"Yes," agreed Rosvel. "Fairies get bored. They may say they'll let you go, but then they'll speed up the crushing process. Certainly."

"Certainly."

"And Noah *must* verbally respond? He can't just nod when presented with the choice he agrees with?" Katalina asked quickly, her voice growing higher. Nerves were settling in for them all.

"Yes," the twins said in unison.

"We're doomed," Mark reiterated.

"Another classic quote from Mark, everybody," said Luna, garnering a reaction from absolutely nobody. "Hey—how come when Noah berates Mark, you guys all agree, but when I do, there's nothing but silence?"

Celeste released a deep breath. "It's funnier coming from Noah. He has a certain charm about him."

"There's a brotherly chemistry between them, too," agreed Katalina.

"We're friends," Mark concurred. "You're... a merperson I am traveling with."

"Gee, thanks." Luna's tone was dry, and Noah could tell this was going nowhere fast. If only he could reign everybody in. Though he had to admit, he enjoyed being talked of so highly by his companions. It'd been so long since he'd had friends, and he'd never achieved this level of closeness before.

"Noah," called Mark. "Say something. Laugh. Cry. Groan. Anything."

Noah attempted to groan, but nothing came out. Wooziness was taking hold, slowly but surely, and he took a sharp intake of breath to coax himself awake. The fairy must've taken a lot more blood than he'd thought.

He wondered if dying was better than drifting in and out of such horrific pain.

As the thought hit, his body shut down, and his eyes slipped shut. His companions remained unaware of his shallow breathing and diminishing state. Before he succumbed to the treacherous tiredness threatening to take hold, he glimpsed the twins one last time. They were grinning, their terrifying teeth exposed.

With no thoughts remaining, he fell unconscious, his head resting against the thick metal.

19

A DOOR TO THE UNKNOWN

HE AWOKE WITH A SNORT.

"Finally," Mark's voice cut through Noah's thoughts. There was a rustling of bodies and fabric against him, jostling Noah further into reality. The first thing Noah noticed was that he still couldn't move his head. He was pressed so hard against the metal that his cheeks pulsed with tremendous pain, and he knew there would be marks in their place whenever he broke free.

If he broke free.

"Noah! I'm so happy you're alive," cried Celeste. Much to his dismay, he still couldn't see her. Instead, he was face-to-face with the twins. The same creatures that were taunting them all but moments ago. "Did you know you snore when you sleep?"

"I did, but that's beside the point. How long was I out?"

"How are we supposed to know?" Mark retorted. "Do you see a way to tell the time down here?"

"It's been a while," Celeste said. "At least an hour or two. How do you feel?"

Everything ached, but it was keeping him more alert than ever, *and he could talk again.* "Better, I think?"

"Good. I'm glad." Her voice was sultry and sweet, with hints of admiration interlaced within her words. His heart fluttered, though his body was still processing the despair brought about by being drained of his blood. He never wanted to feel such hopelessness again. It was far worse than anything he'd ever felt, and Noah feared he would become stuck in such a state if they didn't escape soon.

"The fact you're talking is a good sign," Katalina said. "And now you can finally end this."

He would've nodded if he could. "Right. I completely forgot what the conversation was about before I passed out—with the pain and dizziness and all—but I agree."

"With me," Katalina added. "You agree with me."

"With me," corrected Luna.

"No, with *me,*" Katalina emphasized. "Say 'with Katalina.' 'I agree with Katalina.'"

"This is a mistake," Luna warned.

"I agree with Katalina," he said, though he still wasn't sure what he was agreeing to. "But doesn't Luna have to, as well?"

"I agree with Katalina," Luna said with a sigh. "I told them if you did, I would."

"Then it's settled," the twins said. His eye twitched at how in sync they were. There was something both eery and grating about two people saying the same thing at the same time.

The pair began moving their hands in a circular motion. A

squeak of hinges sounded beside him, and when he blinked, there was a shuffling against his shoulder until all the weight was lifted off him. Noah pried his face off the bars with a startled cry, falling on the rough metal below as the cage emptied.

His cheeks were burning, but he exited the cage without a word, frantically throwing himself as far away from it as possible. Noah took deep breath after deep breath, reminding himself that he was here, and here was okay. His head was on a swivel, taking in the darkened walls and parallel waterfalls.

Noah pointed at the flowing water. "I think the right tunnel could be hidden behind the waterfall."

Celeste followed his finger with a dutiful nod. "Only one way to find out."

"I'm so tired of being in caves," Mark proclaimed, rubbing his eyes with pinched fingers.

"I'll have to agree with you on that one," chimed in Noah. "Add it to the list."

"Falling, running, flying, caves," Katalina rattled off with a finger raised for each item. "Did I miss anything?"

"Fairies," Noah added with a groan. "No more of those, please."

"I feel like that's offensive?" Luna asked, glancing around the room before realizing with noticeable disdain that she was the only differing species aside from the riddling tree twins.

As Noah stood and stretched, his knees became wobbly, and he nearly fell. He kept himself upright with Celeste's shoulder, his chin resting on his chest as he stared at the ebbing ground. When the wooziness passed, he found the eyes of Rosvel. "Thank you."

The twins stared at him with an uncanny emptiness, followed by a moment where their eyes widened; their expressions reset just as quickly. Noah cocked his head, curious of their reactions, but he didn't ask, and they didn't explain.

"Time to go," Celeste announced, grabbing the hand he'd placed on her shoulder. She gave the back of it a quick kiss before turning to the twins with a bow. Then she led the charge toward the waterfall they'd all agreed upon. The water was a glorious, sparkling clear blue and gave off warm, comforting steam as it whooshed into the hole below.

"This is a mistake, I'm telling you," grumbled Luna, crossing her arms with indignation. He wasn't sure why she thought so, because he'd been right. There was a tunnel hidden behind the waterfall.

"Then go that way," Celeste said with a whisk of her hand, as though she couldn't care less what her stepsister did. Their dynamic never failed to confuse him. Arguing every chance they had, undermining each other... yet Celeste asked Luna to come with them. Why?

Luna shot her stepsister a glare, but she did not leave the group. She was considered a delicacy to the fairies, after all. She'd probably be devoured the second she was spotted alone.

Noah looked around for the twins, wondering what they planned on doing next, but they were nowhere to be found. His shoulders slumped. Just like last time.

"It's nice they don't overstay their welcome," noted Luna. "They would be rather irritating otherwise."

"Wouldn't it be nice if everyone was that way?" Mark asked

under his breath, tossing a glare her way. Noah chuckled, patting Mark on the shoulder.

"Be nice. It won't kill you."

"It might," Mark said, but his features softened. "I'm joking. Jeez. Can anyone take a joke anymore?"

"Being rude isn't a joke," Katalina shouted from the front of their group as they traversed the wide tunnel.

"What are we looking for again?" Noah asked, diverting the conversation before anything else offputting was said.

"A room," said Celeste. "A room with a jar, but they didn't explain what the jar looked like, or where this room was."

He recalled the story the twins told, and the constellation of hope. He wondered if he would become a star if he died. If his mother had, too. Was she waiting for him? Was Altair? Perhaps they were watching over Noah and Celeste, guiding them to each other in order to save the planets and fall in love.

Noah felt the sudden urge to look at the sky, but they were surrounded by thick rock walls.

"A jar," said Mark with a scoff. "We're banking our entire existence on a fable and a jar."

"Mark, remember your character growth," Celeste chided, as if he hadn't been rude two seconds ago. "You vowed to be nicer."

He waved her words away. "I'm *joking.* It's called *dry* humor, guys!"

"Dry as in boring, maybe," Luna said, garnering a chuckle from Celeste. Even Noah let out a surprised snort.

Mark looked as though he may yell, but he sighed instead. "I guess I deserve that."

Their walk continued with not a single doorway, fairy, or turn. After a few minutes of endless nothingness, they stopped to regroup.

"Maybe we were wrong?" whispered Katalina. "Certainly something would've come up by now."

"No, Noah was right. We're right. Let's keep going," Celeste urged, allowing the conversation to die as she trudged forth. But Noah was having doubts with the first fork in their path and every new one. He was about to say as much when Celeste pointed. "There!"

She ran toward a door. A tiny door. Much too tiny for any of them to crawl through. Hardly a foot could fit. Noah bent down beside Celeste to inspect it. The door was inscribed with a passage written in another language.

"Fairiel, their language," Celeste explained. "I can't read or speak it, unfortunately."

Noah knew he should've been focused on the task at hand, but all he could think about was how close he was to Celeste. Their faces were right beside each other, nearly cheek-to-cheek. He gulped, hastily standing upright with a stretch while trying to appear nonchalant. She had a natural glow about her, the kind that brought about calmness and joy. Radiant, even in the dim light of the tunnel. "That's a very on-the-nose name for a language."

"Remember the bag of powder the Ruler of the Wind left behind?" Katalina asked suddenly, pulling around her pack and digging out a deep plum bag. She pointed to the inscription on its side. "'For use when the going gets small.'"

Luna snapped her fingers. "I think you're right! It must be shrinking powder!"

"So, what? Now you understand riddles perfectly fine?" Exasperation poured from Katalina's mouth as she threw her hands in the air.

"I mean, it's a small door. We'd have to become small to go through it. Much more obvious than the last one."

Mark rolled his eyes and joined in on the argument, but Noah kept his gaze trained on Celeste. He could see the cogs turning in her mind as she stroked her chin, though she did not speak. Then, without warning, she gasped with a finger thrust in the air. "He knew we would have to come here. He knew about the jar and constellations and, well, all of it."

"So?" asked Katalina.

"*So* why would he give us this powder? Why would he knowingly help us?"

"You don't think he's using us to get to the jar, do you?" asked Katalina. "So he can collect the stars himself?"

"That's something I'd do if I were an evil mastermind," Mark agreed.

"It would make sense. He doesn't want to be held responsible for disrupting the Ruler of the Sky's plans and saving the planets. So he's using us instead," Celeste theorized.

"We should get moving, then," said Luna, taking a pinch of the pink powder and sprinkling it into her mouth. A second later, she shrank, releasing a series of shocked squeaks. She let out a pained moan. "Aw, man! You never said it would *hurt* to turn small!"

"I didn't know!" Celeste argued. "It was a gift!"

"Hardly a gift," groaned Luna. She was doubled over, shrinking slowly all the while, until she was a few inches shorter than the door. Her bubbly voice became a squeal reminiscent of a chew toy his cat would play with. "Well, at least we know it works."

"No way!" Mark said with hands on his hips, kneeling to get a good look at the miniature version of Luna. "I want to try!"

"Now, wait a second." Katalina thrust an arm out to stop him from getting too close. "How are we to know this is safe for our bodies? And how are we going to grow back to our original sizes?"

Celeste cocked her head. "I didn't think of that."

"You're stumped?" asked Mark.

"If this is the only way to get the jar, then we have to do it," Luna persisted with her high-pitched and bubbly voice.

Mark walked over to Katalina, prepared to take a pinch of the powder between his fingers. He stopped himself, however, turning to Noah instead. "Maybe one of us should stay normal-sized. You know, in case things go wrong."

"Huh. That's a good idea," said Noah. "Good job, man."

"Thanks, man." Mark slapped Noah on the back. They stared at each other, a mental game of chicken presented as a staring contest. "I'll volunteer, since it was my idea."

"Are you scared?" asked Katalina, causing a jolt of electricity to course through Noah. He couldn't pinpoint how he felt, landing on a mix of fearful anticipation.

Mark nodded, surprising them all. "If Noah doesn't want to,

then I'll do it, but I don't think you should. We don't know the side effects, and it terrifies me to lose you."

"Would you leave me if I stayed little forever?"

"What kind of question is that?" Mark asked. "Of course not! I'll love you forever and always. You know this."

"*We* know this," came the voice of the pipsqueak.

"I want you to stay behind. Otherwise, if you go, I go," Katalina said as she stared longingly into Mark's eyes.

Mark nodded in understanding and turned to Noah with a shrug. "Sorry. I guess I'm staying."

Their lustful looks suggested they were planning to do something dastardly to each other once the others were gone. With an eyebrow raised, Noah cleared his throat. "Who's next, then?"

"Me!" Celeste's hand was instantly thrust into the air, and she quickly sprinkled the powder on her tongue. He watched as each limb shrunk and she plopped to the ground, his heart shrinking along with her.

Noah sighed. "So, it's me, then."

He saluted Mark and Katalina and took the powder. In seconds, he was staring at the white sole of Mark's shoe, the bag of powder shrinking with him. He quickly stored it in his pack, making sure the bag disappeared around his shoulder.

Noah peered up at the giants before them. Katalina and Mark were barely recognizable by the stature in which they towered above. The tiled flooring was suddenly so close, his thoughts suddenly so far. Was he going to faint? He couldn't tell.

The world was dizzying.

Hands were on his shoulders. "You're going to be okay."

The words echoed in his mind. Logically, he knew it was *her* voice, but for whatever reason, he couldn't place where she was. A light nudge grazed his forehead, and he opened his eyes to see Celeste was leaning against him. Her eyes were closed, a hand wrapped around the nape of his neck, her breathing steady. He could feel her gentle pulse against his skin, and his nerves calmed.

When she pulled away, everything was okay. Though he was still the size of an index finger, and slightly woozy, he could easily fit through the doorway now. Celeste was the one to pull away and put her hand on the doorknob. "Ready?"

They shared a moment of elated yet nerve-wracking silence.

"You guys are so small," came a deep and brooding voice from above. Noah instinctively backed away from Mark's large shoes with a yelp. "Like ants."

Noah shuddered at the thought. "Is the door unlocked? Can you open it?"

Celeste and Luna exchanged a look before Luna put her hands on her hips with a scowl. "You didn't think about that, did you?"

Celeste held up her hands in defense. "Excuse me, but neither did you."

Luna's lips parted, and he could foresee the future argument clearly if he didn't put a stop to it.

"Don't start," he begged. "Please. Just open the door."

"*If* it can open," Luna mumbled.

Celeste rolled her eyes, but as they landed on Noah, the tension in her shoulders dissipated. He gave her a reassuring, close-lipped smile and nod of encouragement. It would all be okay. They would open the door, find the jar, and save the planets. He had to hold on to what little positivity remained, and never let go.

She turned the handle.

20

THE ROOM OF MANY

THE DOOR DIDN'T BUDGE. NOT IN THE TRADITIONAL SENSE, anyway. The vertical wooden panels shifted in the center, melding into various parts of a face. Two eyes carved from wood sprouted, with brows atop, and a wooden mouth below.

"Now, now, young lady," said the door in an accusatory tone. "I wouldn't go around honking your nose!"

Celeste jumped back, releasing her hand from the knob. "Goodness me!"

Noah's mouth hung open. "The door talks?"

"It's Eugene, thank you very much," the door said with a scoff. "*The door.* Who do you think you are?"

Luna gestured angrily toward Eugene. "Would you look at that? The door doesn't open *and* we're stuck at this height. Great plan, Celeste."

"Eugene never said he couldn't be opened." Celeste huffed. Annoyance was seeping from her teeth as her fingers curled into fists. Their endless bickering was making him feel thankful for being an only child.

"She's right. I never said that," agreed the door. Noah wasn't quite used to calling the door by a name, yet. While Celeste claimed magic didn't exist in this world, it certainly felt that way. There were no other explanations for what they continued to encounter. For that, he was sure.

"Can you open?" asked Luna with furrowed brows.

"Of course."

"Why aren't you, then?"

The door rolled his wooden eyes but didn't contest her words. "You could start with 'Hello, Eugene. You sure look dashing today. I need your help.' Or 'how has your evening been?' Doors have feelings too, you know!"

Celeste sighed. "You are dashing, as always, Sire Eugene. Whatever is on the other side of you?"

"Secrets," he said with a broad grin. "To see secrets, you must give secrets. Your deepest secret. I require but one for the admission of three."

"I vote for Luna," said Celeste. Noah nodded in agreement. He certainly wasn't volunteering himself or the woman he wanted to spend the rest of his life with.

Noah raised his hand to stop the inevitable fight before it began. "We'll draw, uh... straws, or something. Longest goes."

He waved Mark and Katalina down, cozying up right next to their ears so he could be heard with his high-pitched voice. Katalina nodded dutifully and ripped up some of the gauze she'd brought from Sundar, rolling the pieces into thin, straw-like cylinders. When she was finished, she turned around and presented them.

Noah hesitated before slinking away, hoping Luna and Celeste could get the hard part over with. "Ladies, first."

He'd rather his fate be chosen by them instead of disappointing himself. Peering over at Celeste, he saw her gauze was longer than Luna's. It would either be him or her.

He grabbed the last straw with a shaky hand, and Katalina unfurled her fingers in a slow, dramatic way. His eyes widened. It was smaller than the other two by a few inches. He was safe. Relief washed over him, though it was absurd to feel so. He didn't have a deep secret lingering in the back of his mind—that he could think of, anyway.

"It's me?" Celeste asked with wide eyes, glancing around nervously. "But I have nothing to share."

"You must have something. We all have something," said the door. Noah honed in on the interaction, curious about what information Celeste might divulge. Nervous anticipation spiked within him—what if she said something that made him look at her differently? What if it was as he feared, and he was just another one of Celeste's many conquests?

"What secrets could a door have?" asked Noah before thinking much of what he was saying. He winced, hopeful the door wasn't offended by such a question.

"You would be surprised by what one observes as a seemingly inanimate object," the door said matter-of-factly. Noah's attention drifted back to Celeste, who was still deep in thought. She looked visibly uncomfortable as she sifted through her memories. "And it's Eugene."

With a shaky breath, Celeste said, "When the news came that Altair passed, and I became one of the last people to know and care about saving the planets, I"—she gulped—"I contemplated taking my life."

"What?" Luna asked with a gasp, her jaw dropping. "Why didn't you tell me?"

"You didn't believe me or Altair. It's a hopeless feeling to know everyone's set to perish, and no one cares or believes it, you know. If the planets are going to end, then why wait? A year of trying to figure out everything alone was unbearable. Why not go early? Visiting Sundar was my last ditch effort to find answers about Altair."

"And if you didn't, you planned on—?" Luna cut herself off when she noticed Celeste's nodding head.

"But, you—" Noah stopped himself short. When they'd first met, she'd told him she was tired of figuring everything out alone. He hadn't realized just how alone she'd felt. "You've always seemed so hopeful."

"Always," agreed Luna. "I'm so sorry I never noticed, and for doubting you."

"I carry the burden of hope in a hopeless journey with grace, I suppose," Celeste conceded. "That doesn't mean it's not a heavy burden to carry."

"It was never a hopeless journey," Noah said. She looked like she might cry, and he wished only to stop the tears before they fell. "You'll see."

A tear slipped, but her quivering lips were replaced with a soft smile.

"Oh, perfect! Marvelous," said Eugene, his excitement unfitting of the scene unraveling before him.

Noah ignored him, keeping his gaze locked on Celeste's. "I —I'm glad you didn't give up."

Her cheeks grew bright pink. "Me, too."

Eugene creaked open, and the trio stepped through. Large candles hanging above seemed to light themselves as they entered. Thousands of tiny trinkets made of various golds and silvers were piled atop each other. There was hardly anywhere for the three of them to stand with all the clutter.

"I used to think about jumping off my planet," Noah admitted, running fingers through his blond hair while looking away. "I'd wonder what the point was of trying. I'd wonder what it'd feel like to gradually choke on the oxygenless beyond and feel every limb freeze until thoughts were squeezed out along with my life."

"No one wants to hear you two bond over a sob story right now," Luna snapped. Perhaps her crush on him was finally waning. "The sooner we find this jar and change back to our regular sizes, the better. What is all this stuff?"

"I knew the minute I saw you that you'd understand," Celeste said, ignoring her stepsister. He hadn't a clue how to respond; his flustered brain drew a blank. Thankfully, Eugene was there to fill in the gaps.

"This is the Room of Many," explained Eugene. He was closed, and his face had moved from the outside of the door to the inside, watching their every move. "A storage closet, essentially. Fairies love their shiny things. What are you in search of on this fine day?"

"A jar," Luna said simply.

"Oh? Got a lot of those."

"One that can hold stars?"

There was an overdrawn pause from Eugene. Noah stated the obvious. "So it *is* here."

"I am not obligated to say. A certain someone will not allow it. I've probably already said too much," said Eugene with a pout. "I'm sorry that I can't be of more help."

"That certain someone wouldn't happen to be the Ruler of the Sky, would it?" Celeste asked with her hands on her hips.

The door did not respond.

"I… I can't believe it. You and Altair were right. He tried telling me so many times, and I didn't listen. Why didn't I listen?" Luna paced, brows pinched together. He tried to piece together a way he could help, but there was nothing, was there? Healing came from within—there were no words that could console her.

Luna turned away quickly, channeling her negative energy toward searching the room. They spread out, but as time passed, so did Noah's hope. They'd found a stash of five jars made of different shapes and sizes. A rectangle, a trapezoid, two cylinders, and a square.

"Isn't a jar typically a cylinder?" asked Luna, pulling those two closer to her. One was a standard, medium size, while the other was slightly smaller. "It *must* be one of these."

Noah picked them up, one by one. They were all empty except the trapezoid jar, which appeared to hold a green vegetable floating in a liquid of the same color. None of them were noteworthy, and his anxiety was growing with each dud.

His fingers grazed one of the cylinders, and he gasped. The world seemed to zoom out as a universe of stars and galaxies zoomed in. There were a series of flashing images, things he didn't understand. Hand-drawn stars, a woman in a red cloak reaching to the sky, her face hidden. Two cats with beautiful tuxedo coats.

The images stopped, everything went black, and then a voice cut through it all. "You're not from here."

He shook his head, though he couldn't tell if it was really moving, and his body felt like it was floating aimlessly in a void of nothingness. "And you?"

A womanly chuckle floated through his thoughts. "I'm from everywhere, dear child. From every time. Every dimension."

"Are you one of the Goddesses?" he asked breathlessly. Was he talking aloud, or was it all happening deep in his mind? He vaguely wondered if this was another side effect of the fairy draining him of blood.

"I am the Constellation of Hope. Alexi was my human name before I joined the stars. Now, I watch over Fortun with the Council of Constellations. We see all." He had yet to glimpse who was speaking, but her voice whisked around his body like solemn notes on the wind.

"What is your purpose?" he asked. "Are you trapped inside this jar?"

"A part of my consciousness is."

"Why?"

"To warn you. There is great power in the stars. To have them is both an honor and a tragedy."

"Tragedy? Why tell me and not the other two I'm with?"

She sighed. "You were chosen as someone trustworthy to wield the power by the Ruler of the Deep. I can sense it within thee, but I cannot say if the other constellations will take a liking to you."

Noah took a determined step forward. "There must be a reason. Why us? Why the Ruler of the Deep and I?"

"All I can tell you is that the Ruler is omnipotent. Far stronger than the rest in his natural form. Beware of the power you hold, for there are those who will stop at nothing to destroy others stronger than them. Those like the rulers—*all* of them—love a challenge. Oh—and remember: activation is key. The stars don't work on their own."

The sound of fingers snapping ricocheted in his thoughts as he yelled, "Wait! What does any of that even mean?"

It was too late. The darkness zoomed out, replaced with the Room of Many. He was standing right where he'd been with the jar clasped tightly between both hands. Luna and Celeste were staring at him with wide, terrified eyes.

"What is it, Noah?" Luna asked. "You look like you've seen a ghost."

He was still processing what he'd heard, his brain overloaded. Constellations not only existed but were *alive,* at least to some capacity, and one of them chose to bestow their trust in *him.* It was baffling, and he still hadn't a clue why. If the Ruler of the Deep was both chosen and turned out to be evil, what did that make Noah?

Worse still, with this newfound trust came enemies. They'd have to be more careful now than ever, especially once they got hold of the stars.

Noah thought back to the shapeshifters. If there were two, there were likely more who wanted to stop Celeste and their group. Then there was the Ruler of the Sky, who he presumed was the most desperate of them all to keep the stars. The Ruler of the Wind was a wild card, and the Ruler of the Soil only ever assisted with their camping needs. That was something, at least.

"This is the right jar," he proclaimed. "We have to go. I'll tell you more on the way!"

He walked toward Eugene, handing Celeste the jar to put in her pack. He reached for the door handle when Luna cleared her throat. "Um... Noah? There's just one minor issue. We're still fairy-sized, and we have nothing to change us back."

"Right," he said with dismay. As his fingers released from the knob, his shoulders slumping, a knock came at the door.

21

HIDE AND SEEK

Noah froze. Luna opened her mouth, but Celeste quickly put a finger up to her own with a shake of her head.

"I hate to inform you," Eugene whispered. "But fairies are knocking on, well, me! They don't know you're in here, but it appears their smallness was already triggered by your other companions. I can't stall any longer, so... hide!"

Noah dived behind a pile of golden pitchers and plates. Celeste and Luna looked to be doing the same when the door creaked open and the fairies flew in.

"Just what exactly is going on here, Eugene? What did you let in?" accused one, their voice rising octaves Noah found unfathomably ear-piercing. He watched the fairies through a mirror propped up on the ground against one of the many piles, noting the one who spoke had long blond hair. Both had clothing made of lime green leaves and see-through mint wings.

He considered himself well-hidden, but it was only a matter of time before the fairies went looking and found him. All they had to do was look in the mirror at the right angle, and they'd see Noah perfectly. Needless to say, his heart was thundering in his chest.

"Don't tell me you let more *bugs* in?" asked the other. This one had short red hair and glasses, which looked rather adorable on a tiny, pointy-eared human. "You know I can't stand those!"

Noah vaguely wondered if the bugs and fairies ever fought, since they were of equal size. The image was quite grotesque and made him squeamish, so he pushed it far from his mind quickly as it'd entered.

"I am bug-free, I assure you," Eugene began.

"Well, *something* is in here!"

The pair grew quiet until only the faint buzzing of wings filled the tense air. Noah gulped, holding his shaky breath as best he could. Where were Katalina and Mark? The fairies were convinced of intruders, but made no note of the two who were supposed to be standing out front. He supposed it didn't matter much now that the trio was now cornered. All he could do was wait.

The waiting did not last long.

A high-pitched shriek pierced through the air. "There! I see one in the mirror!"

Noah gasped, his attention snapping to his reflection, where he could see a finger pointing back at him. Though he knew he should move, his body remained paralyzed, as if he could convince them he wasn't there by remaining perfectly still.

"A human? In *our* tunnels? Even worse," cried the red-haired fairy.

The other gasped. "Not just any human—one of the prisoners! They escaped."

Noah put his hands on either side of his head sheepishly, standing slowly as an admission of guilt. "Please, I am but a lonely traveler passing through the tunnels. I am lost, if you could help me—"

"We saw you in the cage, morsel. You can't fool us!"

"Eugene! Queen Iridessa won't be happy about this," the blond chided with teeth gritting in anger. Noah supposed the fairy was attempting to look menacing, but he looked cute no matter what he tried, like a child attempting to be tough.

The memory of Noah's blood being drained shocked him back to reality. There was nothing cute about these miniature, evil creatures.

"Then don't tell her," argued Eugene, his tone frank. "Ever thought of that? Plus, you missed the two other humans that were camping outside the door!"

The fairies shared another look with wide eyes. The red-haired fairy remained in place, his arms crossed over his chest, while the other quickly fluttered out the door. "Arty is notifying Queen Iridessa as we speak. I hope you enjoy being crushed to death with the rest of your pals."

Movement behind the fairy caught Noah's eye. Luna was tiptoeing toward him with one of the empty jars, just out of sight from the mirror's reflection. Noah shifted his attention back to the fairy. "You know, I've always wondered something. How often are you small versus your regular size?"

The fairy scoffed. "*Regular?* How dare you insult me?"

"I'm sorry. How about I call you bite-sized from now on, instead? Would that be better?"

Luna was closer now, centimeters from trapping the fairy. Noah's taunting provided far better results than he expected, and he slowly inched closer to the mirror to block the fairy's sight of the reflection. She was directly behind him now, seconds away from capturing him—

The fairy gasped, spinning around quickly. It was too late, and Luna scooped him up in the jar, quickly placing the lid over it. Luna smiled triumphantly at the fairy banging against the glass. "I poked some holes in the lid so he can breathe. What a fool to think you were in here all alone."

"What's going on here?" a voice came. Every muscle in Noah's body grew tense at the sight of the blond fairy. What was his name—Arty? "Let him out at once!"

Luna spun around with a toothy smile and a cock of her head. "Hey, he looks like you, doesn't he?"

It took Noah a second to realize Luna was talking to him. Noah looked the fairy over, crossing his arms over his chest to mimic him, an eyebrow raised skeptically. Arty's nose was as pointy as his ears, with gray eyes comically large for his head.

"No," Noah and Arty said in unison. Somehow, their synchronicity was further proof of what Luna pointed out, and it made his eyebrow twitch. He didn't want to be compared to a barbaric species.

"Let us go," Noah continued, taking a daring step forward. "Look, I'm from another planet. It's called Sundar. It's flat and boring and it's colliding with Fortun. If we stay here, we could die, which means *everyone* dies. *You* die."

"Wow, that was a wonderful speech," said Celeste, appearing out of the piles of silver and gold trinkets and tapping Noah on the back.

He jumped from her touch, but quickly recovered with a sly smile. "Don't act too surprised, there."

"Risk our lives for some humans?" asked Arty. "No, thank you!"

"Then risk your life for your friend in here," Noah said with a point toward the jar. "We don't even know his name. I could easily cover the holes in the lid to cut off his oxygen, or shake him up."

Arty frantically glanced between his friend and Noah, perhaps determining if Noah was bluffing or not. He was, but Arty didn't need to know that.

Finally, Arty's shoulders deflated as he ran a hand through his hair. "I already informed the others there were intruders. Reinforcements will be here any second. Please. Please—just let Jet go."

Drat. They'd made a critical error of letting Arty leave the room at all, and now it was too late. There was no telling how much time they had left. Noah tried to think quickly, but it was Celeste who said, "We'll let him go if you tell us how to grow."

Arty sighed. "Fine. If you used the shrinking powder, the effects will be reversed if you sprinkle it over your head. 'Pour on your head to grow tall; pour on your tongue to grow small.' That's common knowledge!"

Noah was about to roll his eyes when there was a knock on

the door. He held his breath, limbs growing stiff. He'd thought they had the upper hand by escaping the cage. It was foolish to think they had a shot of leaving peacefully.

A stillness spread across the room before someone on the other side cleared their throat. "Guys? We tried to hide, but they found us. You need to get out now."

It was Katalina, her voice wavering and dejected.

With little choice, they filed out of the room and released the fairy they'd trapped. He flew out hastily with a smug smile and upturned nose. Though they'd been caught, they'd successfully hidden the jar of stars in Celeste's pack, safe from prying eyes and sticky fingers.

On the other side of Eugene was a cavernous walkway full of hovering fairies and the loud whizzing of their wings. Queen Iridessa and her army of loyal subjects surrounded them, poking Katalina and Mark in the back with a few dozen miniature pokers. Two fairies came behind Noah, preparing to tie his hands with rope.

"No," he yelled as he whipped out the bag of shrinking powder and sprinkled some atop his head. He grew instantly, the fairies flying backward with shocked gasps. Once again, the bag grew with him. Noah quickly bent down and sprinkled the powder above Luna and Celeste. Next, he prepared to run, but his size meant nothing to the thousands of small bodies blocking either direction.

"Clever," Queen Iridessa said, with narrow eyes and lips snarled just enough to reveal her fangs. "But there is only one way out of these tunnels, and you'll never make it there alive."

"Nervous?" asked Mark with a cocked brow, his question sudden and, frankly, unnecessary. "Because you should be."

"Really? Do you want them to kill us?" Celeste asked with a light, humorless chuckle.

A sharp, condescending scoff erupted from the Fairy Queen.

"Mark's right," agreed Noah. "Even if you don't let us go, we'll still find a way out. So do us all a favor and let us go."

"A childish human from another planet full of nothing but gloom ordering *us* on what to do? Telling us we've lost? *No,*" Queen Iridessa bellowed, her fingers curling into fists. "I may have shown mercy before, but there will be no more. How I've longed for the taste of mer blood again."

"Wait," Celeste said with a step forward. "You know about Sundar?"

"Of course. Like I said, the collision isn't set for another three hundred years, but it's always been known." She turned to Noah. "According to my sire, your blood was mediocre, too. I expected a bit more... zest from a species hailing from another planet. How about this? I'll let you non-Fortun humans go if you sacrifice these two."

"No," he and Celeste said in unison.

"Very well. Then die." The Queen's gaze became calculated daggers as she flew a few inches higher, a scepter raised. "Charge!"

No one had to yell 'run' for Noah and his friends to scatter. Though the 'where' wasn't exactly thought out. It was odd how much he craved the dangerous escapades this world provided that Sundar didn't. Even at the brink of death, his heart thrummed with life.

His lips curved upward, and he looked behind him, expecting to see Celeste's galaxy gaze staring back, her hand in his. But his hand was empty, and she was gone, along with everyone else.

"Noah!" Celeste's screams ricocheted through the cavern walls and up his bones. His smile waned, and he dashed back the way he came, stopping at a dense fog of fairy bodies. He swatted at them viciously, ignoring the small stabs of pain where fangs poked flesh. "Noah!"

"Celeste!"

"Noah—" Her voice was growing fainter. He ran through the haze of fluttering wings and bodies, swatting and whacking all the way. Noah stopped at the sight of a massive pile of fairies on the ground and inhaled sharply. They were creating a human-shaped lump, and he knew, deep down, it must've been her. Her groans were muffled by the sheer number of bodies on top of her.

"Celeste, dear Goddesses—" They were draining her blood. They were going to *kill* her if he didn't do something. But what was there to do? He couldn't step all over them because he would bruise and batter her—and commit murder, which didn't sound too great either.

He opted to reach down and pull them off of her by their wings, tossing the fairies to the side one by one. He knew it would only be temporary; the fairies were recovering and flying back into action at record speeds, but it was the only way to get them off. Celeste moaned as she was slowly revealed, her head lolling. "Hang on. Just a few more."

He faltered when he saw Queen Iridessa latch onto Celeste's shoulder. A primal, rage-filled growl released from his ribs that he hadn't known was in him, and he forcefully picked up the Fairy Queen by the wings. She struggled, thrusting her fists and legs frantically, but she wasn't strong enough to break away. He held her up to his scrunched face with a sly smirk before lifting her up for all the other fairies to see. "Stop feeding on her this instant, or I'll pull off her wings!"

The fairies turned away from Celeste's body slowly, eyes glazed over from the feast. The Queen's loyal subjects listened, albeit slowly, and they gradually flew away from Celeste. Noah covered his mouth with a muffled cry as he fell to his knees beside her.

Celeste was covered in small bites that were slowly seeping blood. It was sickening. Noah debated ripping Queen Iridessa's wings off, anyway—it was the least she deserved for hurting Celeste. Bile rose up his throat at the sight of her mangled and bloodied body—no, he had to hold it together. He had to be strong. For her.

"Fine, fine! Just let me go!" yelled the Fairy Queen.

"Tell us how to escape these tunnels first."

Queen Iridessa kept kicking and thrashing and clawing until she seemed to realize Noah wasn't relenting, and her subjects weren't going to attack in order to preserve her safety. Queen Iridessa went limp as sniffles escaped. "The pain, please. It hurts so much. You're going to rip them off. Please, the pain."

"Well, you should've thought about that before terrorizing

my... Celeste! How dare you act a victim when you were going to kill all of us!"

"Alright, already. I'll tell you how to get out of here. Just let me *go*."

"*And* the way out of the forest. To the nearest lodge," Luna demanded, bending to make eye contact with the Queen.

"Yeah, yeah. Whatever you want. Please, put me down!"

"Wow," said Mark, giving Noah a celebratory slap on the back after he released the Queen. "You've been pulling your weight a lot recently. Nice work!"

"Thanks," Noah said curtly; his thoughts were focused solely on Celeste and the pain she must've been in. The amount of blood she was losing. While he wanted to welcome Mark's words, he couldn't stop the anxiety sending a blazing, unbearable heat within him. So, he did what he did best and tried to lighten the mood. "You haven't been."

It didn't work.

22

YOU'VE MADE IT MOTEL

The trees parted, and an open horizon over a barren land stared back at them with tall, mountainous peaks in the distance. He released a sigh of relief at the only obstruction in the open field; a two-story wooden building with a sign that read, 'You've Made It' and the word 'motel' in microscopic letters underneath.

His eyes watered at the sight, and he glanced down at Celeste in his arms, eager to share the view and celebrate with her. However, she was sleeping peacefully with her cheek snuggled into his chest. The fairy bites extended down her arms and legs, and her clothes were ripped in various places where they tried to drink her blood through the fabric.

He and Katalina covered Celeste's injuries with gauze, but most had bled through. He wished he could toss those who harmed her into the shrinking cage, but he knew it was futile to harbor such hatred. What a hopeless feeling to be had.

"The Forest Goddess is watching over us," Luna said gleefully. The other three looked at her with raised brows in disbelief. Luna—happy? He didn't think she *had* that emotion, and over finding lodging, of all things.

Noah looked back down at Celeste. "She didn't seem to watch over Celeste, now did she?"

Her features had long since relaxed after she fell asleep, her brows no longer pinched together in pain as she shivered and sweat all at once. She looked to be in a state of utter tranquility. Her beauty was unlike anything he'd ever seen, her black hair a sharp contrast to her pale skin.

"You know, Noah, if you stare any harder, she might just dream about falling in love with you," Mark said. He was smiling jovially, placing his hands on his hips as he walked toward the motel.

"One can hope," agreed Noah.

"Look," came Katalina's voice. Noah followed her finger, noting a glow above the hills speckling the skyline. The light was faint, yet brighter than when they'd started their journey.

"Finally," Mark shouted with a fist pumped in the air.

They were getting closer to the stars above the hill. His heart thundered at the thought. If only they could continue forth without a single stop. But the sun had long since set, and there was nothing ahead of them except more darkness. Celeste was drained of so much blood that he was worried she wouldn't wake, and the others had heavy bags under their eyes.

With a sigh, Noah said, "Let's go in and get some rest."

"Hey, man," Mark called over his shoulder, an eye on Noah. "I'm glad you're alright."

Mark remained stoic, but Noah knew his words were genuine. For better or for worse, he'd grown to like Mark a lot, and the sentiment appeared to be mutual. The knowledge of this made Noah's decision to stay on Fortun that much harder. He didn't want to say goodbye to any of them. Why must such a choice be made? It was so unbelievably unfair.

"Same to you," Noah said. "I just hope we can say the same to Celeste soon."

"She'll be okay," Mark assured, though the way he trailed off as he turned back around told a different story.

"Do we think this is safe?" Katalina asked. "It could be a trap... right?"

"I really hope it's not," Mark exclaimed. "But better sorry than safe."

"I don't think that's the saying—"

Noah turned. "Well, I'll certainly feel safer here than that forest."

They reached the front door of the motel and barreled inside. From the outside, it looked a lot like the homes of the fairies; wooden planks were covered in navy branches with leaves sticking out from odd places. The inside, however, was an entirely new world. Instead of wooden furniture and a rustic feel, everything was velvet. From the deep purple carpets to the forest green couches and black counters, *everything* was velvet.

There was a fully grown, average-looking human man at the front counter, providing Noah with a sense of comfort. Though this could've been part of the trap. A human used as a front for a hidden fairy operation. He'd have to keep his guard up.

Katalina was already speaking with the brown-haired,

middle-aged man. He was wearing a dusty blue velvet vest with a black undershirt. His mustache was long and twirled upward at each end, and he messed with a curl as his intense stare panned over to Luna and Noah.

"Well, well," said the man, whose nametag read 'Villianet.' "Congratulations, sea dweller. I haven't seen your kind stroll through here in perhaps a decade, maybe two. The fairies love your taste."

"Her taste?" Mark asked. "Why would you phrase it like that?"

"Does your name really have the word 'villain' in it?" Noah asked with a gulp, the question at the forefront of his mind.

"Yes." Villianet shot him a glare. "You aren't the first to point this out. That's why there's a sign."

The man gestured toward the wall beside him, and their eyes all collectively followed.

I'm half-fairy. The boring, human half.
My mother wanted me to be like her and drink other species' blood, but I don't really care for blood (and, no, I don't have fangs). I prefer vegetable casseroles, in all honesty.
My father wanted me to be 'normal.' By human standards, anyway. I just wanted to be an innkeeper and live close to my family :)

"The smiley face at the end is really what sells your kindness to me," Mark said, his voice dripping with sarcasm. Noah about elbowed him, if he had the free hands to do so. "*That's* how I know you won't kill us."

Luna scoffed. “Really? I’d say read the room, but I think it’s become clear you don’t know how.”

Noah’s eyes widened at the state she was in. He hadn’t paid Luna much mind until now, and she looked awful. Her dark blue skin was turning a light, near-white ashy color, and her scales were flaking. Surely, she would announce if she wasn’t feeling well.

“Okay, that’s enough now,” Katalina said, with two fingers pinching the bridge of her nose. “Anyway, we’d like rooms, please.”

Villianet’s eyes narrowed, honing in on Celeste. Noah shifted uncomfortably in his spot, staring down at her beautifully pale, sleeping face.

“This is a place for those who’ve survived the forest. I don’t allow the dead into my motel; I hope you understand. We already have an infestation and she doesn’t look like she’s made it,” said the innkeeper, adjusting his thick, black-rimmed glasses.

Noah’s lip curled in disgust. “She’s made it. Give us a room, please.”

“There are three rooms available—”

“Now, wait one second,” said Mark, wagging a finger toward the innkeeper. Noah cringed before Mark said another word, mentally preparing to be both kicked out and incredibly embarrassed. “If you moved here to be with your family, where is your father, then?”

“That’s an insensitive thing to ask,” Noah said under his breath.

Mark slunk back, running a hand through his thick black hair bashfully. "Right. I-I'm sorry."

The man's eyes softened, saddened. A look Noah knew well, and Villianet's answer was in Noah's mind before it left the man's mouth. "It's alright. I am human, but I gained the ability of longevity of life like fairies. My father passed but three decades ago—he was old, you see. But my mother is alive and well, nearly six hundred years old, and she and all my nieces and nephews live in the forest."

"You *want* to be close to them? They shoved us into a cage that shrunk," Luna pointed out.

The man smiled. "It's not so bad when I have this motel to meet people like you, happening by or surviving the forest." He clapped, defusing the tension. "Now, those rooms."

"Just one, thank you. I'd like us all to be in one room," Noah said, without hesitation or discussion.

"Oh? Have something special in store for us, Noah? Just so you know, I'm flattered, but I have a fiancé—" Mark cut himself off with an *oof* as Noah whacked him in the chest.

"I'd feel safer if we were all together."

"It *was* fun to room with you before," Mark admitted. "Luna, pay the man."

She pointed to herself. "You want *me* to pay? Why?"

Mark crinkled his brows in disbelief. "Because you're the only one with the correct currency who isn't currently unconscious."

"Okay," interrupted the innkeeper, his voice growing impatient. "I understand the lot of you like to bicker, but it is fairly late, and I'm about to have my shift change and go to sleep. Please, hurry it up."

Luna scowled, pulling out a series of floppy, golden bills, and handing them over to the innkeeper; they were much different from the currency he'd seen Celeste use before. With the room paid for and the key handed over, Villianet said, "Perfect! You just reserved the last room! Guess we won't need to do a shift change."

"But didn't you just say there were three—?" Noah trailed off, realizing Villianet wasn't paying him any mind, and was instead taking out a sign from behind his desk labeled 'closed.'

"I hope you enjoy your stay. Breakfast in the morning until eight. Oh, and there's a bar just down the hall that opens at night. There is an infestation down there, though, so be aware of that. Have a wonderful time."

"An infestation of wh—" Noah began.

Villianet walked away with his head held high and a smile on his lips, completely ignoring the question before it was even asked. The lobby grew quiet as not another soul loitered about.

There was a silent exchange of suspicious glances between the group. Mark was the one to break it. "Do you think he's a bloodsucker?"

Noah shook his head. His eyes and arms were insurmountably heavy. "It's a possibility, but I hardly think it matters. He seems harmless, and I'm exhausted—let's just find the room."

No one argued with that.

23

AN AMBUSH

THE ROOM WAS SMALL AND COLORFUL, WITH TWO TWIN-SIZED beds. The blankets were made of dark green velvet, whereas the walls were mint. When they entered, Noah nodded for Katalina to peel back a blanket.

He carefully laid Celeste down on the forest green sheets, ensuring her head rested nicely against the pillow. Though she was sleeping, her cheeks were a faint, rosy color, and she was snoring gently.

"You know, I was thinking we could use those leaves from the hedge maze to heal her. I figure she's trying to save the planets, so she'll *have* to be deemed good," Katalina said, reaching around and pulling some out of her pack.

"I forgot we had those," Noah said, an ounce of hope entering his hopeless mind. "What a great idea!"

"If we crush the leaves into a paste with some water, they

should work," Luna agreed. "But we'd be taking a risk on whether it'll heal her or take her life force away."

Katalina nodded. "It's worth a try. I'll get right on it."

Noah watched as his eager cousin grabbed a cup sitting on the bedside counter and headed to the bathroom. He turned his attention back to Celeste, noting the way her lips were slightly parted, and a light groan escaped them.

"You sure love to stare," Luna stated from behind. She was standing at the foot of the bed, her eyebrow cocked. Was she... judging him?

He looked around for Mark, but he must've gone to the bathroom, too, because now Noah and Luna were alone together.

"The day we met, I thought you stared at me because I was either blue or beautiful or both, but I guess you just stare at anything and everything, huh?"

"What's your point?" Sweat formed along his temples as he realized she was upset. He couldn't fathom why when he showed no interest in pursuing anything romantic, and she was often rude to him. He'd hardly attempted friendship thus far, either.

She sighed, running a hand over the gill atop her head. "I gave you my card, remember?"

He hadn't, and she must've realized this by the look on his face, because she shook her head with a disheartened frown. "She's lucky."

"Why? Because she treats me with basic respect?"

Luna stared at him but said nothing more and walked toward the door. He reached for her, though she was much too far to grab a hold of now. "Wait! Where are you going?"

"On a stroll." Her words came out heated, as though he were the last person she wanted to be speaking to. "I want to make sure this motel is truly safe before we go to sleep. You never know. Especially as a merperson."

"Do you want help? I can—"

She winced again. Was she offended by what he said? He couldn't tell if she was in pain at his words or physically in distress, but she made no further word of it and turned to leave.

Luna took two steps out the door, allowing it to close behind her. The door was inches from doing so, but Noah stopped it just in time and followed her out. "I think you need help."

Her eyes widened, steps faltering, but then her expression turned cold and unresponsive, and she led the way down the hall. Doors lined the walls on each side, and there were no elevators here, only stairs made of smooth brown velvet.

The decor was oddly eclectic, to say the least, and the halls were quiet. Portraits of the innkeeper and his family of five were interwoven into the walls along with a few photos of two children, though he couldn't tell what their relationship was to the motel. They differed from the others, their hair bright blond instead of brown.

When he turned back to Luna, she was not marveling at the sights. She was staring straight ahead, her eyes locked on a mission he didn't quite understand.

"What makes you think there's something wrong with this place?" he asked. "It seems rather homey, and the innkeeper was nice."

"Exactly. Wouldn't you want a secret feasting ground for fairies to seem homey, so their prey lowers their guard and stays?"

Noah gulped. "Wouldn't they attack by now?"

"Not until we're asleep, I'd wager."

A moment of silence washed over them as they made their way to the lower level. Luna sighed. "I meant to say this earlier, but... I'm sorry for the way I held us up in that fairy cage. You were in serious pain and nearly unconscious, and I got in the way. I think I feel... guilty, especially since Katalina was right."

"Oh." He wasn't sure what to say. There wasn't much *to* say. "I hadn't thought about it. So, no worries."

Luna nearly stopped in her tracks, but her brows furrowed, and then she chuckled instead.

"Your expressions don't always match, you know," he pointed out. "I can't figure out what's happening. Are you happy that you're angry? Angry that you're happy?"

"You don't think much of me, do you?" she asked. Hurt lined her voice. He was thankful she was facing forward; he was regretting tagging along, and his sour expression was undoubtably a dead giveaway.

"We're friends?" he tried. "I don't see what makes *me* so interesting to *you*. I'm sure there are plenty more... fish in the sea?"

She stared at him blankly. "That's borderline offensive."

"Right." The squeak of hinges interrupted their conversation, and Luna swiftly put an arm out to stop him. He did as instructed, watching the door with a burning curiosity as someone stepped through.

The person, who was more of a creature than anything, had two exposed long, and hairy legs with hooves. The torso and head were mostly human; he had a thick beard and a mop of fluffy brown hair. The beast's body, however, was abnormally hairy, and he had floppy and long ears like a deer or sheep.

Noah's first instinct was to run, but the human-animal hybrid looked to be faster. So he stared. The beast closed his motel room door, looking over his shoulder at Noah and Luna.

The stranger didn't seem to mind either of them, drifting the same way they were heading and down the stairs.

Luna shook her head with a tsk. "So fearful of every little thing."

"I'm sorry that most of the species we've encountered have tried to kill us." He was surprisingly annoyed by the way she judged every little thing about him. For someone who actively had a crush on him, she was more than a little unkind. "How am I supposed to tell them apart?"

"Well, for one, we're in a motel with rooms instead of out in the wild," she retorted. "Could be your first clue."

"*You're* the one who stopped me from walking like we were about to be attacked! *You're* the one patrolling the halls for danger, and now you're berating me for being safe?"

Noah was beyond confused at how the night was going. His body was fatigued from losing so much blood, and he desperately wanted to be in bed beside Celeste, nestled in each other's arms.

"Looks like it." She sped ahead, glancing at each door they passed with urgency. He quickly followed, realizing he was lost without her. For such a small motel, it felt more like another maze, and he forgot which way led back to their room.

"What is your problem?" He nearly barked the question, her hostility uncalled for. She tensed, but didn't respond. Something caught the side of his eye, something moving under her shirt. But when he looked closer, it stopped. It must've just been a wrinkle in the fabric.

She still wasn't answering. It was nearly driving him mad. He'd thought Luna would need the extra company. Plus, on the off chance she was right, and there were more fairies lurking about, then she wouldn't be able to fend them off alone.

His brows crinkled at the sight of Luna's head on a swivel, bouncing frantically between closed doors leading to motel rooms and trying their handles. The anger left his body, morphing into a bundle of nerves. "Is something wrong?"

Maybe he was just being paranoid, but he could've sworn he saw something move underneath her shirt again.

He blinked, and a hand was around the collar of his shirt in an instant. Noah gasped as he was pulled into a room, greeted by utter darkness. "Who's there?"

"Shh," Luna said, turning on a light with a finger over her mouth. They looked to be in a storage closet with loose cleaning bottles and rags. There was enough room to take maybe five steps each way.

"What—"

"I said, *shh.*" She released a groan; it was a low, guttural sound he hadn't heard before. "I've been holding that in for so long. I was hoping they'd have a spare room like this."

Luna nodded toward a broom behind him. He didn't ask

questions, quickly taking it by the handle. She drew a circle in the air as she mouthed, *Hold it the other way.* He did as instructed with trembling fingers.

Luna blushed before dragging down the shoulders of her loose shirt. Noah shielded his eyes in fear he'd see something he shouldn't.

"Oh, no. No, thank you. Please put your shirt back on. I didn't follow you here for *that*. Sorry. Well, wait, am I? I thought it was clear I like Celeste. Love, even." He trailed off at the sight before his eyes, recoiling to create extra distance between them. "Goddesses. That's not good. Not good at all."

24

WHAT HAPPENED HERE

THEY TOOK SMALL BITES. SO SMALL THEY WERE NEARLY undetectable, and not a drop of blood seeped through her shirt. Luna revealed only her shoulders and back, for which he was thankful. However, there were dozens of bites covering her skin, and there were at least four fairies *still* biting her. He didn't doubt there was more underneath the rest of her clothing.

The fairies were still feeding slowly to not disrupt the flow of the fabric, despite none being there. The small, ravenous creatures appeared to be lost in ecstasy, oblivious to Luna exposing them. Dread filled him as his lips curled in horror. He couldn't stomach the sight.

"More?" Noah mouthed, and she gave a hesitant nod as confirmation.

Merpeople taste the best. The words of the Fairy Queen rang in his mind as he tried to determine how to get all the fairies off without being attacked. He could grab them by the wings, two at a time, but the remaining fae could speed up their draining process before he got them all. They could kill her instantly.

Noah inhaled sharply, thinking of only one solution—the same Luna presented. He'd swipe the broom over them, forcing their hands and fangs off her. Then he'd whack them before they could alert the others.

He aimed for the fairies on her back first. Luna cringed at the nearing of the broom, and he knew he had accidentally hit her by the pained squeak she let out. Three fell to the ground unconscious, their wings bent.

The sound of buzzing whizzed in his ears, and his jaw clenched as he swung at what felt like nothing. He assumed it was a fairy, but they were moving too fast for him to keep up. Noah put all his strength into his next attempt, and the momentum sent him spinning in a full circle. His grip on the broom loosened, and the poor excuse of a weapon flew across the room. Noah landed on the ground, stunned that his swings missed.

A single fairy was hovering over him, holding their stomach while cackling. Noah looked up with shock, wondering if this would be it. If his life force would be taken in a storage closet at a random motel. Luna groaned as she thrust herself toward the broom and picked it up.

He watched as she slammed her shoulder into the wall and whacked another out of the air mid-flight. She shrieked in pain when she moved off the wall, five fairies falling to the ground, their limbs contorted. Noah hopped up, noticing six more fae had unhooked themselves from Luna and were now flying toward him.

He looked around for a weapon. A pit of sadness erupted within at the sight of the crumpled bodies surrounding him. The one who'd been giggling was now among the others on the ground, trying to stand with wobbly legs and unusable wings.

There were no weapons, so he opted to use his hands. He managed to smack a few, though fangs nicked his palms in the process. Noah released a pained yelp before holding his breath, trying his best to remain calm. He didn't want to think about how he could accidentally kill them. He couldn't stomach *murder* on his hands.

There was a long pause as their attackers stopped; Noah and Luna's heavy breathing filled the room. He shuddered while grabbing his chest, desperately wishing his touch alone could stop the fearful yet excited thumping of his heart. "Why didn't you say anything?"

"They threatened me. Said they'd drain me in a millisecond if I told anyone anything. I don't think they were bluffing."

"I'm so sorry." Noah stared at the wall ahead. He hadn't meant to maim the creatures, but none of them were standing, and many of them had bent limbs and wings. He reminded himself that he was left with no choice. "How are you still standing? If they've been draining you this entire time, you should be exhausted."

She shrugged. "I don't think they were in a rush to drink my blood. I think they *enjoyed* causing all that pain, so they drained me slowly. Freaking fairies."

There were no faults to be had in this situation, yet he couldn't help but feel this was his doing. If Celeste had never run into him, had never taken him, Mark, and Katalina on this eccentric adventure, Luna wouldn't have come with. Would she and Celeste be better off without meeting him?

Was he the burden he feared he was?

Maybe that's why Celeste was so hesitant to hand over the notebook.

Maybe he was nothing more than a liability.

"Thank you," Luna said gently as they exited the storage closet.

He wanted to get as far away from this horrific scene as possible, yet he tossed a hand in front of Luna to stop her from walking. "What should we do about their bodies?"

There was a pause. "I'll take care of it. You go on ahead."

He wasn't sure what that meant, but perhaps it was better not to. Noah nodded hesitantly. "Next time, let us know something's wrong sooner. You didn't have to suffer."

"Right," she said with a half-hearted smile. "I'm sorry. It's hard for me to admit when I need help, and I believed their threat. I was going to keep it hidden, but I couldn't bear the pain any longer."

With that, she went back into the storage room to clean up. He stared at the closed door for a moment, debating if he should help, but ultimately decided not to. Noah aimlessly wandered through the motel before eventually finding his way back to their room. Celeste was still asleep; Katalina and Mark were nowhere to be found, but there was a note on the second bed that read—*Went to the bar downstairs. Be back later.*

His shoulders slumped, realizing he'd be alone with Luna once again when she came back. With a sigh, he gave Celeste a quick kiss on her forehead before heading to the bathroom, fully prepared to decompress in the warm embrace of steaming water.

He made it halfway when the motel room door clicked open. In walked Luna, who instantly took off her shirt with a pained moan. She paused mid-step at the sight of Noah staring at her, and her cheeks flushed. He turned away with haste, prepared to enter the bathroom, and slam the door shut. A delicate voice interrupted his plan. "Luna?"

Noah froze, a pit growing in his stomach. If he didn't move, maybe Celeste wouldn't notice him. "Noah?"

He winced, turning slowly toward the bed. Celeste's eyes were slightly open, and her pupils were shifting between him and Luna. "What'd I wake up to here?"

Her voice was so soft, so tender. Noah rushed to her side, knowing just how awful it looked without context. "It's not what it looks like. She began undressing before she noticed I was in here."

Luna scoffed with an added roll of her eyes. "As if I would want a man who doesn't even glance my way."

Celeste flashed him a meager grin before her gaze was lost behind her eyelids. "I'm just kidding, silly. I know you, Noah."

His shoulders relaxed, and he smiled to himself as he leaned down and gave her forehead another kiss. Her trust in him was equal to his in her, and it spiked comfort within him.

While he wanted to soak in such a feeling, Noah couldn't shake his nerves. Her hesitation to hand over the notebook to the fairies paired with his insecurities regarding, well, everything, sent him in a panic. Noah shoved it deep down, trying his best to get on with the night.

Lying there, she looked so peaceful, so content. Despite his doubts, he craved her touch, her voice, her laughter. Suddenly, he wanted to be lying next to her, his arms tightly wrapped around her torso as they laid together in complete bliss.

"Must be nice to be the two of you," Luna muttered, brushing past Noah to the bathroom he was initially planning to use. He sighed, annoyed he wouldn't get the shower he so desperately needed. Though he supposed Luna needed one far more than he did at the moment. At least he had Celeste, and they were all safe for another night.

"Sleep well," he whispered. Her response was a light snore. He walked over to the second bed and tried his best to fall asleep to the thought of her.

25

THE HAUNTED BAR

CELESTE DIDN'T WAKE UNTIL THE FOLLOWING EVENING. THE leaves from the hedge maze were crushed into a deep green paste, and spread over every bite. When Katalina cleared off some of the paste earlier in the day, the bites were completely healed. Celeste was deemed good by the maze, a fact that didn't shock him in the slightest.

Luna, on the other hand, refused to use the leaves. "I'm not interested in what the hedge feels about me," she'd said. This also didn't surprise him.

Celeste's eyes finally fluttered open when Noah was in the bathroom, and when he heard Katalina call his name, he about tripped over his own feet to scramble to her side. His heart skipped a beat when he saw Celeste leaning against the head-rest, awake.

Color was returning to her cheeks, and she grinned as her eyes met his. Luna handed her a steaming cup of warm milk, and Celeste held it with both hands gingerly. A deep pang of joyful sadness ricocheted through him at the sight. She was okay.

Now, two hours after waking, they sat in the motel bar. It was small, with a few high-top tables scattered about, and it was empty save for the group of five. Mark and Katalina had long since gravitated toward the dance floor, where a woman played guitar and sang ballads of love. Luna was chatting with the barkeep at the end of the counter, holding a glass of... something in her hand, leaving Noah and Celeste alone at the bar.

"How are you feeling?" Noah asked, taking a sip of his drink. He'd heavily debated the act, as he always did, but watching Celeste nearly die sent him over the edge. He'd spent the last two days worrying deeply for her, fear never leaving his side. It was exhausting, so he wagered one drink wouldn't hurt.

They were sitting in the center of the bar counter, legs dangling off tall chairs with round, cushioned seats. They were sitting just close enough to feel the electricity between them without touching, and he gravitated closer with each sip.

The ale was thick and warm down his throat, and his nerves tingled as it traveled through him. Celeste chuckled at the visible shudder the sour taste provided him.

She glanced down at her drink—water. They'd switched roles since the last time drinks were involved. "Physically? Better, but every muscle aches. Emotionally? I'm devastated that I missed rooming with everyone."

"You didn't miss much. I spent the whole time worrying about you," he said with another sip. "And I'd offer to give you a massage if I knew how to give 'em," he said with another sip.

"I didn't want to miss anything!" She giggled. "And don't worry—I can teach you."

Something about the combination of her mischievous wink and bite of her lip made him turn red, and he had to look away before he caved and kissed her.

So, he turned his attention to the limited decorations. There were more portraits, either of landscapes or people contained within branch-like frames. Vines with pink and red flowers hung off the ceiling, and birds chirped somewhere from above. Quaint and homey, though the photos gave him a sinister, uncomfortable feeling he couldn't explain.

"And how are you mentally?" he asked, the age-old question Noah always hated being asked. It was odd, being on the other side of the exchange, knowing the dread she probably felt as she filed through the typical things to say. Perhaps she would go with 'I'm fine,' or 'everything's okay.'

Celeste sighed, taking a deep swig of her water, and he noticed her hand was trembling. "I'm nervous that I've slowed us down too much, and we're going to be too late."

He waved her words away instantly, though truthfully, he feared she was right. "What are you talking about? We're so close to the stars. We can see their glow right over those hills, and we have almost everything we need. Come tomorrow, we'll have the stars and be on our way to the Ruler of the Deep."

"Almost?"

Noah nodded. "When I touched one of the jars, I met a constellation who told me we need to activate the jar in order for the stars to work. She didn't explain how... but I'm sure we'll figure it out."

Celeste stared down at her hands with a look of defeat. "See? This is what I mean. There's still so much more ground to cover. We're going to be too late. If only we'd met sooner."

Her lip quivered, and he wrapped a protective arm around her shoulders, pulling her into a tender hug with his cheek resting against her head.

"We weren't meant to meet sooner; we were meant to meet now."

Her eyebrows drew together as she pondered this. Finally, Celeste said, "I can't argue with that, now can I?"

Fingers tapped on a microphone, and his attention drifted to a raised platform near the dance floor, where the female singer had been. A man with curly, ear-length black hair stood in the center of the stage, a spotlight on him. A fuzzy patch rested on his chin, and though his skin was supposed to be auburn, he was transparent, and the tone was washed out.

"Why—that's the legend, Melvious Arkane!" Noah jumped to his feet and nearly spilled his drink. Celeste saved the glass from meeting its demise.

"You're right," Katalina shouted from the dance floor, a hand over her mouth. "But how...?"

"Good evening, ladies and gentlemen... and gentlefish," he said, gesturing toward Luna. She opened her mouth as if to speak, but seemed to change her mind and turned to the barkeep, instead, whispering in his ear. When she was done, he swiftly made her another drink—and then made one for himself.

"Welcome to my show," Melvious Arkane continued, tossing his hands out on either side of him. He was alone on the stage.

No band or instruments. Just him and his boisterous, flailing arms and a crooked, dashing smile. "I'd like to start with my first classic, 'Draegon Eggs Don't Break.'"

Noah released a sharp gasp at the sound of ample applause erupting around them. When he examined the room, there were more transparent people filling the bar and surrounding the tables. The bar was filled to the brim, though it was empty just moments ago.

"What is this?" He turned to Celeste for answers, but she shook her head.

"He was a big singer here," she yelled over the swell of the singer's voice and the erupting crowd. "Rose to fame in his late sixties, but he died a few years ago from old age... wait, how do you know who he is?"

Katalina and Mark glanced over their shoulders at Arkane as they rushed over to the bar, shock etched into their features.

"He doesn't look dead," Noah shouted. Now that Noah scrutinized the room, everyone appeared to be in clothing that differed vastly from each other. There were people in powdered pink wigs, those with bushy hair and shirts with peace signs, and even some in modern ballgowns. Decades of generations littered the crowd.

"Dead?" Mark nearly shouted. "Are you telling me we're looking at ghosts?"

"That's really him?" Katalina asked eagerly. "I had the biggest crush on him when I was twelve."

"Yes, but how do *you* know who he is?" Celeste reiterated.

Noah gulped down his entire drink in one go and called over the barkeep for another. "He was only the best artist of our generation. He sang some of my favorite songs. 'The Rocks Don't Fall Unless I Let 'Em,' 'The Countryside is Broken.' These are classics. Never heard of this one, though. But that's not the important part. You're telling us ghosts are real?"

"That depends," said Celeste. "Did you also hope Melvious Arkane would fall in love with you when you were twelve?"

Noah laughed, eyes welling with tears. He would forever be thankful for having the chance to hear her voice again. After undergoing two days of wondering if she'd ever wake up, she was here. He would cherish every second.

She looked at the ceiling, tapping her chin in thought before continuing. "It's a little hard to explain. For example, the black hole separating our worlds is more of a portal, right? Well, think of ghosts as an added layer to this reality. A dimension overlying another dimension."

"So... they aren't ghosts?" He couldn't say he was following.

"No, they are. Like I said, it's complicated," she said. "I think this might be the infestation the innkeeper was talking about."

Noah stared at her, shocked by the casualness of her tone. Noah never particularly cared for the traditional theory of ghosts. Being condemned to walk the planet alone because something was holding them back from ascending into the afterlife was, well, sad. He couldn't imagine running into his mother as a ghost. It terrified him.

"Do they stay here forever?" he asked. These ghosts didn't seem all too sad or lost, though, so that was something.

The barkeep came over and topped off Noah's drink. He hadn't asked for more, but he graciously accepted and downed it in a single swig. The world tilted with each fresh glass he drank. The image of his mother staring back at him as a ghost flashed through his mind, her hazel eyes haunting him. Locked in a life she never wanted, just like when she was alive.

"These people can pass on when they please. When we die, there is a choice. Some choose to stay. Mostly the rich and famous who can't let go of their legacies... and their groupies tend to follow." The barkeep nodded toward the audience, who were applauding the dead singer.

"His voice is beautiful," Celeste agreed, leaning against the counter. Noah's jaw was growing taut, the ale hitting him with sudden ferocity. He tried to take in the crowd instead of focusing on the nausea consuming him. There were only human ghosts, which brought about a whole new host of questions.

"Spirits gather here often. They latch on to a place and attract more," continued the barkeep. "It's not as unusual as you'd think. Staying away from living crowds is best because it is quite scary for the average person to see a ghost. Villianet wanted this to be a sanctuary for both survivors of the forest and ghosts who wanted to live freely in a world that fears them. It's become a bit overrun as of late."

"Enough of this," Mark yelled with a finger pointed to toward the dance floor. "No more death talk. Let's have some fun!"

With that, he grabbed Katalina's hand and pulled her closer to the stage with an ecstatic swing in his step. Noah and Celeste exchanged a smile of their own before Noah downed his last glass.

"I don't think I can dance right now," Celeste said with a

pout. Right. Her body was tired after losing so much blood. He knew the feeling.

"We don't have to dance to have a good time," he whispered, standing behind her with his arms wrapped around her waist. He was taller than her, gently resting his chin on her head and swaying them from side to side. They watched the crowd, pointing out their favorite fashion statements and eras littering the bar. He opted to go with peace signs; she picked pink, powered wigs.

The song switched to a ballad, one of his favorite melodies by Melvious Arkane, 'The Last Girl on the Train.' Noah sang along softly as they swayed. Celeste's fingers trailed down his arms until their fingers were intertwined. He smiled to himself. Here he was, in the strangest bar, in the strangest motel, with the most beautiful woman in the world.

He kissed her cheek—a light, lingering peck. She followed his lead, kissing the back of his hand as they continued to sway, and warmth spread throughout him. Noah was in and out of a drunken daze, using all his mental capacity to remain balanced.

"I see why you like his music," Celeste said, leaning into him.

He leaned into her ear and whispered, "I'm so unbelievably grateful to have met you." He paused, wondering if he should continue. "And I'm so thankful you're okay. I never want to see you in pain again."

Celeste turned to him, lifting one of her hands to rest on his cheek while their eyes searched each other's souls, only to find their way back to themselves. Noah held his breath, his mind flipping through everything she could say or do, and every muscle in his body grew tense as she leaned in closer, their lips brushing. "*I'm* the grateful one. I couldn't do any of this without you."

She closed the gap between them, their lips meeting tenderly. She tasted like strawberries on a warm summer day. Like a star burning in a setting sky. He never wanted to let go, never wanted his lips to leave hers.

There was applause around them. Vaguely, he heard Melvious say the show was over. The bar was closing up. They weren't allowed to kiss in open areas—the barkeeper was shouting as such over and over as Noah and Celeste ignored him. Their lips were locked in a battle of dominance and need.

"Gross." Luna interrupted the moment, shocking them out of their daze. As she passed, she added, "You better stop that once we get to the room."

Noah pulled away, giving Celeste a final peck on the cheek. A blush dusted her cheeks as her eyes searched his. He thought she might pull him back in, but she said, "You're right. It makes it more fun to wait."

"Does it?" he asked with a curious twinge to his sultry voice.

She stood on her tiptoes, her lips inches from his. "It does."

Celeste gave him one last kiss, and he returned the favor with giddy passion. When she pulled away, he was cold, but she was right. He wanted more, and there was something fun in knowing they could whenever they wanted to, but didn't. A game of chicken.

Noah smirked and whispered, "I can't argue with that, now can I?"

26

At last.

Tonight, he dreamed of her.

They were on the back of a draegon, flying with their fingers intertwined and the wind in their hair. It was beautiful, and he was in love.

A fleeting feeling.

He knew it couldn't last.

He allowed himself to get lost in the dream, his hands trailing her body as every inch of him pulsated with desire. She toyed with the zipper of his jeans, and he released a light moan at her soft touch. His hands stalled as his head tilted back.

His body shocked itself awake, and he realized with an embarrassed blush that he'd moaned out loud. Noah's eyes fluttered open, his mind in a ravenous, lustful frenzy. He noticed movement from the corner of his eye, and his gaze slowly found its way to hers. They were sleeping in opposite beds, and everyone else was still asleep.

She offered him a confused, curious smile. "Having a pleasant dream over there?"

"The best." Noah smiled, his cheeks darkening even further. "Good morning."

27

A SERIES OF HILLS

He'd never seen such a robust range of hills before. There was but one mountain on his home planet of Sundar, and while the mounds on Fortun were grand thus far, they were certainly not *this* grand.

When they first landed on this planet, walking up and down the hills was an odd, three-dimensional experience, but here, the walk was like any other. He was thankful for this. The normality of gravity and physics was something he took for granted, and he relished in this content, non-woozy state.

The thought of Sundar provided a pang of sadness and fond reminiscing. The mountain there was so, so tall when he was a child, with trees and houses speckling the side. He came to learn the mountain separated his life from others; solitude versus city. Noah much preferred the side he lived on, with dirt paths and a beautiful—though terrifying—waterfall off the edge of the planet.

His memories jumped to the seconds right before Celeste ran into him. He was standing at his mother's tombstone, reading the inscription over and over again. *She spent her life looking for the Great Beyond, and there she rests.*

Noah attempted to push down the memory before it began to swirl and destroy the thrill of this moment. He nearly got lost in the idea of never seeing his cat or mother's gravestone again, but he quickly switched to thoughts of Celeste and the stars that were mere hills away. Noah couldn't give in to the sadness anymore; he was tired of the weight it added to his shoulders.

"You okay?" Mark asked, coming up beside him. "You've been pretty quiet."

Noah peered down at the tall teal grass their shoes shuffled through. "I'm just thinking about what happens after we save the planets, I guess."

Mark nodded but didn't speak right away; he wasn't one to talk about sensitive matters unless there was something that truly bothered him. Noah kept walking, looking around for the other three. They were all ahead, waiting at the top and discussing matters Noah was too far to hear.

"You still want to stay?" Mark finally asked, his eyebrows raised. "Even after what those fairies did to the three of you?"

"I think so. If we can stay, I will, but I'm scared of how much I'll lose. Sundar isn't a terrible place to live, by any means. It's just a little broken."

"True." Mark took a deep breath and put his hands on his hips, gaze fixed on the ground. "You know, we really have no idea what will happen when the black hole closes. Maybe there's no choice at all, and me and Katalina are forced to stay here. I've thought about that a lot recently. How we just assumed we'd hand over the stars and the Ruler of the Deep would let us go."

Noah paled. "That hadn't—"

Mark raised a hand to cut Noah off. "Either way, I'd be happy. For the most part. Except if we *can* go back, and you stay here, the two of us won't even be able to call."

"Speaking of, I was wondering if you could do me a favor back on Sundar—"

"Don't you dare ask us to take care of your cat," Mark warned with a wag of his finger. "I'm not a cat person."

"You *think* you aren't a cat person."

"The Goddesses made me allergic for a reason."

"So you could overcome it," Noah challenged with a lackadaisical shrug. Before Mark could retort, Noah batted his eyes, clasping his hands together as he begged, "Please, Mark—watch over Henry for me. Or at least give her to a good friend."

"We *do* need a mascot for our kickball team." Mark shook his head as though he were shaking himself from a bad dream. "You could come back with us. You could join our kickball team, or a rival team just for fun, make friends, *and* not be in danger all the time. We could bike or exercise together, too."

"Well," Noah said sheepishly as he watched Celeste and the other two descend the next hill. He desperately wanted to hear what they were talking about. What was Celeste divulging, and why did she keep laughing? She briefly glanced over her shoulder with a small smile directed at him before disappearing over the hill. "I honestly like it here. It's been fun. So much more fun than anything I've ever done before."

Mark raised a skeptical eyebrow. "That's an insane thing to say."

"Let me ask you this, then. If you were me, and Katalina was Celeste, would you follow her here? Would you want to stay?"

Mark sighed, giving it deep thought as his breath drew on. "Of course. She's the embodiment of perfection. I've never met someone smarter or funnier... or hotter."

"Gross," Noah said with a grimace. "But sweet. How'd you two meet?"

"Went to the same university." Mark smiled, temporarily lost in the memory. "She showed me up in front of our entire mathematics class. Knew she was the one right then and there. I went to school for phone fixing, you see. Math was about the only class we had in common."

"Boys," yelled Luna from the next hill over. The others were walking far faster than Noah realized, and they were already at the top of the mound. "Hurry it up. You'll want to see this."

Mark and Noah exchanged a look before Mark yelled back, "I've hustled enough on this trip!"

"Works for me," Noah said after a loud scoff from Luna. The last hill was of average height, but he couldn't fathom jogging up any inclines after walking for an entire day. "My legs are on fire. I don't think I *can* hustle."

They were nearing the others when Noah grabbed Mark by the shoulder. Mark turned with obvious surprise, and they both stopped walking. "Is there something wrong with Celeste? A reason you don't want me to stay?"

Mark sighed, shaking his head. "It doesn't matter what I say, now does it? Love conquers all, or whatever. Celeste isn't what

I'm worried about, though. After we save the planets, it sounds like something big could happen between the rulers. Something bad. Katalina and I just want you—*both* of you—to be safe."

"So you want both of us to come back to Sundar with you? Is that what you're saying?"

"It'd be safer. I'm sure the planet won't crumble away in our lifetime." There was a moment of silence before Mark added, "And, no offense to Celeste or anything, but what does it say about a person who asks a random stranger on an adventure like this? What if you aren't the first one, and instead one of many strangers and adventures?"

"What does it say about a person who says yes to a random stranger?" Noah asked, cocking his head. Mark's words grated on his nerves; it was a subject he didn't want to touch.

Mark snapped. "Now *that's* a good point. Like I said, you've probably made your mind up already, but there's no harm in asking her to come to Sundar with us. Luna, too. If she can as a non-human."

Noah nodded, and Mark tapped him on the back before they continued up the hill. There was no time to ruminate on their conversation because a bright glow was shining ahead. Noah's heart leapt into his throat. When they reached the peak, he had to shield his eyes.

They made it. They found the stars.

28

A SKY OF STARS

"THE STARS, THEY... LOOK LIKE STARS?" KATALINA ASKED WHILE reaching toward one floating a few feet above her.

"Would they look like anything else?" Celeste mused.

"Careful, Katalina," Mark warned, raising out a hand to stop her from grabbing the star. "Remember what the twins said? We can't go around touching the stars with our bare hands!"

Up close, all the stars had five points and uneven lines, like a crude drawing made by a child, and they glowed a very faint yellow. Every star was the same shade, but differed in sizes ranging from large to small to barely even visible.

"It's warmer over here," Luna noted, rubbing her arms. The heat wasn't obscene, but it was certainly sweat-inducing after a few minutes. While Noah enjoyed the hug of comforting warmth surrounded by the stars, Luna was shrinking away.

"It's part of science to touch things you aren't supposed to," Katalina said matter-of-factly, earning a shake of Mark's head.

Still, she lowered her hand and cocked her head in thought. "Fine. We'll scoop them up with a boring jar. My question is—where is the blue star?"

"And what color could 'hope' possibly be?" Celeste added.

"It's up there," Luna said with a point. Noah followed her finger, but all he saw were more yellow stars.

"Are you sure? I don't see anything," he said.

"Me neither," Celeste chimed in with hands on her hips.

Luna glanced between the other four and the sky. "Huh. I guess what they say about merpeople is true; we can see inside stars. You really can't see that? It's only a few feet higher than the rest."

They all shook their heads. "That's a shame. It's beautiful—crystal clear and shiny, with a small constellation etched in the center. Looks like there's a galaxy trapped inside."

"Does that mean you see the color of hope, too?" Noah asked, fervent anticipation laced within his words. If only having hope led to everything working out.

Luna scanned the sky but ended her search with a shake of her head. "They're all wrapped in yellow except that blue one up there. None of the others stick out much."

Celeste put her hands on her hips. "Interesting. I can't say I was expecting that. I thought we'd see the right stars and *know,* you know?"

"No," Mark said, earning a chuckle from Noah.

Noah examined the stars further, finding nothing more of note, though the enormous accumulation of light dusting the scene was burning his eyes.

"Oh, great." Mark tsked. "Another guessing game."

As Noah continued to walk, he noticed the stars were only yellow at certain angles, and when he moved his head around, they shifted into a twinkling multicolored array of beauty, swapping through every color on the spectrum.

He laughed to himself as he twirled, each star twinkling with a new color. "This is amazing!"

"I must say, the journey was worth it just for this," Luna said with breathless awe beside Noah. "Aside from our underwater operas, this is the most beautiful thing I've ever seen."

Noah's eyebrows raised; he hadn't a clue what an opera was. "I'd like to see an underwater show, sometime. That sounds fun."

"I have plenty more breathing bubbles you can borrow, too."

"Let's do it! After the planets are saved, you, me, and Celeste can see this 'opera' firsthand," he proclaimed. The thought of Celeste reminded him she was not by his side. When he looked around, he saw she was assessing each star she passed with a cute, quizzical expression.

"Wait," he called for her. She glanced his way with a broad grin. He could feel Luna watching him, her expression almost unreadable, if not for the way her eyes welled. Her constant flip-flopping made him uncomfortable. It was obvious what she wanted, what she would never have. Her hope dwindled with each passing moment, and he wondered if perhaps that was why she couldn't see the star the shade of hope. "Let's lay under the stars."

Celeste took a step forward. He was addicted to the sight of her. She was absolutely gorgeous, and he wanted nothing more than to lie under the stars with her. After all, the planets were going to collide if they failed, and he would never have this chance again. He wouldn't pass up any more opportunities and live with regret.

"Don't you feel it would be a waste of time?" she asked, looking up at the sky. "I've never thought to do such a thing."

His mouth parted in surprise. "There is no such thing as wasted time when it comes to you, Celestial."

She blushed, her lips sputtering as she tried to regain her composure. "I know that's the way you see me. But I'm merely human, just as you are."

"Perfection may not exist, but you're the closest to it." Noah would never stop doubling down on such a fact. He loved her so fully, he'd never known such a feeling before. He felt like a broken record, even within his own mind.

"Here," she said with a hand held out for him to take. He did, and they sat in the grass before laying down. The stars were so, so bright, but his vision was finally beginning to adjust. The sky was a deep navy and speckled with indigo and baby blue, and the stars twinkled yellow at this angle, shifting between red, orange and green when he turned to look at her.

"You make me feel special," she whispered, eyes trained on the stars.

He leaned in closer. "You are."

She finally, *finally,* turned to him. His entire body swelled with a ferocious heat at the way her eyes pierced his. He glanced down at her lips while inching forward slowly. So slowly, so surely. Allowing the tension, the agonizing *need* for one another, to bloom.

She smirked in return, jokingly narrowing her eyes. "You just wanted an excuse to kiss me."

He placed a hand on the crook of her neck as he turned onto his side, using an elbow to prop himself up. The stars glowed within her eyes, shining with exhilaration. With love. For this, he was sure. It was comforting to know he would never have to worry.

Their lips were brushing now, to the point he could hardly hold back. "I wanted to lie under the stars *and* kiss you."

She leaned in eagerly before he got the chance to, and their noses bonked. They reeled back from each other, and her cheeks burned bright red in embarrassment as Noah held his nose and chuckled through the pain. "I-I'm so sorry. I-I just couldn't wait any longer!"

When their giggling subsided, their eyes met, and Noah pulled her in. Their lips collided, and their mouths and tongues moved feverishly, their bodies intertwined in the grass. He breathed her in, pulled her close. His hands trailed her back, clawing at her hair and the front of her shirt.

When he pulled away, he was breathless, his chest heaving. He wanted more. So much more.

"Noah, I—I know this may sound odd. We've only known each other for a little over a month, but... I think I love you. I've never had such fun before."

Noah smiled, but he couldn't push down what Mark suggested, or the uncertainty lining his thoughts. He almost kept it to himself, but his true feelings bubbled over before he could stop them. "Me, neither. You're everything I could've asked for. Though I must ask—have you taken many men on adventures? Pevelyn, the Ruler of the Wind, your father all made… comments, and then you didn't hand over the notebook while I was, well, having my blood drained. Are you sure… are you sure you love me? Are you sure I'm not just a novelty?"

She looked away with eyebrows pinched in pain. "I'm sorry about that, truly. It was one of the last things I had of Altair with his handwriting, his doodles, and ideas. I shouldn't have hesitated, but it had nothing to do with whether I thought you were worthy or not of being saved."

Her voice was trembling, a truth behind each syllable that convinced him of her words. He understood, to an extent. If he had something of his mother's to give, he would have difficulty parting with it, too. "I believe you."

"You were the only person I asked to help me save the planets, you know. Of course, I've dated other people. But they aren't a part of my life anymore, and they haven't been for quite some time now. You have nothing to compete with, except maybe yourself."

He wished he could move on easily and accept her words at face value, but he continued to ruminate, jumping from scene to scene, each filled with Celeste exploring Fortun with other men.

But she only asked *him* to save the planets. A complete and utter stranger, who she now claimed to love. He would allow this fact to simmer into his chest, remaining lodged in his heart whenever doubt erupted next. She only chose *him.*

Noah brought himself back to the present by counting the stars before looking back at Celeste. Her lips were slipping from their joyous state into a slight frown. His pain and uncertainty looked to be affecting her, causing a cycle of discomfort, and he decided in that moment he trusted her. He would let it all go. At least, until the doubt inevitably seeped through his thin barrier of positivity.

Even if she had a past, he could be her present and her future. "It's a shame the planets had to be in danger for us to cross paths."

"Fate," she whispered. It was a word that took hold of him so effortlessly he had no choice but to kiss her. He wrapped his arms around her waist with a light moan, fingers trailing underneath her shirt and circling her skin. She followed his lead and ran her hands through his hair before exploring his chest. "I think I know what you were dreaming about the other day."

"Oh?" he purred, nipping at her ear and kissing her neck. He prepared to peel off her shirt, if only to kiss every inch of her before the others noticed they were gone. "Care to demonstrate?"

"Guys!" called a voice. Katalina, he presumed. "I think I found something!"

"Finally," Mark remarked. "And where the fuck did Noah and Celeste go?"

"Language," yelled Luna from afar.

Noah chuckled as their mouths separated, and their eyes found each other. His body was on fire, full of lust and desire, but he said, "We'll continue this later. I'm sure we'll find time."

"If we don't run out." Her voice wavered before she leaned in for a final, quick kiss.

He pulled away. "Honey, even if we were stuck at the bottom of the ocean, I'd still find a way."

29

BLUE STAR, HOPE STAR

"I THINK IT'S *THAT* ONE," SAID KATALINA WITH AN EXAGGERATED point. "I noticed it's yellow like the rest, but only turns green when I tilt my head, whereas the others sift through multiple colors. Right?"

Celeste and Noah rejoined the group as Katalina finished her sentence, which was accompanied by Mark raising an accusatory eyebrow at them. "Finally getting down to it, huh? I never pegged you for a guy who'd do these things outside, though. Maybe you *can* party?"

Classic Mark. Though Noah had to admit it boosted his ego. Mark could be a good friend when he wanted to be. Noah touched his chest. "I can't tell whether to be hurt or flattered."

Celeste squinted up at the star before putting a hand on Katalina's shoulder with a reassuring smile. "I think you're right. At the very least, it's certainly different from the rest. Good work."

Noah tilted his head before nodding in agreement. The star shifted from green back to yellow when he looked straight up again.

"I don't see it," Luna grumbled, and he found that most interesting of all.

"Do you think it's safe to touch?" Katalina asked. "I want to feel a real star! It's warmer here, but they don't seem *too* hot."

"We went over this already, didn't we?" asked Luna.

"The scientist in you never wavers, does she?" Mark asked with a subdued smile before his gaze drifted to Noah. Noah tensed, preparing himself for whatever Mark was going to say. "If this is how you feel toward Celeste, you should probably stay."

Noah was taken aback by his words, quite literally; he took a step backward, his eyes widening. He'd expected Mark to say something rude, but in a funny way, as he was prone to do. But the look in his eyes was serious, his face slack of further emotion.

"Ugh," said Luna, crossing her arms. "Just hammer it in, why don't you?"

"Are you *still* going on about that?" Celeste asked, an argument brewing on the tip of her tongue. "Noah was never going to choose you. Besides, what about the Sky Prince? How could you forget about him? Or do you really only want what's mine?"

Noah's ears perked. He'd forgotten about the conversation Luna and Celeste had weeks ago about the Sky Prince. Celeste mentioned using him to get answers on why the rulers were adamant about the planet's colliding.

Katalina took a step forward. "You have a crush on someone else?"

Luna tsked. "He's a friend."

"A friend you like, and that likes you," Celeste teased before turning to Katalina. "She's always been one to have multiple crushes at once."

Luna said with a glare, "Friends like each other, yes."

"I feel like we're missing context here," Mark added. "Anyway, can we get back to the whole star thing? How are we going to get them down?"

"And we never answered the question of touching them?" Katalina asked.

"You can't, and please don't try," warned Celeste.

Noah marveled at how close they were to some of the stars. One was nearly touching the grassy ground by his feet. Without warning, Katalina kicked it and the star fell from its place in the air. Noah and Katalina jumped back as a soft sizzle sounded. The star burned out, turning from yellow to a charred brown, and continued to roll until it disappeared over the hillside.

Noah and his cousin made eye contact, their shocked expressions revealing the same thoughts; their skin was prickling with intense zeal at the prospect of experiencing something so raw and real.

"Here, I think I can reach it," Luna said. "Who has the jar?"

Celeste raised a hand before pulling around her disappearing pack and taking out the jar in question. Luna was a good few feet taller than the rest of them, even Mark. She grabbed the jar from Celeste and stood on the tips of her toes, scooping up the star.

Celeste thrust a fist in the air. "Perfect! Let's go back to the blue star you saw, and see if we can reach it. I'm sure that's the right one!"

To capture the next, Mark sat on Luna's shoulders since he was the second tallest of the bunch, and successfully scooped up the blue star. This one was much smaller than the hope star; it looked no bigger than the palm of a hand.

Mark tossed the jar to Celeste, and she caught it with a joyful whoop of glee. She met Noah's gaze, tears streaming down her face as he said, "Altair would be so proud."

Celeste's mouth hung open before she smiled and dried her cheeks.

"Oh man, I could kiss you right about now, Mark," Noah shouted, pulling Mark into a tight hug. "But I'll let Katalina do it for me. Thanks in advance."

He gave Katalina a nod of approval, and then scooped up Celeste and spun her around. When he placed her back on the ground, he planted a kiss on her lips. She laughed, cupping his cheeks in her hands as she said, "We did it."

Katalina rubbed her chin. "Though I'm curious—why is no one guarding them if they're so important?"

Noah placed Celeste back on the ground, and she nodded, her face growing serious. "You're right. We should celebrate later. There must be some sort of system in place to keep the stars from us aside from merely moving them. We should go."

"Go where? Back to the Ruler of the Deep?" Mark asked. "And then it's all over?"

"Theoretically," Celeste confirmed.

"Hopefully. Otherwise, everything will have been for nothing," Noah said, anxiety clawing at his ribcage.

"Let's go, then," Luna agreed. "My boat is at the main port. Whatever's next, we have to be prepared."

Just like that, the marveling of their accomplishment was over, and they were pushing onward toward the next goal. They still had a few days of travel before arriving back at the ocean, and even longer depending on if they found the creature where the Ruler of the Deep lived inside.

Their crew speedily jogged up and down the rest of the hills, much to Noah's dismay. Thankfully, it was uneventful, despite the tension running through his veins. When they reached the bottom of the last hill, there was another field of grass and small bushes.

At first, he thought there was a wall in the distance, much too far to make out, but he quickly realized the wall was moving toward them, and it wasn't a wall at all. It was a mass of people.

With each blink, the mass seemed to jump in time, and they were in front of their group within five blinks. It was an army, by the looks of it. The beings were humanoids made of white, puffy clouds. They had mouths without lips, and eyes without eyebrows. The scarlet suits they wore had pastel red hearts stitched into the breast pocket.

No one said a word.

"Um, excuse me?" Celeste shouted with hands cupped around her mouth. "Can we help you?"

"This isn't good," Luna hissed. "It's *them.*"

"Who?" asked Noah.

A vine was thrust from the clouds. Noah watched it unravel

and sway viciously in the wind. He tried to find the source of the vine, but it was too high to see.

"Huh. I think we're being pressured to go up," Celeste said.

"You think?" Mark asked incredulously.

"Oh, man. This isn't good *at all.*" Luna reiterated, shrinking away from the guards, only to bump into her stepsister.

"*Who are they?*" Noah asked desperately. Celeste's lips were a tight line, her eyes scanning the horizon of cloud people standing before them. A guard stepped forward with a fluffy, white finger thrust toward the vine.

"Climb."

30

CLIMB

Noah stared at the sky; the vine disappeared into a thick fog of clouds. His arms ached at the thought of climbing all that way. No harness, no safety equipment, or net on the ground. If they slipped, they'd die. He didn't want to die, as startling as such a realization was, and he didn't like their odds of survival.

"First falling, now climbing," Mark said with a craned neck.

"To be fair, we could climb and *then* fall," said Celeste while giving the vine a firm tug.

Noah pointed toward the clouds, a nervous sweat already gleaning along his temples. "We have to climb this? Without falling? Are you sure the five of us can do something like that?"

Celeste shrugged. "I don't think we have much of a choice. This is the Ruler of the Sky's army. She has guards of hearts and diamonds, and the hearts tend to be ruthless."

"I don't get it," Katalina said. "Why would the Ruler of the

Sky let us find and capture the stars in the first place? Why wait until *after* we got them and not before?"

"She's cocky," Luna said simply. "She knew we'd never be able to escape, with or without the stars."

Noah swallowed nervously. "Right. I don't suppose someone else would like to go first?"

He looked around at the other four before Luna let out a sigh. "I can. Merpeople have excessive strength compared to humans, and the Sky Kingdom is a tad kinder to merfolk than fairies are—it used to be, anyway. I could probably come back down and report how far the climb is, if you'd like."

He crinkled his brows. "But then you'd have to climb down and back up again."

"If it's for the good of the group, then so be it." She grabbed the vine and shimmied up a few inches before the entire thing shook and was pulled up by an unknown force at an incredible speed.

Luna disappeared into the heavy clouds, gone without a trace. A few seconds later, the vine was lowered once more, and Luna was no longer attached.

"Well, there's no screaming or a falling body, so... that's a good sign, right?" Mark asked hesitantly. Noah's shoulders relaxed. Climbing it was one thing, but being pulled up wasn't so bad. He could do that.

Noah grasped the vine and tugged on it. "It's like that fable from back home. 'Climb a vine to get real high; don't watch the birds pass you by.'"

Mark's eyes lit up next as he enthusiastically pointed toward

Noah and finished the rhyme, "'For if you do not look ahead, you may just end up being fed.'"

"Yikes," said Celeste. "Well, there aren't many things up there like that. Though, she *does* have a rogue ecklweckl as a pet that'll eat people from time to time. But being fed would be the least of our problems if we run into *her.*"

Mark took a deep breath, but Noah merely met Celeste's gaze with a small smirk, finding peace in the next stage of their journey. Whatever happened next, he believed in her. He believed in himself.

"Wow, you're *ready* for this, aren't you?" Celeste asked with a twinge of intense eagerness lining her voice. She wanted him to say yes, he realized.

"I'm ready for all our adventures," he said wistfully, wishing he could pull her in for a kiss. There was no time, however; the vine was tugged upward at a speed that made his stomach churn. He whizzed through the air, his ears clogged from the sudden acceleration and change of altitudes.

There was a moment where he thought he was stuck in a cloud, the air thick and difficult to inhale. He felt like he may suffocate within the heavy, never-ending fog.

And then he was there, on the other side.

31

PRINCESS OF THE SKY

It was brighter up here, with a completely clear sky and the usual splashes of purple and pink. The vine stopped a few feet above a wispy cloud. Noah clung to the tendril while looking around nervously for anything to place his feet on. There was nothing but clouds rolling on for miles. After all of their falling, he was becoming scared of heights, and he wagered this was the highest they'd been yet.

"Excuse me," came a deep voice. Noah looked around frantically. Two humanoids made of condensed clouds were standing beside him with diamonds instead of hearts etched into their clothing. They were interchangeable with no defining characteristics that differed from the other. "You must let go."

"I—I can't. There's no ground!"

"Do you not see we are standing just fine? Fool!"

"Fool!" agreed the other.

"Get off!"

"Fool," the other repeated.

"We said that already!" The cloud man bopped his companion on the back of the head. "Your blue friend was escorted that way. We'll be doing the same now."

Noah tentatively dipped the tip of his shoe into the cloud. His weakened arms were shaking, but the cloud didn't feel sturdy enough to stand on. Not at all.

Noah reminded himself it was okay; Luna didn't fall, and these two cloudmen weren't, either. It *must've* been okay, yet nerves held him back. As always. He never failed to disappoint himself.

"We haven't got all day, fool," one of the guards shouted.

With a shuddering, deep breath, Noah used his weight to sway himself and the vine before he jumped, landing beside the guards. He closed his eyes, terrified of plummeting to his death. Noah waited two beats, then opened his lids slowly. He'd landed on his hands and knees. Though his fingers were covered by the thick wisps of a cloud instead of grass, the ground—if one could call it that—was solid. Everything was okay.

One guard snorted, and the other laughed. "Such a silly human, afraid of nothing. Weren't you taught about the cloud kingdom in school?"

Noah shook his head, and the guards stared at him, perplexed. "Gravity is different above these clouds. Not all clouds, but the few that stretch this way and that. Don't go too far either way, and you'll be fine."

They nodded for him to follow, and he did so reluctantly. Noah glanced over his shoulder as the vine was lowered for the next person. The sheer vastness of the clear magenta horizon and the kingdom ahead left him breathless. A pathway made of magnificent marble stone was carved into the clouds, leading to a pale pink castle. His mouth fell open at the sight of thick roots with dark blue flowers decorating the exterior.

Behind the castle were two large white buildings reminiscent of farmhouses on Sundar. As he wondered what they were hiding in said barns, one of the guards looked over their shoulder and said, "Lastly, do *not* go near the animal pens. She'll never forgive you if you do."

Something about the sentiment made his skin crawl.

He was escorted to the front steps of the castle; the area was completely vacant of other citizens or guards. "Where is everyone?"

"Your questions must wait." The guards said no more. Instead, they stared ahead, grabbing his arms and dragging him up the stairs to a set of double doors decorated with the outline of a woman in a long, flowing dress.

"What are you going to do to us?" Noah asked, but again, there was no response. The double doors opened on their own, and the guards shoved him inside. The floor was made of more marble, and there was a spiraling set of stairs in the center of the lobby, leading to a second floor with an open balcony.

"*We* aren't going to do anything, fool."

"Fool," chimed the other.

Luna was standing in front of the staircase. When she turned, her shoulders relaxed at the sight of Noah. "Thank goodness. I was worried they were going to murder us one by one!"

He stepped up beside her and whispered, "Are the Queen and all her subjects aggressive?"

Luna shook her head, eyebrows pinched in worry. "The Ruler of the Sky is known to have a temper. Her partner can be... more erratic, but she makes herself scarce. Not all the citizens here agree with what the Crimson Queen has done, but there's nothing they can do without being sent off the plank."

"The plank?"

"It's a thin platform off the clouds, and they force you to jump off and fall to your death."

Noah gulped. "And since we technically stole the stars...?"

"She has free rein to do as she pleases with us."

The other three arrived one after the other with no issues. Was the Queen sending them separately on purpose, instilling fear by insinuating those who went before them were killed?

When Celeste appeared by Noah's side, he interlaced his fingers with hers and pulled her close. He held her slightly behind himself, using his body as a shield. He knew she didn't need protecting, and yet he felt the urge to give his life to her. After all, they were dealing with a deranged woman who forced naysayers to jump to their deaths.

"Every little detail just gets a tad bit darker here, doesn't it?" Noah mumbled to himself, rubbing the back of his neck. Even a place full of such whimsy had a dark underbelly of terror. He wondered what people on Sundar were hiding.

"It'll be okay. We'll figure it out." Celeste sounded so sure he almost believed her, if not for the scrunched nose Luna offered in return.

"Surrounded by guards?" countered Luna. "After we *stole*

something from her? Not to mention there's a ruler on the premises, no doubt reading all our minds?"

Celeste stared back with rosy cheeks. "Well, when you put it like that—"

"Hello," came a silky voice ahead. Her tone was buttery, words gliding off her tongue like a knife to warm bread, melting instantly. A woman around their age stood at the top of the staircase with her fingers curled around the railing.

Her tan face, arms and legs appeared human, but her long lavender hair and bangs were fluffy and full like the clouds. A silver tiara rested atop her head, and she wore a long, pastel blue and red ballgown with an elaborate lace train following her as she walked down the stairs.

The woman stood with her head held high and a smirk. Her lavender eyes pierced into his soul, daring to drag every ounce of him out. She had power. For this, he was sure, and she was terrifying because of it.

A sharp stab radiated through his back as he was pushed forward. He shot a glare over his shoulder; a spear dug into his back. "Fools! You will bow to the princess!"

"Ugh, is there an off button for these guys?" Mark asked, swatting away the guards and their sharp weapons. He lost, and he, along with the others, was pushed to his knees, face pointed to the ground.

All this skin prickling tension was unbearable. They were kneeling in front of royalty, something he'd only read about in books. He wondered if the authors knew of this place and recounted their memories for Sundar natives. Perhaps they were purely imaginative, and similar ideas spanned universes and dimensions.

"You may rise," the princess said. They did as instructed, and Noah mistakenly made eye contact with her. She countered with a squint filled with a mischievous twinkle, shifting to Mark and the others as she examined the room. She gave off raw power, a confidence that came with the knowledge of being better than everyone else in the room. An aura of domination. "I am the Princess of the Sky. You may call me Sie Mae."

Mark took a deep breath, about to ask something, no doubt, but Noah elbowed him in the side with a shake of his head. "Not *now.*"

"Much like the men here are called 'sir,' women are 'sie,'" she explained. "It's as formal as the word 'princess.'"

Noah nodded along. It made so much sense he wondered why they didn't have such denotations on Sundar. Though he supposed 'Mrs.' and 'Mr.' were close enough. The princess' gaze suddenly shifted to Noah, and she walked up to him until her face was inches from his. He froze, intrigued by what was to come.

Sie Mae moved on to Katalina and Mark next, purposefully stepping between them as she passed, detaching their clasped hands by doing so. She glared at Mark with a cocky smile, and he looked away; Noah could see Mark's hands shaking and temples dripping with sweat. For once, Noah was certain they were all scared.

Sie Mae found her way back to Noah, her eyes narrow as she towered over him by at least two inches. He didn't like the way her eyes assessed him. It made him feel cheap, lesser than, which he supposed was the point of her intimidation tactic.

He glanced over at Celeste, hoping to catch her kind eyes flickering toward him. She was watching, but her brows were pressed together in hurt. Sie Mae was far too close, but he didn't want to cause a scene by backing away. If he offended her, the worst-case scenario was a deadly fall, and he quite liked being alive.

Sie Mae only leaned in closer at this thought, inspecting him even more. She pouted before a corner quirked upward. "Interesting."

"So I've been told," he said before he could stop himself, looking everywhere except at her.

The princess cocked her head at his words. "You have taken something from my mother. She does not take kindly to such actions."

She moved on to Celeste, who was staring at the ground. Sie Mae trailed a finger from Celeste's throat to her chin, tilting Celeste's face upward so their eyes were level. The princess leaned in and whispered something in her ear. Celeste gasped, her cheeks growing red, but Noah hadn't caught a word of what was said.

"But for now," the princess continued as she walked back toward the stairs and turned with hands tucked behind her back. "Consider yourselves lucky. My mother is charitable. She will give you a magnificent last night to remember and a chance to live if you hand over the jar."

"What?" asked Mark, taking a sharp step backward in shock. A guard jabbed him with their spear from behind, and he fell forward onto his knees with a surprised yelp. Noah reached down to help him up, noticing the spear had drawn blood from Mark's back, and his shirt was damp.

"You will attend the ball tonight. All of you. Attire will be provided inside your rooms. You're free to pick whatever you wish to wear. The dancing starts at eight sharp. Do *not* be late," the princess said.

"Where's the Ruler of the Sky?" asked Celeste. Her question made Noah bristle. He was rightfully worried about meeting another ruler, especially if she was anything like Sie Mae, but he crossed his fingers that they would escape before the chance arose.

"And your brother?" asked Luna, garnering a surprised huff from the princess. "Where is he?"

"Still going on about my brother?" Sie Mae asked with a sneer. "Well, you're in luck, too; his brain endlessly pines for you. Even when he lays with others."

"Not something I needed to hear," Luna grumbled, crossing her arms over her chest, blue cheeks darkening. Her squirming seemed to entertain the princess. A fun game providing discomfort to others. He didn't need to meet the rest to know there was something deeply wrong with this family.

"They'll both be present tonight." Sie Mae said no more and turned toward the staircase. She walked halfway up the steps before placing a hand on the railing and peering over her shoulder. "The guards will escort you to your rooms for the time being. Do not try to escape. There is no way to."

With that, she sauntered away. He watched her go, shocked by the events unraveling. They somehow went from prisoners to prisoners again in a matter of days. It wasn't something he wanted to get used to, this feeling of hopelessness.

Noah realized if he believed in fate, then this had to be part of it. Was everything by design, or only a few select things? Was his entire path predetermined?

But what about his mother, then? What would her death mean, or did it mean nothing at all?

He reminded himself to stay focused on the task at hand. It was much too easy to get lost in thought; now was certainly not the time. The guards were separating the men and women, herding Noah and Mark with spears, and jabbing at them as if they were cattle.

Mark and Noah exchanged a look. Ah. Of course, they would be separated from their partners and stuck as roommates yet again.

32

OUTFIT CHANGE

"I EXPECTED THAT TO BE MUCH MORE MEMORABLE," MARK confessed.

Noah and Mark found themselves in a room alone together. There was an enormous closet spanning an entire wall, with suits and tuxedos sorted by every color imaginable, though pastel appeared to take up the most options.

"Meaning?" Noah asked, lying on the bed for a moment to release his tension. His anxieties were making his limbs grow heavy, his heart in constant static shock. Noah's feet hung off the bed lazily, and he felt the pressure slowly leak from him with each light kick.

"We just met a *princess.* She's important in this world, but she wasn't all that interesting, was she? Just a typical tyrant's daughter."

Not like they had any experience with that. They'd heard of such concepts in fictional books, but Sundar only had two ways to live. Freeform, away from the government on the crumbling side of the planet, or adhering to the voting rules on the city side.

The room was a hodgepodge of random decor, ranging from family photos to statues and model ships. It lacked elegance, something he assumed all royalty had, though the room admittedly had character. A home of those who collected odd yet fascinating things.

"Wow," said Mark. He stood in front of a full-length mirror and held up a white tux with black trim. "This just might be my dream."

Noah raised a brow. "You mean the privilege of sharing a room with me again?"

Mark took out a handful of hangers, each with suits of varying colors. "Um, hello? Wearing suits is one of the best aspects of being a man. You look like a fashionable, suave secret agent in whatever you choose, and the ladies love them."

Noah cringed. "I don't need to know the details about what you and Katalina dress up as after hours..."

Mark laughed. "That's not what I mean. Trust me, Celeste will be incredibly into it, too. There's also the bonus that I can take one of these suits for our together ceremony." His smile wavered. "Which you won't be coming to, I guess."

Noah tucked his hands under his head as he stared up at the ceiling. "I will regret not being there, but I'm happy for you guys! I can tell you love each other unconditionally."

"Like I said—if Katalina asked me to help her save the world, I'd say yes just so I could talk to her for a few more hours."

Noah smiled as he finally stood with a stretch and looked over his options. He picked out a navy blue tuxedo. "Thank you. I appreciate it."

He held it up to the mirror, knowing he was going to choose it solely because he hated trying on clothes. Meanwhile, Mark quickly threw on suit after suit. Lavender, rose, grassy green—he tried them all. Still, he opted to go for white at the end, tightening the black tie with a smirk. "This is the one."

Mark's eyes flickered to Noah, who'd gone with the navy blue. Noah held his head high as he tightened the bow. There was something powerful about wearing a tuxedo. He would have to keep this in mind for the *after* part of their journey. Mark followed suit and said, "Nice. We look *good.*"

"You were right—we look like secret agents."

Mark nodded. "Just like in the books, the lady's love 'em. I'd love to save the world in this, too."

"I didn't know you like to read."

Mark shrugged. "I like a lot of things. Suits, books, kickball, biking. Mostly kickball, but there aren't many ways to pass time on Sundar outside of work."

"Why don't you stay, then?" Noah asked, looking at Mark through the mirror. "Convince Katalina. Have a together ceremony here. Sundar has nothing exciting to offer. It's much too small, with nothing new to discover. Katalina would have a field day here as a scientist."

Mark grimaced. "This planet is scary, dude. I like the mundanity of Sundar. Running from fairies and riding the backs of draegons doesn't excite me. I just want to read a good book, go on a peaceful walk, and play sports with my friends. This place is awful."

Noah cocked his head. "Huh. I didn't know you hated it that much."

Mark crossed his arms. "Um, I think I've made it pretty obvious. I don't complain nearly as much on Sundar, I can tell you that."

"I doubt that."

"You would."

They stared at themselves in the mirror before checking their watches in unison, which were also provided with their room. "We still have two hours. What now?"

They stood in silence a moment longer before Noah said, "What do you think the others are doing right now?"

"Thinking about us, I'd imagine."

"Maybe we should go find—"

There was a knock on the door. Their heads turned.

"Who do you think it is?" Mark whispered.

"I don't know, but I'm scared."

"Of course you are."

"Of course *you* are."

Mark held up his hands. "Okay, yes. I'm scared, too!"

Noah led the charge, slowly creeping up to the door. There was no way to see who was on the other side. He took a deep breath, hoping it wasn't someone ordered to kill them.

He pulled open the door.

Noah's chest deflated, and he smiled. "Celeste? What are you doing here?"

Katalina popped out from behind the wall, and he pulled the door open fully for Mark to see.

"Well, I figured we had two hours to kill. Might as well have a look around," Celeste said. She was wearing a dark blue and black ballgown that shimmered like a night sky.

"You have something to show me?"

She grinned. "Perhaps."

Noah turned to Mark and Katalina, who were lost in conversation about how many options of suits there were, and what he should wear for their together ceremony. It was adorable, honestly. Noah couldn't help but feel proud of his cousin and newfound friend. They were truly meant for each other.

"Do you guys want to come?" Noah asked.

Mark shook his head. "Like I said, mundanity. I don't need to see any more of this planet. It stresses me out."

"Fair enough," Noah said, thankful to have time alone with Celeste. It was such a rarity that he thanked every second he had with her. He cherished them as if each time was the last.

Noah turned back to Celeste as she asked, "Ready?"

He nodded, taking her hand. "Ready."

And she whisked him away.

33

A WARNING

As Celeste took him down the hall, they passed Luna and a tall man he presumed to be the Sky Prince. He was tan like the princess, and wore a suit splashed in pastel purple and pink, and his hair was a white wisp atop his head. Noah dragged his feet, slowing him and Celeste down to watch the interaction.

"Luna," the man said, his eyes the color of the stars—a bright yellow. He took her hand and gave the back a delicate kiss. Luna's hands were covered with black satin gloves that extended to her elbows, and she wore a shimmering ballgown of the same color. "A pleasure to see you again."

He glanced over at Noah next with an eyebrow ticked upward. "Ah, your human friend. I've read your thoughts about him, dear."

Luna grimaced as she seemed to shrivel, and Noah shivered at the thought. The Sky Prince turned a nose up at Noah, his lips forming a sneer, adding to Noah's unsettled nerves. He shouldn't have stopped to eavesdrop, but he was so enthralled by such a poignant creature that he felt compelled to. It was beautiful.

"I am not an *it,*" the man declared, but he was blushing, and he turned his head away. The discomfort in Noah only grew. What was going on with these two?

"And you, Sir Octover," Luna said, gaining the Sky Prince's attention and relieving the attention from Noah. "How has the sky been all these years?"

"As well as the sea, I presume. But I must confess, I was saddened you didn't attend the ball last year. It would've been our—"

"It's no matter, Octover. I'm here now." Her voice was a gentle bubbly melody meant only for him. She placed a hand on his cheek and guided his eyes back to hers.

Noah was officially overstaying his welcome. He whispered to Celeste, "Should we continue?"

She nodded, her shoulders relaxing in relief. "I thought you'd never ask."

Celeste gestured for him to follow, and he raced forward to clasp his hand in hers once more. Her touch was tender, taking him back to the day they'd met when she asked him to take her hand. A warmth spread along his cheeks. He longed to be pulled by her everywhere they went. They zigzagged through the halls and down the spiraling staircases as she called over her shoulder, "I want to show you something I've only seen once. When I was younger, around ten or eleven. I hope it's still there."

"What is it?"

"You'll see." She stopped them in the middle of the staircase, her eyebrows pinched in worry. "I must warn you of something before we continue. The princess will ask to dance with you tonight."

"What do you mean?"

"I saw the way she looked at you."

"I'll just say no, then. Easy." He wiped his hands together to emphasize his point. "I only want to dance with you."

She shook her head. "You can't say no. She's the princess of the castle we're staying in. It would be unseemly."

"Unseemly? These people are holding us hostage! I don't owe them anything."

"You do if your life is on the line," Celeste said, her voice trembling. Her fear was palpable, sending goosebumps up his arms.

"Please, sweetheart, call me the Crimson Queen," a deep and demanding voice said from behind. Celeste stiffened, her jaw tightening. The hair on Noah's arms stood on end; he was afraid of turning around.

He did so slowly, his eyes first on the marble floor, before panning up a deep ruby red dress. Unlike her children, her hair was white with hints of pastel pink, blue, and lavender to match Fortun's sky. Her interwoven braids were pinned into a bun atop her head, and a golden crown with glittering jewels rested in front. Her complexion was smooth, albeit worn along the edges, and her eyes were a distant gray. He could see the resemblance to her daughter clearly.

"I rule the sky with my wife. Therefore, I am not the only Ruler of the Sky."

"You won't be the ruler of anything if our planets collide," Celeste said, her chin held up in defiance. "Tell us why you moved the stars. What purpose does that serve?"

"Who says it was I?" The Crimson Queen's smile dropped slightly. "And I would not come into your home demanding answers for things I should know nothing about. Unless you'd like me to ask why you would, say, believe your father when he tells you he's away for business?"

Celeste's eyes widened, but the Crimson Queen did not stop there. "It doesn't matter, because I'm not asking, and you're not answering. You stay in our kingdom until you hand back the stars, and I won't kill you. That is our trade."

Our trade? Noah thought. *She must be mad.*

The Crimson Queen's lips curved upwards. "Why, of course, Noah. Aren't we all?"

He shook his head before he could stop himself. Once again, he'd forgotten she—and her children—could read minds. "No."

"The Ruler of the Deep begs to differ." The Crimson Queen squinted. "I can see the thoughts swirling in that head of yours, boy. There is a deep sadness in you. In both of you. How my ecklweckl would enjoy feasting on you."

The Queen clapped her scarlet-gloved hands. "Now, I must be off to dinner before the dance tonight. I hope the two of you enjoy the yearly ball. It will be your last if you don't comply. And remember, someone's always watching. You can't leave the clouds no matter how hard you try."

The Crimson Queen turned and sauntered away. Two guards with hearts etched in their suits appeared from the shadows, flanking either side of her. She was certainly regal, with an air of utmost importance who no other possessed.

When she was out of sight, Celeste released a sigh. "She is one of few who scare me."

"You did well, though, standing up to her."

"Did I?"

"Better than I did," Noah said, carefully dodging the question. "What do you think they're all fighting about?"

"Power, I'd imagine," she said with a shrug. Noah thought back to all the books he'd read as a child and teen. All the parables led back to humanity being its own destruction. "There is no power worth going to war, is there? What if the Ruler of the Deep is just as evil as she? What if there is no good?"

Her hesitancy was reflected in the tremor of her voice. A highly unusual state for Celeste to be in.

"There's us. There's your brother, and Luna and my cousin and Mark. Plenty of good is out there, but those who are evil tend to gain power faster. It's easier for them because they have no empathy. They'll do whatever it takes."

Celeste squeezed his hand as she took a deep breath. "I'm scared, Noah. I'm scared about what will happen after we save the planets. What will become of Fortun? What will become of us?"

He grabbed her by the arms gently while holding her gaze. "There will always be good, Celeste. Whatever happens, we can face it together."

Once again, he debated kissing her, but he waited. He feared the Crimson Queen was around the corner, taking notes. She could use whatever information she had as leverage and use it against them. He couldn't risk anything happening to Celeste.

"Where were we?" he whispered, their mouths inching closer. "You were about to show me something?"

Celeste nodded dutifully before spinning around, her hypnotic smile and enthusiasm returning. She wasn't an overly vulnerable person, and he cherished this moment of shared anxiety. They were far more similar than he thought. "Right. Come this way."

34

THE RUINS

His mouth fell open as she took him through a metal archway decorated with white vines and red flowers. Beyond the arch was a brick path lit by tiny, glowing bugs and floating lanterns.

The cloud they walked on ended when the path did, like a steep cliffside. Except instead of water at the bottom, there was only air. From here, the path split in two directions. To the left, the brick walkway was replaced by a trail of gold glitter. It led to one of the tall and long buildings resembling a barn.

Straight ahead, where the clouds ended abruptly, was a tightrope across. Noah tentatively inspected where the tightrope led; his eyes landed on another cloud much too far to jump to. He spotted a carousel of faux animals, a Ferris wheel, and various tents scattered about.

He squinted, noting every attraction was painted shades of purple, reminding him of the Ruler of the Wind, and they were all covered with thick green vines and red roses. A surprised smile formed on his lips.

"Is this—" Noah began, but Celeste cut him off.

"—the ruins of an outdoor circus? Yes, yes, it is."

"You have those here, too?" His heart thrummed to life with giddy joy. Noah went to every circus with his mother growing up. He loved the sweet and salty scent of caramel apples and popcorn, and seeing the endangered animal shows to raise money to help them survive. What a beautiful time it had been, then. He'd taken it for granted.

"From what Altair's notes say, it was an idea from your world. You have one every two years, no?"

Noah nodded vigorously. "I adore the circus, and you're telling me there's one here? It's official. I have to stay. I have to stay with you."

Her lips parted in surprise. "Really?"

"Really. I'll convince Mark and Katalina to watch Henry." His smile fell. "Unless... unless you don't want me to."

"What? No, of course I do! It's not that! It's just... you'd probably never be able to go back, you know? Could you live with that? Never visiting your mother's gravesite, or seeing your old town or friends or family? And for what? Me?"

He shrugged. "Is that so wrong? Besides, I think my mother's casket was whisked away in a flood years ago. It's just a symbol, you know? I could make a new one somewhere here. She's always with me like Altair is with you."

She crinkled her eyebrows in concern while looking back at the circus. "I don't want you to give everything up for me. The circus is different here, anyway. These have been ruins for almost a decade. They were once enjoyed by everyone across the land, but at some point, the Crimson Queen went mad, and no one outside the kingdom has been invited since. The cloud dwellers here aren't the biggest fans of the circus, so it ran out of use."

He grabbed her by the waist and pulled her close. Her wavy black and blue hair framed her heart-shaped face, and he lightly tucked a strand behind her ear.

"Don't you see?" he whispered. "I have nothing to give up that I haven't already lost. Mark and Katalina will make decent cat parents. If there's one thing I know, it's that I want to be with you. Do you not want me to stay?"

She sucked in a deep breath. "Of course, I do. I just don't know if I'm... as special as you think I am. I don't want to disappoint you."

"We're all imperfect, Celestial. I love all of you."

Her blush deepened. "You know it's funny... I've thought about going to Sundar to stay with you. It would be pretty neat to live on a flat planet, I think."

He nearly laughed, finding that hard to believe. "If I didn't know any better, I would've thought you were being sarcastic."

She crinkled her nose with a light chuckle. "Of course, I'm not."

Noah stared out at the ruins. "Well, where we decide doesn't matter much to me. As long as we're together."

He could feel Celeste's gaze as she said, "I—I feel the same."

She jumped into action without warning, placing her hands on her hips as she bounced on the balls of her feet. "Now, shall we zipline over?"

"Is it safe after all this time without being maintained?" He'd thought they'd have to walk on a tightrope to reach the other side, but a zipline made much more sense, and sounded safer. As he reassessed the fall between where they were and where they were going, he took a sharp step back. "It might be too dangerous."

"Nonsense. Not for us," she said.

He side-eyed her with a smirk. *Us,* he thought. He about melted right there, her sincerity igniting a pang of desire. He had to do something quick to get his mind off her, opting to inspect the zipline further. Two rubber handles were connected to a wheel attached to the rope. It was at a slight angle downward; all they had to do was push off with enough momentum... and hold on.

"You're right," he finally said, testing the rope with a few tugs. "After everything we've been through, what's the worst that could happen?"

Celeste shot him a mischievous smile. "Noah Everlow. I never would've expected such a thing from you. Well, how can a girl say no to such a brave, handsome man?"

"Handsome, you say?"

Noah gave the back of her hand a quick kiss. He could hardly contain the love flowing through him, the passion begging to burst from his lips. Still, he waited to kiss her until the time was right, and grabbed onto the zipline handles. Celeste climbed onto him, wrapping her arms tightly around his chest and resting her chin against his shoulder. "Are you sure it can handle both of us at the same time?"

She nodded. "It was built to hold up to three. We'll be fine."

Noah pushed off the ground without hesitation, and they zipped through the air. He laughed, releasing a loud, "Woo-hoo!"

His hair whipped in the cool wind as raw adrenaline and exhilaration coursed through him. It was over too soon.

He planted his feet on the ground. The grass was longer than he expected, his shoes becoming lost in the overgrowth. A rustle sounded ahead. Noah tensed, preparing for the worst, but released a sigh of relief when a white bunny popped out. He chuckled at his deflating fear. "Didn't you tell me you were part rabbit when we met?"

She nodded. "I always hoped I'd someday grow a tail and ears. The Ruler of the Wind is lucky he can change his appearance at will."

Noah looked back to where the bunny had been, but it'd long since hopped away. He pictured Celeste with two floppy ears and a fluffy tail, and raised a brow. "You could always dress up, you know. Do you have something like the Pumpkin Festival here? We wear costumes once a year." He trailed off when she shook her head. "Oh, well. How are animals able to stay on the clouds?"

Celeste shrugged. "Who am I to know the why?"

"The girl with all the answers... answerless?" Noah stepped up to the carousel, taking in the craftsmanship of each animal-shaped seat, of which were largely based on animals that were extinct on Sundar.

Every feature was made of ceramic and hand-painted with splashes of pinks and whites. The animals were not painted in the correct colors, at least not to him. A pink lion outlined in black; a zebra with blue and yellow stripes; a shark that was green instead of gray. The paint was fading, however, and the vines were growing heavily along, well, everything.

He reached for Celeste and pulled her up onto the carousel platform. She stumbled and fell into his arms. Noah released a soft groan from the impact of her body and landed with his back against the nearest faux animal—a purple draegon.

Her hands rested against his chest as she looked up at him. Noah's breath hitched when she leaned in, their lips colliding. He pulled her closer with fingers entangled in her wavy black hair, and took in her radiant, flowery strawberry scent.

His thoughts vanished, replaced only with a burning desire that sent him on a quest of her body. Her dress was snug around her waist, so he lifted her leg and hiked up the fabric, caressing and squeezing her thighs gently.

She moaned when they pulled away from each other, and the sound of birds chirping in the distance filled the gaps between their heavy gasps of breath. Noah smiled, his eyes still glazed, and mind in a daze. He whispered in her ear, "Dance with me."

He swept her away before she could say a word, and she released magnificent spurts of breathless giggles behind him. Noah waltzed with her, weaving through the carousel with broad twirls, releasing hands only when a faux animal got in their way.

During the brief moments when their fingers didn't touch, there was a burning hole in his chest, and when they found each other again, he became whole.

Noah pulled her close, kissing her suddenly and passionately as they spun around before releasing her again. They danced to the soundless night; their laughter was the music their bodies swayed to.

When they were finished, they collapsed on the grass beside each other. Celeste snuggled into his arms as they looked up at the starless sky.

"Thank you," he said. "For the perfect night before the planets end."

"No, thank *you*." She sighed, kissing him on the cheek before looking into his eyes. "You're everything I could've hoped for, and so much more. I don't know how you do it."

"Do what?" Every ounce of his being was hooked on each word she said.

"How you can be the most perfect imperfect person I've ever met?"

Noah chuckled. "Is that a compliment?"

"It was supposed to be," she said with a gasp. "But now I see how it could sound otherwise. Hey—'perfect' is in there twice. So, I'd say it's a compliment."

Noah cupped her cheek in his hand and pulled her in again. He didn't want to stop. He couldn't get enough of her. Never enough. When they pulled away, Celeste was grinning, holding his hand and nestling her cheek against it. He wondered if she knew how bright she glowed, even in the darkest hours.

"There's one more thing I want to show you here! The ghost tent is still open for business," Celeste exclaimed.

He supposed he should've been frightened by the idea of a tent full of ghosts in an abandoned circus, but he laughed, instead. He laughed so hard that tears blurred his vision and slid down his temples.

Celeste cocked her head. "What's wrong?"

"Nothing. I—I'm just so happy, I can't contain it. How grateful I am to be here with you." He wiped away his tears and stood up while brushing off his tuxedo. A few yards away, he saw a towering tent that stuck out among the rest. Not only was it ten times taller, but it was painted all black.

Noah gulped at the sight, though the fear was merely temporary. Celeste jumped up and grabbed his hand, pulling him toward the structure without another word.

It was then he knew—he loved her. He would always love her.

Always.

35

AN EMPTY WELCOME

Two hours later, it was time. Noah and Celeste went their separate ways and back to their rooms. Noah was a little disappointed to see Mark wasn't there when he returned. He'd wanted to gush about what Celeste showed him, and about how Sundar inspired something on this planet. A fact Noah still found shocking.

As soon as he closed his bedroom door, a knock came. His brain and heart automatically began working overtime; the halls were empty just moments ago. Was it the Crimson Queen, there to scold him for trespassing? Or the princess, coming to seduce him and ask him to dance?

When he opened the door, there was a guard on the other side. "Right this way, sir."

Noah tentatively followed the guard down to the first floor. The cloudman was wearing a suit with a diamond etched in the breast pocket. He wasn't one of the violent ones, so that was something.

Noah was brought to a set of double doors with cloud dwellers, as Celeste had called them, carved into the stone. He pushed them open, expecting a luxurious room full of people dancing and drinking. The other side was empty.

The doors opened up to a path made of crimson carpet leading to a pastel red curtain hanging horizontally, like a divider between life and death. A brisk breeze sent a shiver down his spine, and he wondered if he should turn around and run off to the circus and the ghost tent within.

The sheer canopy above billowed and swayed with the golden hue of strung-up lights, illuminating an otherwise dark passageway. Most importantly, he was alone. He thought couples would line the walkway, bumping into him with dirty glares. But no, the party was devoid of life. Eerily so.

Noah turned around, and his heart sank at the sight. Or, rather, what he didn't see. The double doors he'd entered from had vanished, revealing a startling darkened sky above a black wall. He touched the damp, black stone. He could only move forward.

A whisper brushed against his cheek, and he jumped at the sudden chatter from beyond the swath of fabric behind him. He spun around with a gasp, a figure suddenly blocking his path. The princess. Her mauve ballgown shimmered in the light and her fluffy lavender hair was tied into an intricate bun atop her head.

Noah's mouth ran dry. He was standing in front of royalty and inside enemy territory. He had to remain on high alert.

Come to think of it—where were Celeste and the others? Why wasn't Mark in the room when Noah returned?

His nerves quickly worked on crushing his windpipes as he stared at her. Sie Mae smiled. "Noah Everlow. I've been waiting for you."

Her voice was gentle, a low thrum of electricity spreading through him, and his nerves seemed to vanish. He couldn't place how or why, and his mind drifted away as he looked past her to the closed curtain and the chatter. He had to figure out how to convince her to spare their lives and help them escape. The only way to do so was by channeling his inner Celeste. Instead of questioning her, he tilted his head with a reassuring smile. "I've been waiting for you, too."

"Oh?" she asked, her eyebrows raised. "You, too, have wished to speak alone?"

He nodded tentatively. "It's a pleasure to meet another ruler and their subsequent children. Your home is lovely."

She waved his words away before extending an elbow for him to take. He looked at her arm hesitantly, wondering if this was the right decision. "You are so cordial and rigid. Please, relax. It is so rare to have company from outside the kingdom these days. I am here to ask you to dance."

Celeste was right; the princess wanted to dance with him. He stared down at the gloved hand she offered. Noah wanted to refuse so badly, yet he knew he couldn't. They had to play their parts. One wrong move and they'd be falling to their deaths, and the planets would collide next.

"I would be honored to dance with someone as beautiful as you," Noah forced from his lips. There was a sinking feeling in his gut—no good could come from this. It would be the perfect night to escape, while everyone was busy celebrating, their eyes on the Queen and her children, but they'd be surrounded by guards and cornered.

Sie Mae scowled. Curiously, he asked, "Was it something I said, your majesty?"

The princess shook her head with a small smile. "No... not at all. Shall we?"

He nodded with a nervous grin. "We shall."

36

TO DANCE OR NOT TO DANCE

Sie Mae pushed the swath of pastel red fabric to the side, revealing a courtyard amidst the clouds. There were two brick walls covered in vines, one on either side of the entryway. Directly ahead, the clouds opened up to a beautiful, deep magenta sky.

A starless sky.

He found it hard to believe there was a jar stuffed with stars somewhere in Celeste's pack. The idea a star could be contained, much less in a jar, was an absurd notion. Hopefully, the Queen or princess thought this, too, and wouldn't deduce where the stars were kept.

The dancing came and went with the princess. Back and forth surrounded by couples doing the same.

All he wanted was Celeste.

Noah watched her dance with others from the corner of his eye. The men laughed as she spoke, and his heart sank each time one stepped closer or offered her another drink. His jaw clenched at the way they looked at her. Revolting. It took everything in his power to stay put instead of marching over there and pushing her seducers out of the way.

"Have you ever considered becoming a prince?" Sie Mae's question cut through his thoughts like a saw to a tree. He winced, and when he turned to her, she was squinting, though her demeanor remained rather diplomatic. He didn't like the way she searched his eyes, as though she was hoping he would agree to whatever she said. "You certainly look the part."

He peered over at Celeste, a pang of frustration bursting at the way one man tried putting his hand on her cheek. She slapped his attempt away, releasing a fraction of Noah's fears. "No. Do I?"

"You do. You have the backstory to make for an excellent king, too."

"Come again? I'm not sure I'm following." Noah was completely blindsided by her line of questioning, or what she was referring to. He hadn't offered her any hints regarding what his past was like.

"Mother can do more than read minds. She can peek into the past. She can even alter it, if she so wishes. Turn dreams into nightmares; love into hate. She told me all about your mother."

Noah stiffened. "I don't want to talk about that."

"Okay. Why don't you want to be a prince? Wouldn't anyone want such a title? And certainly, be a prince of mine?"

He finally looked at Sie Mae. "Well, we don't have such titles on my planet, so it's never crossed my mind. I've read a few books with the ideas of royalty, perhaps, but I've never been one to insert myself into those. So... no. I've only thought of me as me."

Her mouth hung open. "What a strange thing to say."

Noah held back a sigh. Everyone found him so fascinating here, and he could hardly understand why. He was an unemployed, anxious cat guy living in a rundown apartment with no clear aspirations. He was as boring as Sundar.

He spared one last glance Celeste's way. She was as gorgeous as ever, twirling in the arms of another. Though this night was squandered, at least he could stay on Fortun after they saved the planets. They'd find time to dance together again. He would wait a thousand lifetimes to dance with her.

The princess grabbed his chin and pulled his eyes back to hers with a sly smile. She leaned into his ear with a whisper, "It was your fault."

Her voice echoed through his mind as the world seemed to drift away. "It was all your fault she's gone, you know. You did nothing. You still don't. No"—she chuckled—"You do nothing at all except fail."

His vision blurred, and suddenly he was standing at the edge of Sundar with his mother. He was a child, merely twelve, jumping from rock to rock. It was illegal to pass the sign labeled 'the end,' but she always took him there. He laughed with another hop, nearly losing his balance.

Young Noah turned to his mother, looking for approval, or perhaps for her to come out and join him. Her lips were curled in disgust, dark black bags decorating her eyes. Hatred seethed from them.

Noah gasped as the world came back into focus. The princess was staring back at him with a cocked head. "Funnily enough, I can do the same thing as my mother."

He stifled a scream, the feeling of dread seeping into his mind, turning his positive memories into sludge. It was all his fault.

"Stop that," he said through gritted teeth. He couldn't stand the sight of Sie Mae any longer. "How did you become so despicable?"

"Despicable? I only do what Mother tells me to—"

"Okay, and? Do you listen and believe everything your mother says? Parents are just people; they can be wrong. Sometimes very wrong. I should know."

"Yes, I suppose you should."

The princess stared, a gleam in her eyes. Her smile slipped, however, as Noah broke away with furrowed eyebrows. He was shaking with a mix of anger and fear, but he wasn't taking this any longer. How dare she talk about his mother and penetrate his mind? All in the name of what? Doing whatever her mother said? She was pathetic.

"I was supposed to ask for your help," Noah said with a glower. "But you're no ally I'd want to have. Now, if you'll excuse me, I'm going to dance with the love of my life before your family tries to kill me."

Noah started to walk away when she shouted, "I know Celeste has the jar. Your thoughts have made that clear. I could easily tell my mother if I wanted to."

He stopped and turned around, a lump forming in his throat. "Is that a threat?"

Of course, she'd been reading his mind the entire time. She was the daughter of a ruler. He hated how his thoughts were being fed to a stranger; the invasion of privacy both made his eye twitch and his heart sink. A horrid concoction of emotion he wished he could bury.

"You have no hobbies. No interests. All that goes on in your head is saving the planets and *her.* I haven't heard a single thought about the others you came here with, either. They could be in danger, and you'd never have noticed!"

"Hey—I have hobbies," he said with his hands raised. They were gaining the attention of the other partygoers now, and some couples paused to watch. "I read. I go on walks. I stare at my ceiling, wondering where my life is going. These are all quality hobbies I *do* have."

"I'm certainly far more attractive than that girl. So why?"

"Why?" he asked; his voice rose with each sentence. "Because she wants me to be free. To be not just happy, but content with whatever I choose to do. All you want is control. Tell me, is that something *you'd* want? To constantly be walking on eggshells in the name of a title? That isn't love."

There was fury burning in her eyes—perhaps sadness and a hint of embarrassment, too—but he had nothing more to say. He couldn't stomach the sight of her; she was far too vile. Noah didn't bother to check if the princess watched him go; he didn't care. If there was one thing Sie Mae was right about, it was that there was only one person on his mind.

Celeste was dancing with some guy in a black suit with black hair and a dashing smile. Some guy Noah briskly grabbed by the shoulder, as he said, "I'll take it from here."

Her dance partner curled his fists and squared his shoulders. Noah vaguely wondered if he was about to get into his first fight over a woman when Celeste said, "Edgar, this is my suitor. Thank you for the dance, but I'll take his hand now."

Edgar shot a hurt look her way, and she pointed toward Sie Mae. "But it looks like the princess needs a partner."

Noah followed her finger, and his heart tremored at the way the princess was glaring, fumes erupting from her ears. Edgar paled, yet gravitated toward Sie Mae, regardless. Noah chuckled to himself, his shoulders deflating once Edgar's intense aura was gone. He took her hand and whispered in her ear, "Your suitor? I like the sound of that."

He placed his hand on her back as they twirled around the room, their eyes never leaving each other. There was an energy between them he didn't know could exist. Her gorgeous black and blue ballgown shimmered in the moonlight as though she were wearing the stars themselves.

"How should we try to escape?" he asked. "As much I would love to dance together all night, I don't think we have that luxury."

Celeste shook her head. "Do you see a way out? Mark and Katalina are dancing with a circle of guards around them. We have to play the long game until the Queen makes a move or we find an opening."

Based on how much the princess was fuming, they probably wouldn't have to wait long. "I really upset her."

"Good. You look dashing in that tux," Celeste said, drawing him out of his mind. "I could stare at you all day."

Noah chuckled. “I’ll have to remind Mark he was right—ladies love suits.”

“And you, apparently,” she said with a sigh. “Everyone seems to want you. I can’t keep them away, and for good reason. You’re unlike anyone I’ve ever met, and I think others sense it, too. I didn’t know there was someone out there who could make me feel like I’m... home. That no matter what, everything will be okay. I’m worried I’ll have to keep fending off all these women.”

Noah blushed, running a nervous hand through his hair. “Me? I’m pretty sure I was five seconds away from getting punched in the face by the guy you were dancing with.”

She chuckled. “Edgar would never win. He isn’t you.”

Noah leaned in, their fingers intertwined. He didn’t care who saw or what they thought, and kissed her deeply.

37

SHE'S HERE

WHEN HE PULLED AWAY, HE RAISED AN EYEBROW WITH AN accusatory smirk. "Ms. Celestial, are you… jealous?"

His brows rose even higher when a bright red hue overtook her cheeks. "Oh, my—you *are,* aren't you?"

Though he usually found comfort in making Mark squirm, doing so to Celeste was a surprisingly adorable experience. She shuffled, glancing every which way before her eyes landed back on him.

"Of course," she whispered. "First, my stepsister openly flirts with you. Then the same thing happened with the princess."

"Hey," Noah said. "I can't control how attractive I am. You can blame the Goddesses on that one."

Celeste tapped him on the shoulder playfully. "You've gotten cockier."

"Maybe I'm just letting the mask slip."

She tilted her head back and laughed. He meant to lean in and kiss her neck when Luna hissed from behind, "You can't be too showy, you two! They're watching."

She was standing alone with arms crossed over her chest, her dance partner nowhere to be seen. Noah followed Luna's nod toward the princess and Edgar, who were dancing with their eyes glued to him and Celeste.

Noah shrugged. "The Ruler of the Sky was never letting us leave, anyway. Who cares about their rules?"

He leaned in and kissed Celeste's neck, giving it little lovebites as his lips trailed down to her clavicle.

"You two are so gross," Luna said with a grimace, looking over her black gloves like she was checking her nails. Her ballgown was sparkling with silver against midnight black fabric.

"Oh, go judge someone else," Celeste said, waving her stepsister away. "Don't you have a date to attend to somewhere?"

Luna's scowl only grew. "Shouldn't we be focusing on trying to escape before things get any worse? If we're not careful, Mark is going to drink too much, and neither of you even care!"

Celeste's face grew serious. "We're clearly cornered. The princess didn't tell Noah anything, either. The prince may be our last chance. Remember—you need to ask if he knows how to activate the jar."

"That reminds me," Noah said with a snap of his fingers and a point at Celeste. "The princess read my mind and knows you have the stars."

She tsked. "That's not good. Here," Celeste discreetly

whipped around her pack and handed the jar to Luna. "She won't expect you to have it."

The Sky Prince cleared his throat behind Luna. He'd changed from his multi-colored suit into that of deep blue silk with a pastel pink tie. His eyes honed in on Luna, and he reached down to kiss the back of her hand. "May I have this dance?"

"Octover," she proclaimed breathlessly. "Why, of course. I've been wondering where you've been. Listen, we need your help—"

Octover whisked her away before she could finish, and she released a startled shriek. They made an interesting couple—one was scaly and blue, and the other was half-cloud. Noah chuckled. "So much for helping us find a way to escape."

Celeste nodded. "They've always been deeply infatuated with each other. I've never understood why, but they can't be together. The Ruler of the Sky forbids interspecies mingling."

Noah turned back to Celeste. "But that's so—"

"My son is not having ugly blue children with gills," boomed a deep, bone-chilling voice.

Noah jumped, his skin bristling at the sight of the Ruler of the Sky. The party stopped at once, and Octover was quick to bow along with his sister. "I'm sorry for my disobedience, Mother."

She sneered as she entered the room, her bright red dress a stark contract to her multicolored hair. She stopped in front of her son and patted him on the head. "It's okay, Octover. We make mistakes every day, and there's no shame in that." The Crimson Queen met Noah's gaze, her smile only widening.

"Well, there's shame in it if you make as many mistakes as my son, here."

Her backhanded compliment rattled Noah, taking him back to the countless times his late mother would belittle what few achievements he had. He could see the hurt flash across Octover's features, knowing the feeling all too well.

"Now go, boy," the Crimson Queen said with a flick of the wrist, dismissing him. "You are disgracing your family by dancing with this creature. Off you go before I take your little water wenches' life."

"No," he said.

Her eyes widened. "Excuse me?"

"I said no. I may be sorry, but I'm still going to dance with Luna. You can't control who I date, and I certainly won't let you kill her."

He turned to Luna and whispered, "Here."

Luna gasped when he unfurled his fingers. There was a little white fuzzball with eyes staring up at her with a soft squeak.

"Do you accept?" Octover asked.

"I do."

The creature jumped from his palm to hers, and melded into her skin, traveling up to her wrist as a black line through her veins. A small heart appeared with the letters *L.O.*

"I'm sorry for having feelings for another," Luna said, peering at Noah in shame.

The Sky Prince grabbed her chin and brought her eyes back to his. "Darling, that would never bother me, so. I know you will always come back to me." He turned to Noah next with a stern look and flushed cheeks. "In fact, I would love for all three of us to head back to my suite. It would be the most luxurious time."

Noah blushed despite himself, but he hadn't a chance to respond. The Crimson Queen looked as though she may burst, her cheeks turning exceedingly red as she shrieked. "Enough! I will not take this disrespect any longer, Octover. You leave me no choice."

Her voice vibrated off the walls. "All guards to the ballroom this instant! Bring the pre-plank torture devices!" She pointed at her son. "*She never loved you.*"

"I don't like the sound of that," Noah shouted. If Octover was seeing anything like the princess had shown Noah, this wasn't ending well.

"She wants everyone except you," the Queen continued with a wicked grin.

Octover fell to his knees. "Mother—stop. Please—"

"That's enough," shouted another. A woman in pastel pink came forward, gloved hands clasped together in front of her. The Crimson Queen halted her efforts, and her features softening at the sight of the woman.

"Give them a fair trial, sweetheart," the woman said. Her hair was white like the Crimson Queen, but her skin was paler, and her cheekbones were sunken in, as though she were sick.

"The Pink Queen." Celeste bowed her head.

"Come with me," Noah heard the Sky Prince whisper to Luna. He released a groan of pain in between words. "I have something to give you. We don't have a lot of time before she has you all killed!"

Noah and Celeste exchanged a nervous glance as Luna and

Octover disappeared through the ballroom curtain. The crowd of guests stalled their soiree, cheerful laughter turning to sudden screams. The music stopped, making way for the sound of stampeding feet.

"You are ruining our celebration, my love," the Pink Queen insisted, her tone as hollow as her silver eyes. "Torturing our son will only make him rebel harder."

The Crimson Queen shook her head as guards filed in and began surrounding them. There was clearly a voice of reason within their relationship, and the Crimson Queen did not listen to it. "I cannot allow them to go free, my sweetums. First, they steal my stars. Then they bring a sea dweller into my home *and* allow her to seduce my son?"

"No one's forcing him to kiss her, you know," grumbled Celeste.

"A trial will show their true colors. That is why we designed the jury and plank executions."

"I thought they were more progressive up here?" asked Noah to no one in particular. "But the Sky Kingdom hates merpeople, too?"

The Crimson Queen scoffed. "This isn't Merup City, boy. Don't insult me."

The princess pointed. "Celeste has the stars. He thought as much earlier tonight."

Noah tensed, thankful they'd handed the stars off. He gulped at the thought; Sie Mae's smile dropped. Oops. Just like that, he failed their plan.

From the corner of his eye, he saw Mark and Katalina

following the flow of bodies out of the courtyard and back inside the castle.

"Wait, no," the princess began.

"Time to go," Noah shouted as he tugged Celeste away.

The party was over before it'd hardly begun.

38

ONE WORD—RUN

"Guards," the Crimson Queen screamed with a finger thrust forward. "Capture them!"

Noah was already running the way everyone else was, toward the narrow walkway with the billowing canopy above. They reached where the door was supposed to be; in its place was the stone wall and the option to go left or right. Mark and Katalina were there, waiting for the next move to be called.

Celeste nodded for them to follow her down the left corridor. "They're trying to confuse us, but I think this is the right way! Keep going!"

Luna was still gone, lost on another floor with the Sky Prince. Come to think of it, *why* did they split up? Was it always the royal family's plan to seduce Luna and Noah, only to coerce them into handing over the stars?

"How are we supposed to get down from the *sky?*" Katalina

cried. Another brilliant question with no apparent answer. They were, at this moment, wholly doomed. He didn't dare peek over his shoulder to check if the guards or queen were following with their long spears and aggressive poking.

"There's a slide on the farthest cloud," Celeste called back. "The only issue is the amount of guards we'll run into from here to there."

His tuxedo fabric was thick, making his body sweat prematurely as they raced down the hall. Noah desperately wished he could blink, and then miraculously be where they wanted to be. But it was never that easy, was it?

They were heading down a peculiar hallway he had yet to see. Most notable was the spiraling set of stairs leading up to an open roof, climbing high into the open sky. At the bottom of the stairs was Luna with Octover's arm out for her to hold.

"Run," Celeste yelled through hands cupped around her mouth. She passed her stepsister by the time either could react.

"Seize them," cried the guards, who were closing in rather quickly. They skidded to a stop when they saw Prince Octover holding Luna's arm and bowed. "Sorry, sir, but the Crimson Queen has requested you hand that woman, and her friends, over."

Octover squared his shoulders and let go of Luna. He stepped up to the guards, leaving his polished shoes directly below their faces. "You dare bark orders at me?"

Without warning, he kicked upward, knocking straight into the nose of the middle guard. The man's head snapped back, and he fell in a sobbing heap with his hands over his gushing nose. Octover made quick work of the other two, but reinforcements were already arriving. Octover wouldn't be able to fend off all of them alone.

The Sky Prince turned to Luna and gave her a peck on the cheek. "Please, hurry. Be safe, my love. We will see each other again."

She gasped as he drew a spear and prepared to fight his own guards. Noah grabbed Luna's wrist and dragged her along, her body a stone he lugged with difficulty.

"Did he end up telling you anything?" Noah asked. When he turned around, Luna was watching the Sky Prince. Octover, in turn, was watching them go with furrowed eyebrows in obvious dismay. He was thrust back into action, however, when a guard swung a fist his way.

Noah focused on their path ahead, much too terrified to see what happened to Octover next. They had to escape, and fast. Luna's voice was hard to hear over the shouting in their wake, and it took Noah a moment to comprehend what she was saying.

When Noah finally pieced it together, he smiled to himself. "He gave us the way to activate the jar. Do you think we can do it?"

He was breathless, the hallways never-ending.

"Maybe." Her tone was anything but reassuring. "He gave us everything we need. Even the hair."

"The hair?" Noah realized his hand was still wrapped around her wrist, and his palm was growing clammy. He released his grip quickly, hoping Luna didn't read too much into the action.

"Hurry, Noah," cried Celeste. He couldn't see her, but her voice was near. When he turned the corner, the front doors were staring back along with the Queen, princess, and a few dozen guards.

I cannot let you leave with that, stated a voice fading in and out of his thoughts. Noah jumped; the Crimson Queen was inside his head. Perhaps all their heads.

And why's that? another voice boomed back. It took him a second to realize it was Octover, though the prince was nowhere to be found.

You know why, the Queen stated, a snarl in her voice. *Why would you help them?*

You know why, the Sky Prince quipped back.

The Crimson Queen tsked. *I will wipe every memory you have of her.*

I wouldn't let you.

"Excuse me, but can't we talk instead?" Mark asked as he rubbed his temples. "All these voices in my head are giving me a migraine."

The Crimson Queen merely stared at him before turning her attention back to her son. "I hope that water wench is worth the drama."

He expected Luna to make a witty remark, but all he saw was a lump descending her throat as she swallowed, a sheen of the faintest blue sweat running along her forehead. Luna must've wanted to impress the woman on some level. This *was* her almost-boyfriend's mother, after all.

"Ha," cried the Queen. "Something from that filthy water impressing me? Don't flatter her kind."

"I thought the skies worship the mermaids?" Katalina challenged.

"Stop with this nonsense. Why would I worship mermaids?" the Crimson Queen asked. *When* I'm *the one who should be worshiped?*

Noah rubbed his chin. "Something to do with your need for the planets to collide, perhaps?"

"Oh, but only a sliver, child," she said before turning her voice back into thoughts. *And who said anything about wanting the planets to end?*

"You want the planets to be saved, but you won't let us use what we can to save them?" asked Celeste with curled fists. "What's so important about the blue star? My brother's research never mentioned it or the star the shade of hope."

"Enough," the Queen's voice ricocheted against the walls, and a hush fell over the room. "We aren't here to discuss your trite little plans. There are none to be had. You will not keep those stars. I forbid it, and as the person who moved them, this means I have the authority to use our plank—guards!"

"If the Ruler of the Deep gets the blue star," Octover began behind them. When Noah turned, he saw the prince with tattered clothing and a hand covering his bleeding stomach, though he didn't appear to be in pain. "Then what happens?"

"Octover," the Queen snapped. "Do not ask such things in front of our prisoners lest you plan to become one."

The guards exchanged worried looks, but no one moved. Tension clung in the air; Luna's hands were shaking at her sides. She was scared. Perhaps of what Octover would say—or what he wouldn't.

Just when Noah thought the staring contest would go on forever between the mother and son, Octover said, "Fine. Then I'll say it. Keeping the blue star in the sky maintains peace between the rulers. If the star is ingested by someone deemed worthy, they become indestructible. My mother has never failed to hold that over the other rulers' heads, so she gets away with things the others can't."

"Like...?" asked Celeste hesitantly.

"Like denying the Ruler of the Deep funding for a sea show or ruling over so much sky they can't build a Merup City II."

"So, the Ruler of the Deep wants to be undefeatable?" Celeste asked with a cock of her head. "Why?"

"Yeah, he seemed nice enough," Noah added. He'd let them live and gave them answers. He was far more helpful than some of the other rulers.

"Nice? He almost drowned you and all your friends," the princess said, wagging her finger at him. "I'm lucky I didn't take a chance on you."

"But he didn't," Noah argued, though that wasn't the highest praise he could give someone, he supposed.

"I don't understand," said the Crimson Queen. "I banished the Ruler of the Deep to live inside that wretched sea creature and proved to the constellations that it was a just action. He'd become too powerful. Why, then, would they choose the lot of *you* to protect? The Ruler of the Deep will take on his true form again and control everything on our lands, and in our seas and skies!"

"Why do you speak like this, Mother?" Octover asked. "Why do you always act like you aren't in the wrong? You must accept you weren't chosen by them. You've taunted and tortured all of your dissenters!"

"Whose 'them?'" asked Katalina. Noah was thankful for this; his mind was trying desperately to keep up, but failing miserably.

The Crimson Queen rolled her eyes. "The constellations, of course! The Council lives inside the blue star. Together with the star the shade of hope, the Ruler of the Deep can increase the likelihood of whatever he desires! The Council are the only ones with the power to save everyone, and they didn't choose anyone to trust except that stupid fish."

"So you're saying the Ruler of the Deep is... bad?" Mark asked after a moment. Noah couldn't figure out who was the good guy or not anymore—maybe no one was. He shuddered, knowing but never wanting to know how right the thought was. It was as Celeste feared.

"That's why you've never actually used the stars and hold it over their heads," Celeste deduced with a snap of her fingers. "You *can't* use the blue star to rule over everyone, because the Council doesn't like you."

The Crimson Queen let out a ferocious huff of anger. "Enough. I will not be poked and prodded by a group of mere mortals. It is a mistake to give the Ruler of the Deep those stars. Hand them over."

She snapped her fingers, and a guard passed her their spear. "My wife begged me not to use my powers on you, so we'll just have to settle this the old-fashioned way!"

She started thrusting it at them with a scowl that quickly

morphed into twisted glee. The Queen aimed at Celeste next, but Noah pushed her out of the way at the last second.

He ducked. The staff of the spear was above his head, and he grabbed it with a sharp tug. The Crimson Queen lost her grip, and he quickly twisted the weapon around on her.

The Queen backed away with a hand over her chest in disgust. "How *dare* you turn a weapon on me, boy! And to think I let my daughter dance with scum like you! Guards, now, you fools!"

In seconds, they were swarmed. Octover was slowly becoming lost in the mix, but Noah could vaguely see the man pull out a small bag. He unwrapped the twine and pinched what looked to be a powder in his fingers.

Octover tossed the powder at the floor as he shouted, "By the powers that be, scatter thee!"

The guards were tossed from their spots in an instant. Noah exchanged a startled look with each member of their group before they all took off running past the Crimson Queen and out the door.

"Why would you help them?" he heard the Crimson Queen ask. She sounded genuinely hurt by Octover's actions, but Noah did not hear the answer.

Outside, there was a steep drop-off a few feet ahead, but the clouds seemed to extend as far as the eye could see from left to right.

"We aren't making it to the slide. It's too far; there are too many guards," cried Celeste. "I don't know what to do!"

"This way—to the back," Luna shouted with a sweeping

motion of her hand. He wasn't one to question how she knew where to go, though he could take a guess. All he could do was follow.

39

THE DRAEGON PEN

THE RUNNING DIDN'T STOP UNTIL THEY REACHED A SIZABLE building painted white with splatters of red haphazardly tossed across as though the Queen couldn't decide what color she wanted the barn to be. To reiterate that fact, there were cans of paint scattered in front of the door.

"Get inside," Luna ordered. "Hurry!"

Instead of hinges, this door had wheels connected to a track above meant to slide open and shut. His fingers trembled as their group clamored inside and shut the door behind them.

On the other side was a thick, surprisingly heavy latch used as a lock, and it was taking longer than necessary for him to push it into place. He was taking *too* long; they wouldn't make it. "I need more help!"

Mark jumped into action, reaching over Noah's shoulders and slamming the lock into place. Noah scrambled away from the door, taking a stunned second to rest, sitting on the cold, damp floor. He jumped at the sudden rumbling of bodies desperately slamming into the door.

Noah tilted his head back to look at the high ceiling in contemplation. The days they had left were growing slim, and now they were once again like animals trapped in a cage. Thankfully, the lock was strong, and the door didn't budge. After a few more failed attempts, the rattling stopped.

Mark put his hands on his hips triumphantly. "Ha! They can't even get into their own building!"

"Fools," decreed the Crimson Queen from the other side. It wasn't an insult out of anger nor directed toward her subjects. In fact, he could hear the smirk in her smug voice. There was pride oozing from her, the arrogant pride one had when they knew they won. "They won't last an hour in there. Take your posts, gentlemen. We'll either be hosting an execution or hearing one."

The sound of scattering feet filled the taut air until only his deep breaths remained. They were surrounded by enemies with no way out. Instead of finding a sanctuary, they'd cornered themselves. The Crimson Queen had all the guards she needed *and* had the advantage of being in her own kingdom.

"What does she mean by that?" Mark asked, rubbing his chin in thought.

A low, gruff huff came from behind them.

"Uh, guys," Luna said, her voice uneven. "We might have a problem here."

Noah turned slowly, afraid any sudden movement would upset whatever was going to attack them next. He hadn't a clue what he was expecting to see—an ecklweckl, a derithia, a crew of fairies? Something that could tear them to shreds, at the bare minimum?

He nearly fell to his knees at what stood before them. It was none of the above, yet exactly as he feared. Not just one draegon, but an entire barn of draegons. There were clear dividers between each one, and room above for their enormous faces to poke through, all of which were facing their crew.

Noah wasn't the only one trembling; Luna cowered, shuffling toward the door in which they came. She relaxed when her skin met the cool metal.

"I didn't think this would be the way I go," she said, her voice quivering. "Burnt up or eaten by draegons. Oh, sweet Sea Goddesses, if I'd known, I'd have told my mother I love her."

"No sad talk," interjected Noah. The draegons' necks were chained to the walls, hindering an attack—though they could easily breathe fi—

"You'd think the Queen would put muzzles on them or something," Celeste pointed out. "I mean, they could easily burn their captures alive, right?"

He cocked his head with a smile. "That's exactly what I was thinking."

"That's exactly what we were *all* thinking," Luna added with a tsk. She was endlessly confusing to him. She clearly had feelings for the Sky Prince, yet she continued to act jealous of Celeste. He supposed what Celeste said was right—Luna wanted what she couldn't have, even if she didn't really want it to begin with.

"Why don't they melt off their harnesses and escape?" Katalina asked.

"Maybe they like being imprisoned," suggested Mark.

"That's ridiculous." Luna shook her head. "Draegons have many metals that affect them negatively. They probably *can't* burn it off."

"And if they tried, they'd risk burning themselves," Katalina added, pointing to the hay littering their clawed feet. Noah examined the draegons as she spoke. The nearest was orange, a scratch covering a closed eye. Its other eye pierced into Noah's soul, forcing him to look away. There were at least fourteen more draegons staring back.

Inspecting the walls, he noticed a stairway spiraled up to another platform. It was a thin walkway, suspended in the air, with no railings to lean on. There were dozens, a network of balancing beams leading to the very top, where a rectangular hatch was etched into the corner. "It's okay. There's a way out. An emergency exit, I'm guessing. Somewhere on the roof."

"If we can get up there without being killed," Luna contested. He supposed her worry made sense; she was a merperson surrounded by fire breathers. But while he expected them to attack, they were much like Elora—the draegon they'd met the first time they'd visited Mermain City—watching the intruders without a care.

Their enormous eyes were bright with curiosity. It must've grown boring in a barn. Did they communicate telepathically, like the merpeople and sea serpents? He couldn't be sure—their blank stares gave nothing away. Surely they didn't sit in absolute silence for days and weeks on end?

"Let's just go up and hope they don't burn us to a crisp," Celeste whispered, nodding toward the spiraling staircase.

Noah followed, taking soft steps up the stairs with nervous precision and his head down in fear of accidentally making eye contact and provoking one.

A sharp gasp came from behind; Mark, no doubt. His voice confirmed it. "They're watching us."

"They're probably curious, and bored," Celeste said, though she sounded uncertain. "Draegons don't harm people unless given a reason. I guess we aren't a good enough reason."

"How could you possibly know that?" Luna asked. "Just how many draegons have you met?"

"I *read,* Luna. Something you could learn to do for once. With such a long life, you could've read all the greatest hits by now, and written one of your own."

"Why must you attack me every chance you get?" Luna shouted, tossing out her hands. Noah froze, shocked by her sudden switch. "You call me names, look down on me, and now you're attacking my intellect—again! Did you invite me just to rub in how much you hate me? I'm sorry for not believing you and Altair in the beginning—I believe you now. I don't know what more I can do to prove it to you."

Celeste's eyebrows creased in confusion. "Don't act like you haven't said the same—and worse—to me. You flirted with Noah, knowing I liked him. This hasn't been the first time you've lashed out against me. But, no, I still wanted you to come. I still love you despite it all."

Luna withdrew after that, which everyone appeared thankful for. The fighting was becoming too much. No longer was he afraid of the draegons looming below, but instead of the anger hanging in the air between the stepsisters.

The staircase led to a series of thin walkways without railings. The emergency hatch lever looked to be only a few beams away. The first beam leading there was especially long and narrow, meaning they'd have to go across one-by-one and rely solely on their balance.

Mark muttered obscenities under his breath as he paced. To his credit, Mark was trying his best to keep his anxieties under control. A bout of anger or misplace humor would not be uncommon from him right about now, yet he continued to merely mutter.

Noah would dare say he was proud of the guy.

He stared down at the captured creatures below, their scales an array of colors, though all except one were red.

"Doesn't that angry one look a lot like Elora?" asked Noah with a pointed finger.

The others looked, but Celeste was the one to chuckle. "They all look like her. Most draegons look the same."

"Most, but not all. She's the only one that's red."

"Why would she be here?" asked Celeste. "She wouldn't leave one horrid situation for another. Elora is safe and sound, flying about somewhere with her freedom."

"Why are *any* draegons here? Locked up in a cage?" Luna asked with a look of disgust. "Why do such an awful thing?"

"I thought you didn't like draegons?" Celeste accused.

"Of course, I don't like fire breathers. That doesn't mean they deserve to have a life like this."

"We'll free them," Katalina agreed. "Like we did for her."

"Maybe she'll fly us to freedom again," Mark added. Noah held his breath at the thought of the wind whipping through his hair. The feeling of being totally and utterly free, of fresh air sneaking into his lungs and coiling around his ribs. He would love nothing more than another go at it with Celeste by his side.

A roar came from below, disrupting their conversation and jolting the staircase every which way. Noah yelped, holding onto the last part of the railings before the beams took over their path.

"I don't think I can do this!" Mark shouted. "I don't have any balance at all."

A gust of fire burst from the left—the draegon nearest had turned red, and now they were all changing. Curiosity must've told the creatures something nefarious was afoot. Though the palace guards were no longer banging on the doors, there were still five strangers exploring their pen.

"Look—the fire isn't burning away the metal," Katalina shouted. "We'll be oka—"

Another fireball sent the staircase rocking. Luna screamed, clinging to the railing with dear life. Though the metal didn't melt, the blast of fire was enough to knock the staircase off its hinges. The structure quickly became unsteady, dangling in the air with a low moan of metal begging to break.

"You'll have to," yelled Celeste. She wasted no time jumping onto the balancing beam and running across. "If we don't hurry, they'll knock us all to the ground!"

Noah sped over next, wishing he could do so swiftly, but he hobbled and held his breath the whole way.

For once, Noah didn't stumble and fall. He reached the other side with a fist tossed in the air and then ran across two more. The red lever was on this side, and he pulled it so quickly that his entire arm pulsed with pain. The roof opened slowly. Much too slowly, and they still had to climb all the way up there. There were at least two more beams, this time at an incline.

"The draegons are still shackled," Luna began. "How are we supposed to unlock them all?"

"Guys," Mark yelled, his hands out in front of him as if to stop everyone. "The fire breathing stopped."

In fact, the barn was oddly quiet. The platform Noah and the others found themselves on was connected to the wall. He crept toward the edge carefully, hoping a stray fireball wouldn't come hurdling toward his face.

Noah held his breath at the long snouts, and big round eyes pointed up at him. No, not at him, but at the darkened night sky above. Freedom was staring back, mocking the chained creatures.

Looking around, he noticed a beam leading downward toward a thin platform big enough for one. And there, with a squint, he saw another lever, this one painted white. Noah pointed. "There, I think I see something!"

He took a step onto the beam as Celeste reached out to stop him. He glanced back at her with a look of understanding and determination. "Please, Celeste. I can do this."

Her eyes burned bright with love and light, and she whispered, "Be careful."

She let go, and he shimmied down the beam, his body carefully balanced in the center. If he looked below, he would see just how high up he was and have a panic attack. So he didn't look, and instead focused on the lever ahead. Goddesses, he hoped this lever worked.

"You're going to get yourself killed, dude," Mark called.

"Only if you keep distracting me," Noah yelled back, though he was shaking from head to toe.

A roar sounded from below as shackles shifted. There was growing unrest among the draegons, freedom looming over them like a cruel joke.

Fire shot at his hand as he reached out to pull the lever. The heat grazed him, and the fireball shot through a part of the roof that hadn't opened. A few screams came from above as guards fell in a blazing heap. Noah gulped. He hadn't expected them to be waiting on the roof, too.

"Why are they shooting at me?" he screamed, looking down at the terrifying fall. He would break bones at best and his neck at worst. "What is going on?"

"Pull the lever already," Luna yelled.

He reached out to do so, but noticed a hint of ash at the base of his feet. Ash? From the disintegrating ceiling, perhaps? When his eyes panned up, he saw something—another lever poking out the side of the platform. It was hidden, the same color as the metal, and had no labels.

As a test, he reached for the original lever again, only to be shot at. He smirked. So, they wanted him to pull the other one, then. He did as the draegons appeared to instruct, closing his eyes in case they incinerated him, anyway. Best to die without knowing.

With a pull of the smaller lever, a series of roars erupted, along with the clanking of metal-on-metal. Peering over the platform, he saw the chains were falling off. They must've seen a worker perform the task before, guiding Noah in the right direction.

He watched the draegons change back to their neutral purples, and blues, and greens. Only one was still red, staring directly up at him as the rest slowly unfurled their wings and began taking flight. One by one, they passed Noah with a thankful nod before disappearing into the sky. There was not a moment of hesitation as they zoomed toward the freedom they'd longed for.

Guards shrieked outside as fire shot at them.

His eyes did not leave the remaining red draegon. He couldn't believe it. It really was *her*.

40

ELORA RETURNS

"Noah, where are you going?" Celeste grabbed him by the wrist to stop him. He'd successfully made his way back to the others with no issue, but he was heading down instead of up. Toward danger instead of safety.

He looked back, their eyes locking. Her mouth fell open at the certainty blazing inside him, and Celeste let go as she said, "It's her, isn't it? Elora."

"Oh, wow," said Mark. "When I made that joke about her flying us to freedom, I didn't really think she'd be here."

"If I'm guessing, they had about all the living draegons in here," Luna estimated. "There were, what, ten? Twenty? That sounds about right."

"Oh?" asked Katalina. "That doesn't seem like a whole lot for an entire species. Are they going extinct?"

"No. In fact, I think their numbers are growing by one each

year," Celeste said. "Draegons don't procreate often. Draegonologists learned they like to keep their numbers small."

"Thank the Sea Goddesses for that. The less fire breathers, the better," Luna added.

Noah clamored down the stairs as they continued to talk above him, his eyes glued to the draegon waiting at the bottom. Why was she waiting? Surely, she could've left by now, or at least flown up to meet halfway.

As he neared, Noah was reminded how small he was compared to her. She towered above him like a medium-sized house, her eyes narrow and horns twirled to a point on either side of her head. She was a majestic beast, and Noah tentatively reached out to pet her side, feeling the roughness of her scales beneath his fingertips.

The scales were sappy, and a slight sheen was added to his fingers when he pulled away. Her scales appeared to shift like sequence, turning from red to a deep purple.

"What's happening?" he yelled.

"I don't know," Celeste and Luna called in unison, with Celeste adding, "Purple means comfort, though! So that's a good thing, right?"

I remember you.

Noah jumped at the sound inside his head. He spun in a quick circle before landing on Elora. The voice sounded feminine and aged. Ancient. He wanted to ask how old she was, but he couldn't gauge how appropriate that was for such a giant, fire-breathing creature.

Bewildered, Noah thought, *I was told you couldn't communicate with us!*

Of course, I can. Humans are on the lower end of sentient beings, you know. Even bugs have more brains than you.

Thanks for that, Noah thought dryly. *After we helped you escape from that dastardly cave and everything.*

Ah, Elora said. *That's where you're from!*

She seemed much too excited by this. He didn't know how to handle such a thing. Looking around, he realized he was the only one being spoken to. First the Ruler of the Deep, now Elora... why was he always picked as the one to figure everything out?

There aren't many blondes here. Maybe that's why, Elora responded to his internal querying. While he wasn't sure he'd ever get used to this constant need to be on guard about what he was thinking, he surely enjoyed the flutter of adrenaline it created.

What are you doing here? he asked. *Do you like being held against your will?*

She snorted; a noticeable puff of air fell upon him, followed by a grotesque smell. The others remained upstairs, peering down at the odd interaction. To them, it looked like Noah was standing there, staring at Elora and wasting their time.

Elora huffed again, her foul breath sending him reeling backward. *We were drugged and taken in the dead of night while we were sleeping. They want us for something, but the Queen and her guards block out their thoughts. I presume they are preparing for a battle of some kind.*

Aren't you supposed to be stronger than that?

Elora appeared to shoot him a glare. *The Sky Kingdom is*

strong. As you can see, they have indestructible means. We were at peace once and mistakingly revealed our weaknesses.

What changed? He feared he already knew the answer.

One of us helped you. Perhaps the Crimson Queen found it necessary to punish us all.

Noah's muscles tightened, his jaw clenching. *This is our fault?*

The Crimson Queen will stop at nothing to take the stars you now have. It's the only way to keep both control and peace. In a way, I have helped newcomers disrupt years of peace.

"That's ridiculous!" he exclaimed aloud.

"Noah?" called Mark. "Are you alright down there? It sounds like you might be having a mental breakdown."

"I'm talking to Elora," he shouted. "She's more sentient than we thought, and she's claiming the Sky Kingdom enslaved all the draegons because she helped us reach the city and the stars."

"That's ridiculous," yelled Celeste, slamming a fist against the railing in front of her.

Noah admired her equal fervor toward the cause at hand. "Right. That's what I said."

"No—the fact you're talking to a draegon is ridiculous. Like I told you, they aren't sentient!"

It is okay if she believes this, said Elora. *We prefer to be underestimated.*

He neglected to remind the draegon of the position she was in. So far, those who underestimated the draegons were largely proven correct. They were clearly easy to capture for such a large species.

"Help us escape," Noah continued aloud, hoping the others heard his demand as well. "We'll stop the Ruler of the Sky from using you in her silly wars. Once the planets are saved, we'll do whatever it takes to help your kind and stop the Ruler of the Deep if he's truly as evil as everyone says."

Elora tilted her head. *What a demanding one you are. The Ruler of the Deep* would *like you.*

What's that supposed to mean?

But she didn't answer, shaking her head instead. *Our wings can sense when the end is near, you know. A few weeks ago, the tides shifted. The air grew thinner, colder. We've known.*

Yet you're not trying to stop it from happening? Something about this notion frustrated him. Why give up? Why accept defeat so willingly?

Is our demise not our fate? she asked, her voice resigned. She bowed her head and lowered her wing, signaling for him to climb aboard.

A smile crossed Noah's lips. Most of the draegons may have given up, but Elora was still willing to help, even at the cost of her freedom. For this, he was surprised yet grateful. "The end of the world isn't fate, Elora. No—in fact, it's fate we met on this day, at this moment, because without you, we would be in the hands of the Crimson Queen. Without you, we wouldn't be able to save the planets."

There was a long swell of silence as she took flight with Noah clinging to her back, heading toward the others.

We shall see.

41

STAY INN

ELORA DROPPED THEM OFF AT THE EXIT SLIDE ON THE FARTHEST end of the Sky Kingdom. The ground was littered with burnt spots and fallen weapons. It looked as though the draegons disposed of every captor they spotted.

Until we meet again, Elora said with a final bow of her head. They waved as she flew away.

Noah peered down at the purple slide disappearing into the clouds below with a series of twists and turns. The inside looked like a void of nothing leading to nowhere.

"Um, I know I jumped off the edge of a planet into the unknown, but I might have to pass on this one," Mark said. "My fear of heights is extremely high today."

"Just do it so we can get out of here," Luna grumbled, pushing him out of the way and preparing for the plunge. "It leads down to a foam safety pit, so don't worry."

With that, she gave herself a solid push, disappearing into

the darkness. Noah gasped at the sight. She was there and gone so quickly. Not a sound erupted. Celeste followed suit, releasing a series of electric yells as she went down. Noah looked at the other two with a shrug. "Guess it's my turn."

He tossed himself down the slide without hesitation, releasing surprised screams all the way down, his body moving at an impossible speed, the rush intoxicating. The way down was smooth and exhilarating, only to end abruptly with a bone-shattering pain ricocheting through his legs.

He'd landed on a pile of foam squares meant to cushion the blow, but the agony was unimaginable. He released another scream as he tried to waft through the foam squares with stunned legs.

Celeste and Luna had already escaped the pit, and now stood along the side with hands extended to Noah. They fished him out by his armpits, and he tumbled to the solid, teal grassy ground. He laid on his back underneath a starless sky while catching his breath.

Noah smiled to himself, his ears popping after such a high and sudden plummet. While his body was still radiating with pain, he felt free. Safe. Though he supposed an enemy could come down the slide and declare Mark and Katalina prisoners. The Crimson Queen must've known where the five would escape from. In fact, he found it surprising the slide was unguarded. Was the Queen *that* cocky, or did the draegons really kill and scare everyone away?

Mark and Katalina's screams quickly followed before they plunged into the foam with shocked groans of pain. Noah and the other two helped the pair out one by one, concentrating only on the act of doing instead of fearing what was to come next.

Mark fell to the ground as Noah had, running a shaking hand through his thick black hair. "I-I guess it wasn't so bad."

"It was awful," Katalina moaned beside him, snuggling into his side. "I hope we can go back to Sundar."

"There is no time to take a break—her guards could slide down any minute," urged Celeste, already leading the way with Noah and Luna in tow. "If it's the hearts, we'll never make it out alive."

From there, they walked for another two hours through flat fields of flowers and grass before stumbling on a tiny town. There were streets of spaced-out farms and homes with an occasional market or church littering the spaces between.

"Finally, a proper lodging site," Mark stated with a stretch, a yawn escaping him. The lodge had a tiny sign that read, 'Stay Inn.' Noah chuckled at the name. It was adorable.

"This feels like a place you would own," he said to Celeste, and she laughed along with him.

"Funny enough, it is. Surprise," she shouted with her hands tossed dramatically toward the two-story inn. White-framed windows were spaced out against a brick backdrop, and the front door was pastel blue.

His mouth hung open. After everything she showed him, he shouldn't have been surprised by such a fact, yet he was all the same. "Really? Is there anything you can't do?"

She laughed again. "No, silly, I don't really own it. I'd have saved the world by now if I was rich. But owning this place sure would be cool, would it not?"

The rooms here were far smaller than those at the castle, with two twin beds like the 'You've Made It' motel. The walls were painted gray with red stripes, and there were two communal bathrooms.

"I wish we could've spent a night at that beautiful castle," Katalina said with a pout as they entered. "Our entire room had heated flooring!"

"You two could always stay," Celeste suggested with a singsong voice, plopping on the bed. Noah sat beside her, leaning back on his palms. "I'm sure we could get on the Crimson Queen's good side eventually and spend the night. *Or* the Sky Prince could sneak us all in for an evening."

Katalina shook her head vigorously. "No, no. I couldn't leave my family. I've already been away too long. My mother must be worried."

"Yeah, we couldn't do that," Mark agreed with his arms folded over his chest. "Though those heated floors were nice... on second thought, maybe we *should* stay."

Noah raised a brow with faux astonishment. "I can't believe you're thinking of leaving your precious kickball team for... for me."

"For heated flooring," Mark corrected.

"And you," Katalina quickly added. "And you."

Luna slapped her hands together. "Alright. I don't know about the lot of you, but I need to shower and sleep. I declare a bed. Celeste—you may sleep with me."

Mark ran over to the second bed, lying on it quickly. "Katalina and I will sleep on this one!"

Noah's shoulders slumped as he looked at the carpeted

flooring. There were specks of dirt scattered about from their shoes, and the carpet was rough. "Really, guys? *I* have to sleep on the floor? I'm basically *the* savior of the planets. What has Luna done? Or Mark or Katalina?"

Luna scoffed, but it was Celeste who met his eyes and said, "Hey, there, mister. You wouldn't *be* here if not for me. Don't let the power get to your head. I'm sorry. If Luna wasn't my stepsister, I would choose you."

"And I'm not letting Katalina sleep on the ground," Mark contested. "Or myself."

Noah sighed. It was going to be a long, restless night, wasn't it?

42

THE EVIL LEAGUE OF SHAPESHIFTERS

NOAH AWOKE TO THE SIGHT OF A DINGY CONCRETE ROOM. HE WAS groggy, his vision blurred as he tried to wipe the hair from his eyes. His arms wouldn't budge. He wiggled, but the chair he was tied to and his body stood still, pressed against four others. There were thick ropes tied around his ankles, wrists, and midsection.

When Noah stopped thrashing, he looked up and froze. There was a crew of tall, gangly shapeshifters standing around them, their feathers made of sandy grains that continuously shifted. The two directly in front of Noah were staring back blankly with their black, beady eyes and pointy beaks.

"Dad?" Celeste and Luna exclaimed in unison.

Noah peered around the shapeshifters. There he was. Sir Rigulas Relanda, standing on a stage a few feet away with a dozen more shapeshifters on either side. He was dressed in a white suit lined with red.

The air was sucked from Noah's lungs at the sight, which meant whatever Celeste was feeling was much, much worse.

"Why are you standing up there?" Celeste asked, dumbfounded. "Are they holding you hostage?"

Her father adjusted the cuffs of his jacket with a pointed glare. "Hostage? My dear child, do I *look* like someone who would be held hostage?"

"Didn't you hear me before?" The Crimson Queen appeared behind the man, her hand on his shoulder. She was in an immaculate, regal white dress covered in red rose petals. Come to think of it, Sir Rigulas was wearing the same colors as her. The royal colors of the Sky Kingdom.

While Noah was sure the Crimson Queen had mentioned Celeste's father prior, he couldn't remember the exact quote. Something about him being away on business. Stumped, he cocked his head. "What purpose could you have to help these creatures?"

"Against your daughters, no less," Luna yelled.

Before their father could respond, the shapeshifter in front of Noah squawked, bending down to be eye-level with him. Its beady eyes brought about a pit of despair deep within, and Noah looked away before the darkness grew.

The bird grabbed Noah's cheeks and pinched them while pulling his face forward. He released a surprised gasp as his eyes once again met their lifeless black gaze. The creature smiled, revealing rows of sharp teeth dripping with titillated saliva.

His thoughts spiraled into the memory of the shapeshifter pretending to be Celeste all those weeks ago. Noah, with no other plan, tricked the shapeshifter to reveal itself by kissing it. The grotesque image was seared into his mind, even now. Perhaps forever.

"Leave him alone! What is the meaning of this?" Celeste asked, her lips curled in disgust. "You better not give some stupid spiel about how you want the worlds to end for the greater good of society or something, either!"

Sir Rigulas blinked in return with a tilt of his head. His lack of a reaction made Noah squirm, his hands shaking as he tried to untie himself to no avail. The shapeshifter let go of his face with a shove and Noah's head snapped to the side. His neck cramped from the sudden movement, and he groaned, spit involuntarily spilling from his lips and onto the floor.

"Maybe he's one of the shapeshifters," Mark suggested. Though it wasn't a bad guess, a voice inside Noah told him Sir Rigulas was really there, on the side of evil. The Crimson Queen was also present, and she would never allow herself to be captured and copied.

"Very good, Noah," the Queen said, her nose turned upward. "We are ourselves, working with the shapeshifters. Did you truly think you could escape me so easily?"

"We should've kept traveling," he muttered under his breath before stating loud enough for the Queen to hear, "And gotten as far away from you as possible! You're clearly not fit to rule. Insane, even."

"I would've found you regardless of where you ran," the Ruler of the Sky stated smugly. "I have minions everywhere. That's how a queen gets things done. Insanity is the way of balancing between creation and destruction."

Noah blushed, embarrassed by the way she countered every thought he had. He hadn't an argument and remained silent in hopes the conversation would pivot to someone else. Once again, he was not making a good impression on Celeste's parents.

Sir Rigulas hopped off the stage with his hands tucked behind his back and began pacing in front of them. "Haven't you ever wondered *why* the planet is the way it is?"

"The way it is?" asked Celeste. "It's always been the way it is because that is how the Goddess created it to be. There is no other explanation."

"There is—sometimes things just happen. Nature just is. The planets *need* to end, girls," urged their father. Celeste's jaw clamped shut as sweat trickled down her temples. "Don't you see? It's unnatural to have access to more than one world. To *know* of another world far beyond our own, but with beings like us.

"The black hole leading to this other dimension is a blot on what the Goddess created, an abnormality that shouldn't exist. Do you know what happens if *more* of these black holes pop up? If we welcome *more* creatures here? Our planet becomes corrupt. Balance is lost, and we become nothing. We can't allow for that."

Celeste's eyes widened as his words sunk in, and her mouth sputtered like she may say something, but she didn't.

As if to torment her and Luna further, Pevelyn walked in from the side door beside the stage. She, too, wore an elaborate gown, though hers was solely white with a red and white flower pinned in her hair. Noah could hardly keep up, and yet the unrelenting truth was crystal clear.

He and Celeste were never *supposed* to meet. If there was no black hole, their planets wouldn't even be in the same solar system. They were from different dimensions entirely, which only raised more questions likely to never be answered. But—"How do you know that? How do you know the black hole connects dimensions?"

Pevelyn pinched the bridge of her nose between two fingers, her tone blase. "There have been others. Other black holes, that is. They've never induced a collision before, but we still shut them all down."

"How?" asked Celeste as she leaned forward, anger and adrenaline getting the best of her. "*How* do you shut them down? With your little shapeshifter buddies?"

Pevelyn sneered. "We're not at liberty to say."

"But the shapeshifters impersonated you," Katalina pipped up. "Why would they do that if you're working together?"

Pevelyn cracked her neck with a narrow gaze matching her husband, a look Noah found incredibly unsettling. "It's obvious, isn't it? To distract you from the shapeshifter disguised as Celeste."

"So, what? You were going to impersonate me, so I would make my friends give up? Is that it?"

Sir Rigulas offered a toothy smile. "That's my girl. Always so smart. Too smart, I'd say."

There is no need to worry. The Crimson Queen cut into Noah's mind. *We're going to win, and the planets will collide. Look at it this way—all your suffering will end.*

My suffering?

I see the pain in your deepest thoughts. You've lost your mother, she stated. *You should be thankful; you'll be reunited with her soon. You're lucky my wife begged me to spare you and our son from my reality warping abilities.*

The Queen trailed off, her voice echoing through his thoughts as the world around him was lost and replaced. He was standing out beside a long tea table, Pevelyn and Luna on either side. Celeste, Mark and Katalina were standing with Noah, staring at him expectedly.

Well, what now? asked Mark. *Why don't you know anything? You're useless!*

No wonder your mother left you, came Katalina.

And lastly, Celeste. She was holding her stomach, blood slipping through her fingers. Her brows were furrowed with hurt and disgust as her lip quivered. *I believed in you, and this whole time you were leading me nowhere.*

"Enough," he yelled aloud, breaking away from the Crimson Queen's horrid reality. He wasn't sitting back and letting her fill his brain with distrust and demise.

"I am in no rush to die," he shouted. "There are still so many things I want to do. You're the one making a mistake. Condemning your children, guards and subjects to die."

"It's no matter, boy. Eventually, everything turns into suffering. Why not let nature snuff it all out until there is no more suffering to be had?" the Crimson Queen pondered with a sigh. What Celeste told him was true—the Queen had gone mad.

"Noah?" Celeste's hesitant voice brought him back to reality, reminding him how needed he truly was. He wasn't leading them nowhere. Right? He turned to her and gasped at her beauty. Even in fear, even with tears clinging to her puffy, red face, he could not look away. "I—I'm scared to ask them something."

He wasn't entirely sure which reality he was in, yet no matter what, he was hooked on every word. "What is it?"

Celeste shook her head, her voice a harsh whisper. "They were trying to stop me. You don't think they did the same with—?"

"Did you try to stop Altair, too?" Luna's voice was sudden and sharp, though Noah couldn't see her face from this angle.

"The League of Shapeshifters did what had to be done," said Pevelyn.

Celeste let out an involuntary wail at her words. The sound of a heart breaking from the inescapable, irreversible truth.

"The *evil* league," Mark corrected under his breath.

"We never imagined the Ruler of the Deep would fall back on his promise," said Sir Rigulas. "Once the planets end, we'll all be together again. Altair is waiting for us, honey. Don't you see? Disrupting nature is a sin."

"Everything we've done has been for the greater good," finished the Ruler of the Sky.

"Uh, I'm pretty sure killing is a sin, too!" Celeste lashed out, her binds holding her in place, though her chair rattled and scraped against the concrete floor. The sound was mixed with her desperate grunts and sobs. Her shocked horror was bleeding into Noah, and he felt his eyes well with tears. "You had your *son* murdered! You should be ashamed! The Goddess would never accept you into her kingdom!"

"How could you?" Luna cried. "How could either of you—?"

"For the greater good," Pevelyn and Sir Rigulas said in unison.

"He knew too much," added Pevelyn. "And wouldn't stop trying, no matter how much we pleaded. He brought about his own demise, just as you are."

"And now that we've told you everything, sweet beauties," purred the Crimson Queen. "You'll meet the same fate. No need to wait for the planets to collide—we won't take any chances here."

"You said we could keep them alive until they surrendered," their father cut in.

"No arguing," the Queen snapped, and Sir Rigulas cowered with a bow. Pevelyn followed suit as they said in unison, "Yes, your majesty."

There was no longer hesitancy in their voices or actions. The trio had long since decided what they were doing was justified. Noah could hardly believe it; Celeste was staring at the ground with dejection. For the first time, it looked as though she were giving up.

No matter how hard he struggled against his binds, Noah couldn't break free. Worse still, the crowd of shapeshifters grew until the group was surrounded by at least a dozen more.

Every shapeshifter was locked onto one target—a group of five who were in way over their heads.

43

MARK'S MOMENT

THE CROWD OF SHAPESHIFTERS ATTACKED IN ONE FULL SWOOP. Twenty-four or so with blank, beady eyes above sharp beaks, prepared to rip them to shreds. His heart plummeted. Not a single one of his friends was free from their binds.

There was nothing more to be done. Today was the day he would die. And here he thought it was fate to meet Celeste and save the planets. Noah closed his eyes, waiting for the pain of pecking to penetrate his flesh.

"Not today," Mark yelled. Noah turned his head in time to see Mark was standing, fending off the powerful claws of the tall gangly shapeshifters with his thick muscles and broad shoulders.

"Quick—reach into my pack and take out the shrinking powder," Noah shouted. Mark did as instructed, clutching the small purple bag in one hand while using the other to rip off the string. "Taste this!"

Mark pulled out his pinched fingers and quickly tossed the powder toward the creatures. A smirk crawled onto Noah's lips as the shapeshifters with beaks agape instantly shrank. Mark kept throwing the dust until all the birds accidentally ingested it and turned small. They were as small as the fairies but without wings, and they squawked and squabbled while frantically running around with flailing arms.

"I'll use this on the three of you next! Don't think I won't," he threatened Pevelyn, Sir Rigulas, and the Queen once all the shapeshifters were taken care of.

"How did you escape—?" the Crimson Queen began.

"I'm strong. That's how. Now I'm going to untie my friends. We're going to save the planets, and *none* of you are going to get in the way. Got that?" he asked with narrow eyes.

The three stood speechless as Mark untied Celeste and Noah, and they helped free the rest. Katalina popped up and slung her arms around Mark. "That was amazing! I've never seen something so hot!"

"You," Celeste boomed, her fingers curled into fists as she stepped up to confront her family once more. "How dare the two of you! I'll never forgive you for what you've done."

"She's right; I'm disgusted by the sight of you both. I *hope* we don't see either of you in the afterlife," added Luna, tears slipping from the corners of her eyes as she trembled.

"Girls, you don't mean that—" their father began, but Luna cut him off.

"I'm moving out first thing, and I'm never coming back. I can't even begin to understand how either of you could do something so… so rancid."

A flash of sadness crossed Celeste's gaze, but she swiped a tear away and allowed her expression to harden. She was so strong, even in moments she didn't need to be.

"Let's go," she said, turning without another word. If there was one thing Noah understood, it was the feeling of betrayal that came with parents who caused disappointed. His father abandoned him when he was young, and his mother abandoned him when he was a young adult.

Neither daughter said more on the matter, and the group drifted toward the set of double doors leading out. This entire experience was jarring, and all he wanted was to leave as quickly as possible. The room was suffocating, the emotions too heavy to carry.

Mark reached for the knob when the doors shook. Startled, he jumped back, and the others followed suit. An overwhelmed scream was lodged in Noah's throat. He wondered when the panic would consume him, and his body would short-circuit. There were too many things getting in their way. The end was far too close for all these hold-ups.

The doors burst open, knocking off their hinges and flying haphazardly through the room. Noah dropped to his stomach, covering his neck with both hands, his face pointing to the ground. He only looked up once the blast subsided, though the ground began to rumble.

"What's that?" shouted Mark, cowering in a corner with his body shielding Katalina. The rumbling was growing harsher, louder. Noah turned his attention back to whatever had knocked down the door. A squad of guards with diamonds etched into their clothing were placing the large log they'd used on the ground while another crew waltzed in with weapons. Their uniforms were embellished with hearts.

The Queen brought all her reinforcements, by the looks of it.

"All of this for us?" asked Noah.

"Somehow," the Crimson Queen said through gritted teeth, but she soon smirked at the sight of a gigantic beast. It ambled in with humongous feet that made the pebbles jump from their places and sent a thunderous vibration up Noah's spine. The creature was fuzzy, with red and white striped fur, and it had two little antennas sticking out of its head. It was rather cute, though when it snarled, its teeth were pointy, and drool dripped from them.

Noah gulped. "What is that thing?"

Celeste took a surprised step back, though she didn't provide an answer. It was the Crimson Queen, who said, "This is my pet, the ecklweckl."

44

SOMETHING'S IN THE AIR

"You should give up, already," said the Crimson Queen, stepping up to the—*her*—ecklweckl. She gave it a pet in the furry space between its large, round eyes, which looked to be made of yellow, reflective glass. She kept her composure as she placed her hands behind her back and clicked her heels together. "You've already caused such a ruckus."

He wasn't expecting such a turn of events, though he supposed he should've expected the unexpected by now. But in a world of wonder, how did someone so horrifically destructive exist?

"Give up?" asked Celeste. "I don't believe in such a thing."

"Did you not hear anything I've told you?" the Queen asked. "The planets colliding is a mercy compared to what the Ruler of the Deep will do."

"Whatever the Ruler of the Deep has in store, we can beat

him," Noah added confidently. "He's outnumbered, and he'll never reach the skies—"

"Don't underestimate him," snapped the Crimson Queen. The ecklweckl came up beside her, pawing at her hand. She turned away to pace in the other direction, ignoring the creature. "That is how he wins."

The ecklweckl's face turned upward as its toothy mouth opened, releasing a heavy bout of laughter. Noah gasped as he watched the ecklweckl evaporate at the edges before disappearing into the wind altogether.

The Crimson Queen shrieked. "What have you done with my baby?"

"It can't be," Celeste said, a hand covering her mouth.

"Or can it?" asked the wind.

"I can't believe I'm actually happy to hear your voice." Noah looked around; he saw nothing but hazy wisps—and a very upset queen. He smiled to himself. Somehow, they had an ally with no other motive except survival.

"Xyrus! What are you doing here?" The Crimson Queen looked to be bursting at the seams, her entire face growing a bright red. "We have a pact."

"Do we?"

Noah couldn't be sure where Xyrus' voice was coming from anymore. Xyrus encapsulated the entire room; he was both inescapable and untouchable. The perfect mix.

"Does it matter when death looms over us all?" He appeared for the briefest of moments, standing on one of the exposed air ducts above, looking down at them with a smirk. He bowed while taking off his top hat, his purple cat ears sticking out of his thick, black hair.

The Crimson Queen angrily grabbed one of her guard's spears and directed the spikes toward Xyrus. A beam of light sparked from the tip like a bolt of lightning. It was rather beautiful, but it was aimed at the Ruler of the Wind's chest. It was aimed to kill.

Xyrus dissipated from the inside out as the beam struck. Shockingly enough, it looked to be incredibly hard to defeat a man made of essentially nothing. As they watched Xyrus jump around, it became increasingly obvious he was simply showing off. Just what they needed.

Noah's doubt settled in when something whizzed past his cheek and toward the guards. A hot flash of pain vibrated through him, and when he reached up, there was a light cut with blood pooling at the edges.

Paper cranes, the same that'd attacked Noah and Celeste in the hedge maze, were slamming into the Queen's guards. The men whacked them away with yelps of fear, gradually running out the door and away from the impending paper cuts.

"How dare you," screamed the Crimson Queen. "Come back this instant and fight, you cowards!"

But they were long gone.

Xyrus reappeared in front of those who were left; a lone queen, Pevelyn, and Sir Rigulas. Their expressions mirrored each other. Shock at what the humans and merperson before them had accomplished. The biggest accomplishment of all, he felt, was gaining the trust of the Ruler of the Wind.

"Why are you helping us?" asked Katalina. Noah looked

Xyrus up and down. The man was dressed in the same light and dark purple suit without the top hat on, his purple cat ears perked and tail swishing with amusement. Xyrus was, unfortunately, still incredibly handsome with a confidence that suggested he knew he could have anyone he wanted.

"Well, *almost*," Xyrus responded, making Noah jump. "Almost anyone."

"Is that why, then? You're trying to steal Celeste from me?"

Xyrus chortled before his eyes turned to slits. "No, of course not. I don't care much for mortals. I just don't want to die, and this black hole situation is looking worse by the second. I'd rather fight the Ruler of the Deep and Sky than not fight at all."

Celeste nodded with equal conviction. "After all this is said and done, I would love nothing more than to fight in a war with you against the Ruler of the Deep."

"Me, too," Noah added, interlacing his fingers in hers for further emphasis. After everything they'd been through these last two months, he was content. Death was inevitable; he was going to treat it as such. He was going to live every day like it was his last.

And he was going to do so with her.

He wondered if she saw the love and determination in his eyes. If she could sense the peace she presented him, even in the face of danger. The spark she alone ignited.

"Honestly, I didn't care until I felt the black hole trying to suck me in. As I am the wind, I am everywhere, barring the ocean and space, of course." Xyrus trailed off, taking a deep breath like he was announcing a grave discovery. "I have a lot of life to take and to give, but I don't like this unavoidable tug of despair, like utter doom is awaiting me. Suffocation, like a fire snuffed out."

"You can feel yourself dying," Katalina guessed. A harrowing thought to have. Noah wondered if that was how his mother felt before she took her life. A fire snuffed out by her thoughts until there was nothing left.

Xyrus nodded. "It's not a pleasant feeling. Each day, it hurts a little more. I thought perhaps I could ignore it and let someone else figure everything out, but... well, the Crimson Queen was about to kick your asses."

"Language," Celeste and Luna said in unison before sharing a hearty laugh. They both wiped tears from their eyes, and he wondered if it was because of the joke or if they were thinking about Altair. Noah wished he could've met him. Someday, he reminded himself, they would all meet again.

So he hoped, anyway.

"This is nonsense. You know what's going to happen," the Queen roared, as she took a step forward.

"I do not think the death of everyone and everything is the solution," Xyrus said sternly. He snapped his fingers, and his top hat appeared. He twirled it for extra measure before he bowed and placed it atop his head. "I will help you against the Ruler of the Deep once I know the planets are safe. You cannot dictate the demise of entire populations."

His eyes shifted to Pevelyn and Sir Rigulas. "Do you *really* want to be responsible for mass, irreversible destruction?"

The couple was silent at that, their gazes purposely avoiding their daughters. Noah couldn't grasp their reasoning for killing their son. He was sure, in that moment, that he hated these two people so fully, so unforgivingly, because they'd hurt someone Celeste loved. Even if she were to one day forgive them, he never would.

"You're afraid," said Xyrus with a tip of his hat. "That's okay. But that doesn't mean you can just give up. Let them go. Stop this self-destructive sham."

Xyrus and the Crimson Queen glared at each other until she finally looked away. "Fine. I hate that you're right and you know it. Someone needs to knock you down a few pegs."

The Ruler of the Wind guffawed. "Says you, of all people."

Their hands clasped together in a stern shake when the ground shook. It started as a shallow, distant rumble before the pebbles below danced at their feet. Something big was coming.

45

THE ECKLWECKL MAKES AN APPEARANCE

THE DAY WAS ALMOST SAVED—AND THEN THE REAL ECKLWECKL barrelled in. The creature looked exactly as it did when Xyrus was impersonating it, with the same fuzzy red and white stripes and two thin and long antennae atop its head. It was cute, if not for the rows of large teeth within its nefarious grin.

The Crimson Queen sneered, her eyes twinkling with excitement as she swiped at Xyrus' like he was a fleck of mud on her sleeve. She ran to the creature, wrapping her arms around its thick, fuzzy neck. "Finally, my darling! I'm so glad nothing bad happened to you!"

Noah's eye twitched at the altercation. They were running out of time to save the planets, and these fools were squabbling over things that could be solved *after*.

The Crimson Queen released the beast and pointed angrily at Noah and the others. "Kill them!"

The ecklweckl lazily ambled forward on four legs; it was

easily taller than Noah by at least two feet and looked down at him with a cock of the head. Its tongue flopped out from the side of its mouth like a dog. Noah turned to Celeste. "This thing is adorable. Should I be scared?"

Celeste and Luna were equally pale. "I'd take a step back from it, Noah."

"Immediately," Luna agreed.

He didn't, however. Instead, he let the creature stop directly in front of him. Noah had gone up against a plethora of creatures; surely he could handle one more. The ecklweckl bowed with its eyes closed, as if it were waiting for him to do something.

Noah placed his hand on its forehead tentatively. His palm sunk into the fuzzy fur, disappearing within the thick strands. He couldn't explain why he felt compelled to do so, like a force was pulling him closer.

"Are you crazy, Noah?" shrieked Celeste, trying to take his hand off. Her fingers were curled around his wrist, and she froze. Come to think of it, he couldn't move, either. They were both latched on like statues.

"*I will let you go,*" the voice said. It wasn't just any voice, it was *Noah's* voice, but his tone was lower and gruff. Primal. He couldn't control his mouth as it continued to move. "*If you tell me a joke, and I laugh.*"

A bolt of pain reverberated through Noah's body as memories that were not his filled his head. A tiny version of the ecklweckl was pushed off a cliffside by its mother. All the others were dark purple, but he was not.

A young girl climbed the rocks at the bottom as she played

with her siblings, finding the creature battered and bruised. The girl took the creature in, befriended it. The ecklweckl stayed at her side as she turned from princess to queen.

It was utterly painful, the love the ecklweckl felt. Another memory flashed through his mind, this time of the Crimson Queen telling the ecklweckl the planets must collide. That life will end. Noah let out a scream of pain as he fell to a knee, his hand releasing along with Celeste's.

"Oh, my! What's happening?" cried Celeste. She knelt beside him, holding his shoulders while trying to search his eyes. He could barely look at her, his vision doubling, and mind swirling. Noah couldn't get words to release from the back of his throat.

"Someone tell a joke," sobbed Celeste. "I-I can't think of anything!"

"Me, neither," Katalina called. Noah began gasping for breath that would not come. The connection to the ecklweckl was too strong; he could feel his life force being sucked out of him.

The Crimson Queen chuckled. "He'll die any moment now. Say goodbye to your pathetic little savior."

Celeste shook Noah vigorously, but he couldn't keep his eyes open. Clearly, he'd made a mistake. She threw her arms around him and squeezed him tight, her entire body shaking with grief.

Noah could vaguely hear Mark over Celeste's deep sobs. "W-Well, this isn't a joke. But one time, I finished a book only to realize I was reading it backwards."

"*What?*" asked the creature through Noah, his confused voice muffled against Celeste's shoulder. "*How does one do that?*"

Mark's cheeks became flush as sweat slipped down his temples. "It didn't have a cover, so I didn't know which way was the start, and while the chapters were stylistically counting down, I thought they were counting up, so I accidentally read it back to front."

Stunned silence filled the room.

A heavy laughter suddenly erupted from Noah. He threw his head back, completely consumed by the thoughts and words of the ecklweckl. It felt like his brain was becoming one with the creature. Like he was being eaten away from the inside out.

"*That'll do just as well.*"

The ecklweckl turned away sharply, and this one singular movement seemed to cut the connection between them. Noah released a sharp yell before his body grew limp in Celeste's arms.

The creature began retracing its steps out the door, shaking its fur and bumping its head against the Queen as it left.

The Crimson Queen sighed as she fell to the ground dramatically. "I suppose it's no use. You've made it this far, haven't you? If not even my ecklweckl will kill you, then who I am to keep trying?"

"Really?" Celeste asked, disgust lining her voice. "You'll save us based on what your creature thinks, but not out of the goodness of your heart?"

"I should've known The Ruler of the Deep would come out on top, eventually. I can't win." *He knows how to use my power against me.* The Crimson Queen shook her head solemnly with a dismissive wave of her hand.

Noah took a step forward. He wasn't finished with her just yet. "Is that why you fear him so much you'd rather the planets end? Because he can make you see your own delusions?"

She shot him a glare. "When we were kids, the four of us got along pretty well. It's a shame all good things end, but he became drunk on his own power. Insistent that he was better than us as rulers. Maybe he was right, but he threatened my family. Like I said, I'm doing this for the greater good. I had no choice but to trap him in that other realm. But, of course, I should've known he would escape."

Each word came out as a tortured sigh, and he shuddered at the implications of her uneven voice. The Ruler of the Deep was full of so many unknowns. He didn't know who to trust, fully believing they were both on their own levels of insanity. Perhaps there wasn't a right choice, and they were doomed no matter what.

"Get out of here before I change my mind. You, too, Xyrus."

Noah looked around, but Xyrus was already gone.

46

REVELATIONS

Noah and Celeste walked side-by-side behind the others as Luna led the charge to their next destination, the night sky speckled with glowing bugs. They'd been on the side of Fortun with the ocean for quite some time now, but they still had a few more days of travel until they made it to the port.

"I can't believe Mark saved us twice back there," Noah said. They walked beside a trickling stream with medium-sized rocks that kept the water in place. The damp grass his shoes sloshed against was a light orange instead of teal.

"I know—it's a good thing they came along, isn't it?" Celeste watched the couple ahead of them. Luna was at the front, alone. Noah wondered if the Sky Prince was thinking of her, and she of him. "And Katalina is so funny. Secretly, I hope she stays."

Noah nodded along. "I've thought similarly of Mark."

"Well, we don't know what will happen when we hand over the stars. If the black hole closes immediately, they might just be stuck here without a choice. I find that to be the most likely theory."

"Why haven't you said anything about it?"

"I don't want to frighten Katalina and Mark. Going home is their biggest motivation. They clearly don't want to stay."

He cocked his head. "So you omitted the truth for the greater good... just like when you told us Sundar had a higher chance of survival. That only twenty-five percent of the planet was going to be destroyed, when really it was going to be completely obliterated. You promised you wouldn't lie again, but you did."

"I told you I'm not perfect," she grumbled, avoiding his gaze.

He took a deep breath. "Well, it's no matter. Mark and I discussed that possibility already. I guess we'll see."

She nodded. "I hope we can choose. I just want them to be happy."

"Say, I've been wondering for a while now," Noah began, changing the subject. "But why did you ask Luna to come along? It's obvious you don't get along all too well."

Her tone came out curt. "That's just how siblings are. You wouldn't understand. You're an only child, are you not?"

He hesitated, surprised by her defensiveness. "Yes, but—"

"I don't want the planets to collide without a goodbye. She's the only family I have left. We argue. So what? We still love each other."

"I'm sorry for asking," he said as he looked away. Her father and stepmother admitted to playing a part in her brother's death, and she'd been abandoned by her biological mother when Altair died. Luna was all she had left. Noah should've kept his mouth shut. Instead, he dredged up sour memories.

She sighed. "No, I'm sorry. The pressure is just getting to me, I fear. There isn't much time left at all."

"Look," Katalina interrupted. Noah followed her pointed finger to a white and black building off in the distance.

Luna turned to the group with her hands on her hips, an enthusiastic smile painted on her lips. "There it is! I knew it was somewhere around here!"

The white building had the number eleven painted in black beside the door. They'd stumbled on a small farming community, by the looks of it. There were fields spanning miles beyond the building, with similar barns speckling the small hills.

"What is it?" asked Katalina. Her eyes glistened with curiosity as Luna smirked. "A place with food?"

Luna nodded, and Katalina clapped with a broad grin before skipping through the field. She came back and grabbed Luna's hand. The merwoman chortled with surprise before mimicking Katalina's movements.

"I haven't seen Luna this happy in a while," Celeste said beside him, her voice wispy and light. He couldn't pinpoint her emotions. Perhaps she couldn't, either. "It's truly astounding what being away from home can do to somebody."

"Meaning?"

"Meaning she and I were so lost in the routine of our lives, becoming complacent and comfortable instead of happy and challenged." She met Noah's green eyes. "You're obviously different, the way you said yes to me. I think you longed for a challenge."

"I longed for happiness."

"One and the same," she countered. "They can be, anyway."

"Sundar had neither." He watched as the two women disappeared down a hill, only to arrive at the barn door. Mark was somewhere in between, in no rush to join as he seemed to enjoy the breezy, fresh air. "What will be our next challenge after we save the planets?"

"I'm sure one ruler will want our help after all of this is said and done. We might save the planets, but we're also inadvertently starting a war."

"You'd want to stop the war, too? Instead of running off to an unknown land while they squabble amongst themselves?"

She nodded, crinkling her eyebrows in confusion. "Of course. I always finish what I start. I hope you'll help me, too."

He laughed, though he didn't feel too good about an impending war. "Just one of the many reasons I love you. You know how to keep the adventure going."

"And I have an answer for everything."

"That, too." There were a million other reasons, of course. Like how he couldn't keep his eyes off her, or how he could listen to her voice and laughter endlessly. Even if she'd whisked other men away, she'd chosen him as her future, and he'd chosen her. That was all that mattered.

"Now, where does this here barn led to? Another dimension?" he teased.

"Even better—breakfast."

Did he even need to ask why they'd be serving breakfast at midnight?

47

BREAKFAST AT MIDNIGHT

CELESTE PLOPPED INTO THE BOOTH ACROSS FROM THE OTHER three. Noah scooted in last beside her. They hadn't kissed since the ball in the Sky Kingdom, and his body yearned to move closer until their legs were touching underneath the table, and his hip was grazing hers.

They had yet to change, each in their respective ball attire. The dresses were notably battered, along with Mark's white suit, but Noah's navy tuxedo was still in surprisingly good shape.

There was limited seating in this establishment, and most were filled. It must've been a popular place, though he was surprised given how far away from civilization it was. The tables were checkered with gold and silver, and there was a sign tacked onto the front podium that stated, 'No royalty allowed.'

"Finally, some food that's not entirely dessert or dry," Mark said while rubbing his hands together eagerly.

"Or extravagant at the expense of our lives," agreed Luna, propping up her menu while using her index finger to follow along with each item.

"The choices here remind me of home," said Katalina, her stomach growling. "They have Fresh Silk soup!"

"Cakeburgers remind you of home?" asked Mark, pointing at one of the many pictures. Noah turned to the page in question; there were singular slices of vanilla cake and frosting atop a meat patty as though they were buns. Noah wouldn't have classified it as 'appetizing' to look at. "What the fuck is a cakeburger?"

"Langu—" began Luna and Celeste, a tradition that never seemed to escape them.

Mark held up a hand. "Don't remind me."

"I… I've never had Fresh Silk soup," Noah said sheepishly. It was a delicacy on Sundar, something he nor his mother could ever afford. But Katalina and Mark could. As he expected, the pair gawked, their mouths hanging open in awe.

"Never?" cried Katalina. "We're ordering five!"

"We don't have the money for five," corrected Celeste. She slammed her elbow down in the center of the table with a wag of her finger. She stared each of them down, her voice stern. "We can buy an appetizer each and *one* entrée."

"An entrée we have to share?" asked Luna, her tone condescending. "No way. This is my favorite place to go. I'm *not* sharing. Here. I might have something."

She reached into her endless pack and pulled out a few dozen slips of their currency, of which were called quentiles, if he remembered correctly. They had a symbol that looked like a square with the bottom edge missing. Celeste's eyes widened at the wad of paper in Luna's black-gloved hand. "Where did you get that?"

Luna smirked. "I snuck it from Mother's room in case of an emergency. Good thing she turned out to be a terrible person, huh? I was regretting my decision for so long. I still can't believe she did what she did."

"I can't, either. Altair didn't deserve such a cruel death. *Nobody* does." The anguish in her voice was made apparent by the tears sliding down her cheeks. Instead of going on about her sadness, Celeste tossed herself over the table and hugged Luna with a tight squeeze, a groan escaping from her stepsister. Celeste was crying, but she was also smiling. "You're a genius!"

"Alright, that's enough," Luna gasped.

After Celeste let go, Luna opened her mouth to say something more, but Celeste cut her off. "I'm sorry about your mother."

Luna's jaw clamped shut as her eyes diverted from Celeste's. "It's okay. We'll make up in time. This isn't the first disagreement we've had."

Celeste nearly let go of her completely. "This is hardly a disagreement. She aided in the murder of Altair. How could you downplay such a thing?"

Luna shook her head. "She's still my mother. I can't just abandon her."

"Abandon *her?*" Celeste argued. Her voice was rising, and he could tell she would burst if the conversation wasn't quickly changed. Her anger was unparalleled.

The moment was saved by the server as she dropped off

their appetizers. Noah stared down at the Fresh Silk soup. It was a pale, cloudy white with a roasted marshmallow floating atop.

"Yum," he said, hoping to end the brewing fight. "This sure looks delicious."

Celeste released a deep breath as she continued to glare at her stepsister. "I suppose it does."

Mark rubbed his palms together before digging his spoon into the soup-filled cup. He devoured the appetizer in seconds with a satisfied rub of his stomach.

Noah was going to miss Mark and Katalina. So, so much. He vaguely contemplated going back to Sundar before shaking the notion away. He had to remind himself of what was important —Celeste was his *fate,* and he would follow her to the end.

Mark pointed to the Fresh Silk soup with a moan of euphoria. "You need to try this, man. It's next level."

Noah stared down at it. "Are you sure this is classified as soup?"

Mark reached across the table and grabbed his shoulder lightly. "It's the end of the world. What have you got to lose by trying some?"

"It's *not* the end of the world," Celeste corrected with a snap of her fingers. "That's just a strong possibility. Mark is right, though. You'd be missing out."

Noah smiled. "Alright, I'll try the soup. For you."

Luna rolled her eyes with a huff, but added nothing more.

Mark waved his arms in front of Noah. "Um, hello, I'm right here? You could try it for me?" He pointed at Katalina. "For *us*?"

"Yeah, Noah. I'm hurt," Katalina cut in sarcastically.

Noah sighed before putting the spoon to his lips. The texture was divine, melting in his mouth instantly.

A moan escaped his lips before he could stop himself, an involuntary plea of pleasure. When his eyes met Celeste's, she laughed. "That was the cutest thing I've ever seen."

"This is the most delicious thing I've ever *tasted*," he said, adding with a wink, "Aside from you, of course."

"Yuck, Noah's flirting again," Mark said with a dramatic thumb thrust Noah's way.

"I think it's sweet," Katalina contested. "Though it *is* gross that it's my cousin who's saying it."

"Oh, it's gross, alright," agreed Luna.

Though the food was delectable, Noah couldn't keep his mind off what was going to happen next. There was only one week left before the planets collided. If they messed up even the slightest, everyone was doomed. *Everyone.* The pressure was almost too much; no wonder Celeste was cracking.

Noah raised a finger to summon the server for a drink, but Celeste placed a hand on his shoulder, and whispered sweetly into his ear, "After, we can finally rest. Please don't drink tonight. We need our energy. Wait until we win and truly have something worth celebrating—our lives."

He lowered his hand and reached for the glass of water already at his spot. She was right. Though he desperately wanted to escape his fears and excessive thoughts, drinking wasn't the solution. Being with her was. Noah blushed at his thoughts before pressing his forehead to hers. "Thank you."

The conversations became lost between recaps of their

adventures and how there was no escaping boredom, no matter where one lived. Eventually, reality always hit.

"I'm dreading wearing the same drab clothing back home," said Katalina with a dramatic hand to her forehead. Those on Sundar only wore muted colors, and self-expression was discouraged. Dying one's hair was especially forbidden.

"Then bring something from here to stand out," Luna suggested, though it sounded more like a demand than anything.

"Yeah, don't settle for boring," agreed Celeste, creating an X with her arms.

"Hey—I like the clothing on Sundar. I could wear black every single day," Mark interjected.

"Maybe it's easy for you to wear muted shades year-round. At least a colorful coat would do," Katalina argued.

Noah sat back and watched as the group bickered, a grin crossing his lips. He loved every person—and merperson—so deeply that a harrowing pang erupted at the thought of what was coming next. Fate brought him more than Celeste—he was given a new family. He wished he could freeze this moment forever.

But there was no forever. Not here. Not ever.

48

THE COUNCIL

AFTER BREAKFAST, THEY DECIDED TO REST. THERE WERE NO INNS here, so Celeste summoned the Ruler of the Soil's help to build a campsite. Noah and Mark built a tiny fire, something Noah was finding more and more joy in doing.

Sleeping outside was oddly peaceful for him despite the creatures they'd met, and he wouldn't mind doing so more often, but without death looming over them. In fact, he was becoming increasingly eager to hand over the stars. To wake up everyday next to her, happy and healthy.

Luna hid out in the tent while the pair worked on the fire; Katalina and Celeste went out looking for fresh water to drink. Eventually, Luna called out from inside the tent, "Alright, should we do the chant Octover suggested? The one to awaken the council? We must be less than a day away from the ocean by now."

"Do you really think the constellations are inside one of

these stars, with consciousnesses and everything?" Noah asked. It sounded far-fetched.

She nodded. "Octover seems to believe it. Therefore, I am inclined to as well."

"What's the point of this again?" came Mark. "Do we really have to meet with them? I'm pretty sure they'll be as unhinged as everything else on this planet—no offense, Luna."

"It's certainly eventful here," Celeste said as she and Katalina arrived with jugs of water.

"We have to activate the jar in order to make the stars work, and if we're lucky, the constellations can expedite our adventure," explained Luna. "We could be near or far from the beast holding the realm where the Ruler of the Deep is."

"The nevelo we found the first time," clarified Celeste. "If the constellations are real, then maybe they can take us there... or at least show us a path."

"Octover said we must all hold the jar and say these words —'*Bind us to thee, we beg to free. The hour is near, of this I fear. Find us here, and take us there.*'"

They all collectively stared at her. Celeste cocked her head with a cute, scrunched up nose. "Really? That sounds a bit silly."

Luna's cheeks turned a deep blue. "Well, I didn't come up with it!"

She pulled around her endless pack and searched inside. Triumphantly, she fished out locks of Octover, the Crimson Queen, and Sie Mae's hair. "The Sky Prince was the only pleasant part of that experience. He collected the hair weeks ago, but didn't know what to do from there. He was scared his mother would find out and punish him."

"Are you *sure* we have to do this?" Mark asked. Luna held the jar in the center of their circle. "We still have, what, four days left?"

"Two," corrected Celeste. Noah's body froze. Not even he'd realized just how little time there was left before the planets collided. He could've sworn they still had a week left. But two days? Doom was setting in.

He put his hand on the jar with little more thought. If it meant reaching the Ruler of the Deep faster, he would do whatever it took. The others seemed to have similar thoughts because they all followed his lead and repeated the chant together.

The world around them drifted into a mist, his body becoming weightless and floating in the air. No, *sucked* into the air; the wind was knocked from his lungs, and his desperate gasps for breath seemed to fall short.

Just when he thought his lungs may give and his heart may stop, a white light crept toward his pupils. The world came back into focus, though it was no longer the world, but a nebulous void of darkness and stars. Noah squinted; the haze of a million hand-drawn stars speckled his vision as he floated in the nothingness of space.

"Of all the beings who are hundreds of years old, children were chosen for this?" a male voice echoed. Noah glanced around, finding his three companions—Luna excluded—floating alongside him. They were all facing a figure created by dozens of stars in the shape of an arrow, though it wasn't the constellation speaking.

Seven two-dimensional figures watched the group from above while floating around them.

Noah propelled himself in a circle until he found the man who spoke; he had a human face with the snout and mane of a lion. They weren't all human-animal hybrids, however. There was also a wielder with beautiful braids, though half her body was unmade, and a man covered in fabric with only his eyes exposed.

"What's happening right now?" Mark asked; the fear in his voice was made even more apparent by the way he flopped and flailed around in his spot.

"I think the blue star absorbed us," Celeste said.

"And to call us children? We aren't children," Mark argued. "I'm twenty-four! Katalina is twenty-three. Noah and Celeste are... I honestly don't know. Luna's over five hundred!"

"Twenty-two," he and Celeste said in unison. They shared a startled smile. After all this time together, he hadn't asked when her birthday was. He wondered how close in age they truly were.

"In the grander scheme of the universe, you most certainly are," the wielder declared, before turning her pointed gaze at Celeste. "A good guess, Celestial, but not quite. It's a bit more... complicated than that."

"It can't be any more complicated than an evil league of shapeshifters, or a dad and stepmother who arranged for your brother's murder," Celeste countered, her lips quivering.

The constellations were silent at that, stunned at such an

outburst. Finally, the initial lion man said, "Yes, well... complicated more, still."

"We're in the spaces between space," explained the wielder, her angelic voice like a song drifting in the wind. "The ether beyond any planets or ripples in time and dimensions. The spaces between everything and nothing."

"Who chose us?" Katalina interjected. Her words hung in the air, a momentary hush falling over the scene before a round of laughter took hold.

Noah's attention snapped to a big-bellied draegon with wings and the body of a serpent joining in. "*You* weren't chosen!"

Celeste flung a finger in the air triumphantly. "So it's me, then. *I* was chosen."

"No, darling," said the lion man with a snort. "Your *brother* was. As was the Ruler of the Deep. You just so happened to follow in his footsteps and help those we *did* choose."

Noah pointed to himself, a tad disappointed by this development. "So I'm not chosen, either?"

Another round of laughter shook the scene. Noah's frown deepened. "By the Ruler of the Deep, perhaps. Certainly not by us, though."

Noah felt reality smack him in the face. He'd thought that maybe, just maybe, he was special. But no, he was another nobody. At least he and Celeste could be nobodies together.

The half-draegon turned to Noah. "We wouldn't choose children to protect the planet unless they proved themselves exemplary. The Ruler of the Deep's scales are far more ancient than even the mermaids or draegons. He's the eldest creature still living, and the only one who can activate us."

"Did you... did you know Altair?" Celeste asked, almost entirely ignoring their words. "If you chose him?"

While those who'd been speaking looked at her like she was a speck of dirt, all seven constellations nodded. "We see everything. Though they never reached the stars, we have other ways of communicating. We spoke to him and his team in dreams, telling them of the path they were meant to lead. We did not disclose our natural states as constellations, however, nor did we give any hints about what to collect or who to visit."

"We provided them with a calling," agreed the bow. "A way to prove themselves. We did not think others would act against us."

"Why Altair and his team?"

"A curiosity burned inside them more so than anyone we'd ever seen."

"Including me?"

"Your brother asked the same about you. He wanted you to be part of his team, but we did not sense the same desires within you at the time," said the wielder. "You were different, then, and didn't take any interest in helping him. You just wanted to travel the world, not save it. Is this correct?"

Celeste's fingers curled. "I just wanted Altair to be happy, even if I didn't fully believe him at first. I wanted him to find whatever fulfilled him. He was always so sad."

"I'd be unhappy if I knew the world was ending, too," Mark said under his breath. Celeste shot him a glare, and he mouthed the word, 'sorry.'

"There is something we must tell you," said the arrow. "The black hole may close, but it's highly likely the Ruler of the Deep will have the ability to open it again if he so wishes."

"He'll have Sundar hostage," Katalina pieced together with a gasp.

"And the rest of Fortun, as well. We are powerful, especially in the rightish-wrong hands. Please forgive us for whatever may come. He is the only one strong enough to activate us."

Celeste gulped, taking an astral swoosh backward by moving her arms as though she were swimming. "There is no right answer, is there? Either the worlds are ending, or the Ruler of the Deep becomes *the* ruler of Fortun and Sundar. He'll have total tyrannical control."

Noah shook his head, grabbing her shoulder. "We'll cross that bridge when we get there. For now, he's the only way to save everyone."

"Or slowly destroy everyone in a much more devastating manner," Katalina proclaimed with a stroke of her chin. "This is worse than we thought."

Later, he would be left to wonder what was worse; a slow, inevitable demise, or a quick one. For now, he met his cousin's gaze and said, "We still have to try."

The constellations seemed to whisper between each other. When they finished, they turned to Noah. "It looks like the Ruler of the Deep may have picked a good one, after all. We wish you the best of luck. We will activate when the time is right."

"Thank you," said Noah, preparing to add something declarative and hopeful in an otherwise hopeless situation, but when he blinked, space had morphed back into a sky. Not just any sky—it was lime green with cotton candy colored clouds. His brows crinkled as he sat up, leaning against his elbows. The others were scattered around the deck of a ship he didn't recognize.

Mark sat up beside him with a sudden snort, his head whipping from side to side until he spotted Katalina. Then he smiled softly, scooting over to kiss her forehead before snuggling into her side with his arms wrapped around her.

Noah scanned the deck until he saw Celeste, who hopped up and reached for her stepsister's hand. "How did we get here? And what happened to you while we were visiting the constellations?"

Luna shrugged, scratching her scalp. "I guess I wasn't worthy enough for them. I was forced to watch as the four of you slept. Then I blinked, and now here we are."

Celeste glanced over the railing at the pale blue waves. "Huh. That's a bummer, but you didn't miss too much. They were all a tad arrogant, honestly."

"I found it confusing," Katalina added. "Do you think the Council *wants* the Ruler of the Deep to take control of the planets, and that's the real reason they chose him?"

Noah shook his head. "There's no point in wondering now. They chose Altair, too. Maybe they hoped the Ruler of the Deep would have good intentions, and their hope was misplaced."

"What if the shapeshifters are right, and the collision of the planets is for the best?" Luna pondered.

Celeste tsked, surprise lining her voice. "How can you say that after everything we've been through?"

Luna looked like she had more to say, but she clamped her jaw shut and looked away. With a sad smile, she said, "You're right. The best-case scenario is that we all survive, and the Ruler of the Deep doesn't try to control us all."

Noah didn't like it. She didn't sound relieved to be closer to saving the planets. In fact, she sounded devastated by such a notion. What would become of the merpeople once a big fish took control? Her tone filled him with dread as Celeste said, "I agree. We should hurry. The end is coming."

The tremble in her voice did not help soothe his worries.

49

THE DEEPER, THE DARKER

"LUNA?" NOAH ASKED AS HE TURNED TO SEE SHE WASN'T HOLDING a breathing bubble packet. He and the others were preparing for the plunge, taking off any excess clothing. He peeled off his navy jacket and rolled up the sleeves of his sheer white shirt, the fabric already clinging to his sweaty and toned chest. "Aren't you coming with us?"

"We might not come back after this," agreed Celeste. "Once the Ruler of the Deep has the stars and they activate, well... we have no clue what's going to happen."

"I know," Luna said with a bittersweet smile. The kind that quivered at the corners, threatening to fall. She pulled out the jar of stars from her pack and tossed it to Katalina. "But, you see, I've never been a strong swimmer with my legs, so I can't go any further. And, if I were to be honest, I don't want my last memories to be underwater."

"But you've helped us all this way," Noah urged. "Your last

memories *won't* be underwater, because we're saving the planets, remember?"

She shook her head. "Thank you for your enthusiasm and kindness. Few give merpeople a chance outside of worship. We're often seen as gross. Not fish enough to stay in the sea, but not human enough with our gills and blue skin. Sadly, the fact remains that I cannot physically continue."

"So this could be... goodbye?" Katalina asked. "How sad!"

"Well, not for Celeste or I, because we're both staying," said Noah.

Mark shrugged. "And I didn't really talk to her all that much aside from the occasional insult. So... it's not *that* sad."

"Naturally," said Celeste.

"The shapeshifters would've stolen your identities if not for me, you know." Luna crossed her arms over her chest. "Among other things."

Katalina and Mark took turns hugging Luna, uttering their very possible last goodbyes. Noah saluted her. "Thank you for everything. I'll see you shortly."

Noah moved on to Katalina and Mark next. They hadn't a clue how it worked, but they assumed the black hole would suck them back to Sundar. Probably. Hopefully. Henry needed someone to look after her, after all.

"It was fun, man," Mark said as he wrapped Noah in a tight embrace and patted him on the back for extra measure. "You were a downer for a minute there, but you really grew on me. Thank you for, uh... taking us with you on this adventure. I'm proud to call you my cousin-in-law."

Noah sighed as they pulled away from each other. "You're

probably one of the most maddening and funniest people I've met, and I'm going to miss you."

"Woah, there. You're going to make me blush." Mark chuckled, putting his arms between them for emphasis. "Though I will say, I'm disappointed you won't be at our together ceremony."

"I know. I wish I could go, but I know it'll be beautiful." Noah turned to Katalina last. "Thank you for coming with us. We couldn't have done it without either of you."

She twirled a brown braid around her finger bashfully. "I'm not sure how true that is, but... thank you, too. It was far more fun than I could've thought! There's so much to discover here. But, Noah, are you sure about this? We only just found each other; I don't want my children to grow up without you."

Katalina was right. They'd likely never see each other again once they handed over the stars. The idea of this sent tears to his eyes. Still... he couldn't go back. No one on Sundar compared to Celeste, and he'd rather choose love over family, as heinous as it felt to admit. Celeste was everything. He would always choose her.

"I'll miss you and Mark, but I need this. I need her."

Katalina nodded. "I hope you don't regret it."

Though it looked like she had more to say, she took a step back without another word.

"Oh, Goddesses, this is it, isn't it?" Mark asked, his hands suddenly shaking as he wrapped a protective arm around Katalina's shoulders and pulled her close. "Are you ready?"

Noah's mind was reeling as he spun around to find Celeste. Of course, he wasn't ready. He would never be ready. He gravitated closer to her, putting her cheek in his palm. “In case we fail, I hope you know I love you.”

They stared into each other’s eyes. She was gorgeous, yet fear reflected in her gaze, a hint of sadness among it all. He moved closer, wishing he could free her of her anguish. If only his lips alone could provide a cure.

Celeste chuckled. “Of course, I know, and I hope *you* know how much I love you, too. We won’t fail. We have each other. And when all of this is said and done, we can go back to the city and get that ice cream you liked so much. Go on dates you could only dream of.”

Of all the terrifying things they’d encountered, of all the rotten things he’d felt throughout their adventures and his life, everything was made better by her presence.

“You’re what I dream of,” he whispered into her ear, his lips brushing her lobe. Celeste pulled him in, and they kissed with gentle precision, a dance of swirling tongues and light moans. “I’ll always love you.”

“Alright, lovers. As much as I don’t want to be that guy, we’re running out of time,” Mark sounded from behind them. Noah smirked, disrupting their flow, and pulled away from her luscious lips.

They got down to business, jumping into the water one after the other before securing their individual breathing bubbles around their noses and mouths. His clothing was heavy on his limbs, and he tried to soothe his panic with deep breaths.

Down they went. There were no arguments or snarky comments to be had; everyone was too focused on survival.

A sunken ship full of flowers, vegetables and vines was settled in the sand, cracked in half with growth along the wood. As they neared, a blinding whiteness took over the sunken ship and washed over their senses, and then the Ruler of the Deep was there, staring back. He must've sensed the stars were near.

Small red, yellow, purple, and orange serpents danced around, twirling and giggling like children discovering a new game.

You came back, the Ruler of the Deep exclaimed. Surprise lined his voice, perhaps shocked they could steal from the Ruler of the Sky and get away with it.

Of course, said Noah. *We're not sitting back like your fellow rulers and watching our planets end.*

A bellowing laugh erupted within Noah's thoughts. *Very good. I knew you were the right choice. Now hand over the stars.*

50

GIVETH THE STAR

What exactly do you plan to do with them? Katalina asked. Noah couldn't help the tension building within him. Why'd they give *her* the task of handing over the stars when it clearly should've been Noah, who the Ruler of the Deep favored? Or Celeste, who the Ruler already knew. But no, they gave the jar to the person who primarily opened her mouth to ask too many questions.

Noah shook away his judgment. Wasn't he supposed to be the bigger person? Wasn't he supposed to *like* his cousin now that they'd made up and spent months of their time together?

Or was it okay to simply co-exist with family? To love them wholly, but know you will never truly get along? It made him feel guilty, this pang inside. They were so close to the end of their adventures, of their life of grandeur and excitement, and he knew he should've wanted to go back to Sundar, no matter how boring it was, because the rest of his living family was there. He *should've.*

Was it bad to want more than what he had?

Was it bad to drop everything for a woman?

Or was that the curse of life—that there were no right or wrong answers until a decision was seen through? There was no way of knowing without doing. No wonder he had so much anxiety.

It matters not. The ruler released an animalistic growl before adding, *You will be off on your planet away from all this. Why do you care?*

Noah's eyes widened. So the ruler *would* let them go home.

I don't want to be the cause of destruction on another planet, argued Katalina. She wasn't wrong. Noah, Celeste, and Luna were staying on Fortun, along with an abundance of other species. It *did* matter.

Would you use the stars to control Sundar, too? Katalina continued. *I'm not giving them to you if you plan on hurting everyone I love.*

The Ruler of the Deep stared at her blankly. *Control is a strong word. I prefer 'reign.' But no, I have no use for your trite planet. It's nothing compared to this one. The Ruler of the Sky has trapped me in this body. These stars will set me free, and then I'll finally be able to see the world again.*

Noah glanced over at Celeste. He never thought he'd be the one to doubt everything when salvation was staring back. There must've been a reason the Ruler of the Sky trapped him here to begin with. Noah couldn't shake the feeling that all their adversaries had been right.

He understood, in that moment, his true feelings toward Katalina. She was often right, but he hated to be undercut so swiftly. Noah thought so surely the Ruler of the Deep wouldn't betray everyone's livelihood that he never even considered the notion. He looked between Katalina and Celeste. *Maybe you were right and we shouldn't do this.*

It matters, but it doesn't, said Celeste. Her inner voice was oddly calm. *I have to see this through to the end for Altair.*

Exactly, agreed the ruler. *I have been trapped beneath the waves within this nevelo for nearly a thousand years. Do you not think I deserve to see the sun again?*

Noah took a deep breath. He didn't have an answer. The breathing bubble was shrinking by the second, and the Ruler of the Deep was no longer a reliable source to keep them alive if the bubble popped. There must've been a reason. *Why did she trap you down here to begin with?*

The Ruler of the Deep remained stoic as he swirled around Noah and the others. *She views me as a threat. I can control more than water; I can control time and space. Something that lousy excuse for a queen could only dream of doing. But that isn't here nor there.*

I just want everyone to survive, thought Katalina, her voice lined with resignation.

There was a pause, an eery lull until the Ruler of the Deep finally exclaimed, *There are no survivors in life. There are those who make the orders, and those who succumb, but in the end, we all die.*

This is a mistake, Noah thought. Katalina stared down at the jar with crinkled eyebrows before looking at the others. He could see the wheels turning in her mind.

Do not fear the inevitable, urged the Ruler of the Deep. *Embrace it.*

But you'll be omnipotent, Noah countered. *I can't be responsible for unleashing an indestructible being.*

If not you, there would always be another.

Noah disagreed. If not for them, there would be no one, and the planets would collide.

I was already omnipotent, the Ruler of the Deep continued. *Just within this realm instead of the next. I want them all.*

But why?

To prove myself worthy, of course. To prove myself once and for all to the constellations and Goddess alike. They have looked down on me for so long when they should know by now I am their equal. Nay, more than their equal. Do I not deserve to be free? Do I not deserve to be one with the greats?

Noah wanted to scream obscenities at the creature, but Celeste's thoughts overtook his own.

Do it, she said, her words directed at Katalina. Her tone left no room for interpretation.

You'll promise to leave Sundar alone? Katalina urged, and the beast nodded.

If that's what it takes.

Noah pushed forward, swimming toward her with his hand out to take the jar, his panic settling in. *No—stop! You don't need to prove yourself! You could help us and be free without harming anyone.*

The Ruler of the Deep stared blankly. *I was willing to go peacefully after the first hundred years. Even the second and third. But they've kept me here alone, surrounded by pieces of myself in the form of tiny sea serpents. Tell me—does jealousy and lower status warrant tossing someone into an eternal prison?*

Noah was a few more thrusts closer to his cousin, but he knew he wasn't going to reach her in time. And really, what was he stopping her for? He didn't want to die, either. *Why must we be doomed either way?*

I know. Katalina released a deep sigh, turning to Noah as he neared. *I'm sorry. We've already come all this way, and I'm not ready to die. This is the only choice we have.*

Deep down, he knew she was right, but there was something off in the way the Ruler of the Deep conceded so easily. The Ruler was leaving something out, of which Noah was sure. Noah didn't believe him, but he also didn't have the jar. He had no control. Maybe none of them did.

Katalina tossed the jar toward the Ruler of the Deep, who snaked around the object in quick zigzags. Noah was too late. The sea serpent's tongue slithered from his grinning mouth, eyes wide with joyous hunger. His small companions swam around him, their laughter filling Noah's head until it was all he could hear.

It's okay, thought Noah, though he wasn't sure if he was telling the others or himself.

No matter what the Ruler of the Deep tried to do to Fortun and Sundar, he and Celeste would be ready. They would fight him, and they would win. How hard could it be to defeat a big fish?

The jar burst, and the two stars erupted from the shards, illuminating the darkened depths. Noah shielded his face, a piece of glass striking the back of his hand. The wound burned against the saltwater.

The stars wrapped the Ruler of the Deep in a bright, neon blue light, melding into his skin and becoming one with his scales. He was glowing with a radiance that was impossible to look at for longer than a second, and Noah could've sworn the serpent was transforming. The light became too blinding, and he had to look away.

A chuckle rumbled through his thoughts. *The stars are complicated creatures. Sometimes it requires more than one to create a miracle. Behold! There are no greater fools than those who crave life, for they fuel those who crave death.*

Noah's eyes widened as he watched the Ruler's tiny serpent minions get zapped by his power, becoming nothing more than dust floating to the bottom of the ocean. He reeled backward, a scream lodged in his throat. The Ruler's body was expanding as the energy built within.

Noah was thrust backward, his body twirling and twisting haphazardly in the water. His eyes were closed until his body slowed, and when he opened them, he realized his breathing bubble had popped. Panic settled in his gut as he screamed, water rushing into his lungs.

It was all happening so fast. He never expected it to end like this. They just wanted to save everyone, but now they were saving no one.

Whiteness took hold. He no longer knew which way was up.

There was no up.

Everything was gone.

Every*one* was gone.

He was as he began—alone.

51

THIS IS THE END

There was a moment where he came to, floating in an endless, blinding white light. He shielded his eyes with a squint. Noah was no longer underwater, and his lungs were no longer filling. His thoughts were jumbled, and he wondered where he was going, or if there was anywhere left to go.

The light that'd consumed him dissipated into darkness. He was floating in a vast nothingness now, facing a circular hole ahead where Celeste was on the other side.

Noah gasped at the sight of Celeste across from him. She was golden along the edges, her black and blue hair floating. She was still in the deep depths of the ocean, her breathing bubble dwindling. Her eyes were filled with tears, and some had already worked their way up, floating as bubbles to the surface. He wondered if she was truly there, or if this was a dream. Or perhaps it was worse, and she was watching him die.

He took a deep breath that seemed to take forever, cupping his hands around his mouth while doing so.

"I'll always love you," he shouted, hoping she could hear him. Even if she didn't, he hoped she could read his lips and sense the weight of each word as it exited his body. He tried to move a muscle, to push himself toward her, but the blinding white light wouldn't let him.

He was swallowed up, and when he opened his eyes again, there was an orange and red sky staring back. He laid against soft sage grass, a bunny eating flowers a few feet from his face. The sun was crumbling, though it appeared to be slowly putting itself back together, as if gravity reversed itself.

Noah pushed himself onto his elbows, taking in his surroundings. A lone, gigantic mountain stared back with homes littering the side. Two other bodies were spread out on either side of him, groggily sitting up, but she was gone. The beating of his heart drowned out the guttural sob that erupted from his throat. A harrowing cry he couldn't control, sorrow blurring his vision and corrupting his thoughts.

Though the state Celeste was in had looked dire, he knew she would manage to escape somehow. That was just who she was. She was likely alive and well, but on a planet that was not his, and he didn't know what was worse—knowing someone was dead, or knowing someone was still there, but never within reach.

52

He'd heard so many stories about love. How it whisked people away, picked them up from their places, and carried them to the ends of Sundar with forever by their side. How no matter where he was or what he was doing, he would long to be with her. Heart-aching emptiness. Always empty, always aching. Before her and after, but never during. He took the during for granted, and now it was all too late.

So this was what it was like to be in love, huh?

Utterly destructive.

Gut-wrenching.

Air-sucking.

Pain.

FIVE YEARS LATER

THE SUN FELT BRIGHTER THAN USUAL TODAY. HE RAISED AN ARM to shield his eyes from the heavy rays. A thick film of sweat had long since formed along his temples and back, and he held the bike at his side up with two greasy palms. His attire did him no favors as he rolled up his navy sleeves. His pants were black, along with his shoes, each clinging to his hot limbs.

Noah contemplated buying one of those battery-run miniature fans that connected to the front of his bike, but he hadn't gotten around to it yet. They were fairly new to the market, and he'd seen many of them within the last few weeks. He cursed at himself for visiting his mother in such disarray.

He stood at her grave with a bundle of assorted flowers clasped in his other hand.

She spent her life looking for the Great Beyond, and there she rests, her tombstone read. It once filled him with rage, but now he only felt relief that she was probably off in her version of paradise, finally happy for once.

Noah placed the flowers in front of her tombstone with a sigh that would've once been categorized as sad. While the sorrow would never leave, her absence forever a stain in the spaces surrounding his very being, he now knew how to live. To hold and understand the pain. *Feel the darkness,* Celeste's words echoed in his mind, *but don't stare into it.*

Thoughts about Celeste couldn't drift on for too long. They always enacted a pang in his chest that reverberated through his lungs and robbed him of air. It'd been five years since they'd saved the planets. Five years since he'd seen her face and heard her voice.

He couldn't say for sure why he walked the familiar side-walks toward Altair's tombstone. He didn't stop there often, finding it too difficult to manage his emotions. All thoughts led back to Celeste, and not a single woman he'd met since could even remotely compare. It was devastating, yet comforting, knowing he had the privilege of feeling such love, no matter how fleeting. Gratitude helped stifle the pain.

There was no quote or date on Altair's tombstone, merely his first name, surrounded by the five other stones of his companions. Noah wondered if they were truly buried here, or if Celeste had made these in honor of them. "Well... your research was right. We must've done it. It's been five years and nothing's crashed yet."

Katalina suggested speaking out loud during these sorts of moments. It was supposed to be therapeutic to vocalize his feelings or something like that. "Our planet is still crumbling, though the sun and moons seem to be fine now. So that's something."

He paused, unsure of what to say next. Maybe this was silly, and he should've gone on his way. "I wish I could tell you how Celeste is doing. I wish I knew. But I can tell you I'm doing alright—I have a stable job at a bookstore, and make far more money than I've ever made. Oh, and I moved into one of those nice, big apartments on the other side of the mountain."

It had two bedrooms and bathrooms, and he'd gotten Henrietta a companion—a tiny black puppy. He knew it was foolish, but he hoped his pets would fill the void of eternal loneliness in his heart. Honestly, Pongo—short for Pongolio, a popular board game on Sundar that he, Katalina and Mark played weekly—and Henry filled the void relatively well, cuddling with him while watching movies, going on walks together, and having dinner by his side.

His pets were a bright light in a sea of mundanity.

"Noah." His body froze at the sound of his name. It couldn't have been, yet it sounded exactly like—

He shook his head. It must've been a trick of his mind, no matter how real it sounded. The black hole was sealed; this was a dream. Yet he looked over his shoulder, anyway, disappointment settling in before his brain could register what he was looking at.

Who he was looking at.

Noah couldn't peel his eyes from hers, couldn't say her name nor say hello. Her galaxy-speckled gaze was as glistening as ever. She was wearing a pastel blue windbreaker lined with white, and her hair was tied in a high ponytail. Her hair was longer now, and she'd dyed every single strand hot pink. She was unbelievably stunning.

"Celeste?"

Her smile was radiant, and he could tell she wanted to lean in, to say hello with more than mere words, but she pulled him into a hug instead. He was shocked by her soft touch, his body temporarily frozen as she swayed him. Slowly, he wrapped his arms around her, releasing a trembling breath.

"Is it really you? But how...?"

She pulled away all too suddenly, her words coming out breathlessly. "Well, after you, Mark and Katalina got sucked away, the Ruler of the Deep let me go. But it was as the Ruler of the Sky feared. He took a new form and conjured an army. Fortun's been in shambles. Everyone told me not to see him again. They said he was mad with power, or something, but I didn't care. I figured he was my only way to Sundar, so I visited him, and he actually agreed to help me."

"Why?"

She beamed brighter than the sun ever could. "Because of you. You really impressed him back then, you know. He said he was doing you a favor by sending me. For giving him the stars, and everything. That's why he hasn't opened the black hole to take over Sundar, either."

He held onto her every word with bated breath, even though he knew this was nothing more than a dream. Yet her touch felt so *real.* Noah stroked a hand along her jaw, a thumb over her cheek. She leaned into his touch, swaying as she grabbed his hand. "And?"

"He let me come back here. I had to collect another star, of course. Luna was a big help. So was the Crimson Queen, actually. She's been holding her own against the Ruler of the Deep fairly well, though she lost an eye."

She scratched her chin in contemplation before snapping her fingers. "Oh! You'll never believe it! Luna and the Sky Prince got married! She's a princess, now! The people were furious at first. And, well, they're in hiding right now because of the Ruler of the Deep. I fear for Fortun, but I couldn't stand being away from you any longer."

"Celeste," he said, grabbing her shoulders. "You're here."

He chuckled through the words, his eyes searching hers. She was as beautiful as the day they met. And they met here, of all places. "I'm having the strangest feeling, like I've lived this moment before."

She leaned forward and whispered in his ear, "How have you been all these years?"

He smiled, though he knew she couldn't see. Every part of his body was aglow with electricity as he shook his head with another chuckle. "Good. I've been good."

"Oh?"

"I've missed you. Things have been fine, but nothing has compared to what it was like with you." His words lingered in the air as they held each other. He was afraid she would disappear if he let go, and the dream would end. "This is a dream."

"I suppose you'll find out in the morning."

"Yes, I suppose I might." His words trailed off as he leaned in and kissed her, taking in every inch of her lips. She was so incredibly *real* that he didn't care if she wasn't. When he pulled away, he simply said, "Wow."

Celeste's cheeks were rosy, her eyes wide and bright. "I couldn't be away from you, Noah. I just couldn't. I'll never be able to go back, but I don't care. It wasn't nearly as fun without you there."

"You risked your family to find me? Your life?" She nodded, and he leaned in to kiss her again with fingers tangled in her hair. What a preposterous thing to do, risking everything for a man, yet he was determined to do the same on Fortun all those years ago for her, before he was sucked away.

He pulled away when her stomach growled, and he smirked. "Hungry?"

She nodded, and Noah gestured toward his bike, patting the seat before slinging his leg over. "Here, get on. I'll show you my favorite restaurant. We can play board games while we eat. There's an amazing selection of sweets, too. Trust me—you'll love it."

Celeste giggled, taking in their surroundings. "This is a strange place for a meet-cute, is it not?"

She glanced down at his seat, climbing on with a wobble. They laughed together as she got settled behind him, her arms firmly wrapped around his torso. She laid her head against his back, setting off a flutter in his ribcage as she said, "Lead the way."

IF YOU ENJOYED THIS SERIES, PLEASE CONSIDER LEAVING A REVIEW TO SHOW YOUR LOVE AND SUPPORT!

CHECK OUT THE PAPERBACK EDITIONS:

TURN THE PAGE FOR A SNEAK PEEK OF THE EPIC CONCLUSION OF THE WORLD BEYOND DUOLOGY

ENJOY THE WORLDS OF FORTUN AND SUNDAR?
CHECK OUT MORE BOOKS BY ANGELA FUNK

THE FORSAKEN DESTINY TRILOGY

FIVE STRANGERS.
ONE DEADLY EXAM.
NO ESCAPE.

A DARK ACTION ADVENTURE FANTASY

ACKNOWLEDGMENTS

I am unbelievably thankful that I have had the privilege of time to work on my novels and now I can say I've finished my first series! This is such a huge milestone and I am so grateful to everyone who continues to offer support. I am surrounded by such amazing friends, family, and artists who give me the courage I need to keep writing.

As someone often plagued with anxieties and depression, having my characters and amazing supports surrounding me does more than you'll ever know.

First, thank you so much to my beta reader and close friend, Hayley Whiteley (Author of *Ink & Ore)*! I did not get many beta readers this time, and that's okay because I trust your judgement so fully! Though we're in different states, we have worked together to give each other advice and support! You are so talented and I can't wait to continue to do great things together!

Thank you to all my amazing ARC readers as well, who stuck with me through both books or joined in on the fun later. Ashleigh Carter (Author of *The Variance*) is another great friend who helped me throughout the process. I couldn't have done it without you! I am endlessly amazed at how many of you enjoyed this series, and it's so exciting to have gathered such a stellar team, and I would be nowhere without you!

There are so many incredible artists to thank, from my cover designer to the character artists. Thank you to my amazing cover designers, Hannah (@HSBookCovers), who created the paperback covers, and Ann (@OnyxCatArt), who created the e-book and hardcover versions over on Etsy. They both made my books come to life in unique ways and were incredible to work with!

I would also like to thank the amazing Akar (@akarstudio) over on Fiverr for the planet designs, and the gorgeous artwork of Noah and Celeste at the start of the book was done by @SYKOSAN. A special shout-out to a new artist I've worked with, @sophienova793, who drew the character art of Katalina and Mark at the end of the novel! They are all such amazing artists and I love their work so much! While @AzukiArts and @shinkxart are not featured in this book, I am so amazed by the work they did on my characters and their work is located over on my Instagram!

Of course, I would not be where I am without my soon-to-be husband, Caleb. He has been my biggest and brightest support and he has given me the confidence I need to grow. I am so lucky to have you in my life and to have someone to travel with and do such amazing things together. Thank you for reading my novels and for being the best support anyone could ask for. I love you!

My family has always been an amazing support in my life and with my writing career. I'd like to thank my father, Jon, my mother, Tasha, and step-mom, Kristen, as well as my half-sister,

Emily, my grandparents, aunts, and cousins, have been incredible supports throughout this journey and I'm continuously amazed and blessed by the support you have all given me throughout the years. Liz, Sam, Sophie and Izzy are amazing cousins and step-cousins and I'm so thankful to have you all in my life!

My best friend, Carissa, has always bought my books and has been a great maid of honor and lifelong friend! You know she's a bestie for life when she stays in the ER with you until 6:00am! All my other closest friends have been great supports throughout my journey. Thank you so much, every single one of you is awesome!

The road is long, and the journey has only just begun. Thank you so much for giving my books a little ounce of your time and I look forward to the future!

ABOUT THE AUTHOR

Angela Funk is the author of the action-adventure fantasy, the *Forsaken Destiny trilogy*, and the sci-fi romantic comedy, *The World Beyond Duology*.

Born in Brookfield, Wisconsin, she relocated to Iowa to attend the University of Iowa for Creative Writing. Plans slowly devolved, as they do, and she graduated with a B.S. in Therapeutic Recreation, instead (it's a long story). She currently resides in Iowa with her cat, Rory, and her fiancé, Caleb. Outside of writing novels, Angela works full-time with children with autism and enjoys hiking, painting, and watching anime.

Author Website

https://www.angelafunk.com/

instagram.com/authorangelafunk

goodreads.com/angelafunk

www.ingramcontent.com/pod-product-compliance
Lightning Source LLC
Chambersburg PA
CBHW020248030826
48979CB00030B/2653/J

* 9 7 9 8 9 8 9 8 5 0 6 5 5 *